# The Marshal's Lady

ALSO BY SARAH STAMFORD

*THE MAGNIFICENT DUCHESS*

# The Marshal's Lady

## Sarah Stamford

E. P. Dutton · New York

Published in the United States by Elsevier-Dutton Publishing Co., Inc., 2
Park Avenue, New York, N.Y. 10016

Library of Congress Cataloging in Publication Data

Stamford, Sarah.
The marshal's lady.

1. Oudinot, Marie Charlotte Eugénie Julienne de
Coucy, Duchesse de Reggio, 1791–1868—Fiction.
I. Title.
PR6069.T2M3   1981          823'.914          80-23290
ISBN: 0-525-15320-9

Published simultaneously in Canada by
Clarke, Irwin & Company Limited, Toronto and Vancouver

Designed by Wendy Green

10 9 8 7 6 5 4 3 2 1

First Edition

*For Judith Lavinia Mack*
*from her affectionate godmother*

This novel is broadly based on the life of the Maréchale Oudinot, Duchesse de Reggio. For the great liberties I have taken with her character and conduct I humbly beg pardon of her shade.

*"Eugénie, will you marry Marshal Oudinot?"*

*The words were no sooner out of his mouth than Monsieur de la Guérivière was appalled that he had blurted out his question instead of the tactful speech he had carefully prepared. As, angry with himself for his impetuousness, he groped his way to a chair in darkness lit only by glimpses of the moon moving fitfully through the clouds, the gasp of astonishment he heard was succeeded by a silence so deep as to be almost palpable.*

*"Why are you all sitting in the dark?" he muttered. "Let me ring for candles."*

*"No, no, we are better as we are," his wife replied hastily.*

*Perhaps Christine was right; better to leave Eugénie in the kindly dark to recover from the shock he had given her.*

As was their usual habit after dinner the de la Guérivières, her mother, the Comtesse de Coucy, and her younger daughter, Eugénie, were strolling along the banks of the River Ornain, which divides Bar-le-Duc, the ancient city of the Dukes of Lorraine, when he was approached by Pils,

Marshal Oudinot's soldier-servant, with the request that Monsieur de la Guérivière visit the Marshal without delay.

"Continue your walk without me," he bade the ladies. "I suppose the Marshal wishes to see me on some urgent matter of business, but I do not expect that he will detain me long. However, as night will soon fall I advise you not to linger before turning for home."

While he strode away with Pils the three women obediently made their way back to the de la Guérivières' house in the Rue du Bourg, none of them willing to hazard a guess why Monsieur de la Guérivière had been summoned to the Marshal at this unusual hour. In silence they took their places in the salon but, despite the gathering darkness, no one called for lights.

When Monsieur de la Guérivière entered the great entrance hall of the Hôtel Oudinot he found the Marshal awaiting him, his foot impatiently tapping the black-and-white marble tessellated floor, but he greeted his guest cordially before leading him to a study whose walls were covered with maps. The Marshal invited Monsieur de la Guérivière to be seated although he himself remained standing.

When, after a brief silence, the Marshal began to speak his guest was astounded to discover that something very different was involved from the matter of business he had expected.

"The lengthy absences from Bar my career obliges me to make have left me little leisure or indeed opportunity to attend to my personal happiness. On the rare occasions when I am able to occupy one or other of my houses I am increasingly conscious of the absence of the warmth of a real home only a family can give. For some time I have been anxious to marry but, until recently, I failed to find a woman who possesses the qualities I am seeking, good birth, excellent education, sound principles and simple, modest tastes." Almost as an afterthought he added, "As my own income is five hundred thousand francs a year I am not concerned with the size of my wife's dowry."

These confidences from a man with whom his relations,

--◦◦[ ]◦◦--

though friendly, had never been intimate embarrassed Monsieur de la Guérivière, at a loss to understand in what way Marshal Oudinot's marriage plans were any concern of his. Surely this preamble was not leading up to an offer to Madame de Coucy, of suitable age and birth, but he quickly realised that he was very wide of the mark in thinking of his mother-in-law.

"The woman I wish to marry," said the Marshal emphatically, "must be young enough to adapt herself to my habits and temperament, but she would not find me a domestic tyrant."

He paused to light his pipe and take a few turns about the room before facing Monsieur de la Guérivière with the same resolute look he wore when leading his grenadiers into battle.

"I have decided that your young sister-in-law exactly meets my wishes. She knows, of course, that I am considerably older than she is but I can truthfully say that I am much younger than my years—on that score she need have no fears. As the Maréchale Oudinot, Duchesse de Reggio, she will naturally share my social position in Lorraine and all the advantages of my good standing with the Emperor."

Amazement robbed Monsieur de la Guérivière of the power of speech; he sat mumchance as Oudinot concluded:

"Instead of addressing myself directly to Madame de Coucy, I considered it best to ask you to act as my intermediary. Will you, therefore, acquaint her and her daughter of the desire I have formed?"

Monsieur de la Guérivière gathered his wits sufficiently to stammer his thanks for the honour the Marshal was doing his family; he might rest assured that his flattering offer would be considered with all the attention it merited, though he felt obliged to stress that he could not himself answer either for his mother-in-law or for her daughter.

This he perfectly understood, the Marshal informed his guest as he accompanied him from the study, adding his regret at not being able to receive Mademoiselle de Coucy's answer in person.

--◦❦ ❧◦--

"An old wound persists in troubling me so tomorrow I leave Bar to take the waters at Plombières. My cure cannot be deferred as I must shortly return to Holland to resume my command of the army of occupation, but I shall instruct an estafette to stand by to bring me news of Mademoiselle Eugénie's decision for which I earnestly hope she will not long keep me in suspense."

The two men shook hands and the door closed behind Monsieur de la Guérivière, who walked slowly down to the massive ornamental iron gates. He could not avoid feeling irritated by the Marshal's confidence that his totally unexpected offer of marriage would be accepted since his go-between did not share that assurance. Her son-in-law's doubts were based on the character and opinions of Madame de Coucy with which he was now very well acquainted. Much he had observed for himself, still more he had heard from Christine.

As he approached the Rue du Bourg Monsieur de la Guérivière's pace slackened. He realised that the task he had assumed was fraught with difficulty as Madame de Coucy's pride in the family lineage might well cause her to reject with scorn a marriage between her daughter and the son of a brewer, Marshal-Duke of the Empire though he might be.

While the de Coucys belonged only to the provincial nobility of the Franche Comté, that eastern part of France for centuries a battlefield, theirs was an ancient family distinguished for many generations. Their fortune was small, reduced still further by the havoc wrought by the Revolution, but they counted as greater riches the many quarterings on their coats of arms. Even were Madame de Coucy prepared to degrade her daughter by permitting her to marry out of her caste, another factor Monsieur de la Guérivière must number in his calculations; her implacable hostility to everything and everyone connected with Bonaparte and the Imperial régime, an enmity made more bitter by the illusions she had once cherished about him.

Madame de Coucy convinced herself that, when General Bonaparte became First Consul, his intention was to restore

Louis XVIII to the throne, a conviction which became certainty when the General made peace with the Pope and the Catholic religion again became the religion of France.

"You will see," she exulted to her friends, as unshakably royalist as herself, "it will not now be long before Bonaparte acts like that General Monck who restored Charles II to the throne of England."

Humming the old royalist songs, *"Vive Henri IV"* and *"O Richard ô roi,"* as was her habit when restoration of the Bourbons seemed to be in the air, she mounted to the attic where, carefully preserved in an old trunk, were the panniers and lappets she had worn at Versailles and was now hopeful of wearing again. How cruel had been her awakening from the dream of taking her daughters, Christine and Eugénie, to make their curtsey in their turn to the King and Queen! By the time Eugénie could toddle Louis XVI and Marie Antoinette were dead.

All the hopes Madame de Coucy had been cherishing vanished when, on December 2, 1804, General Bonaparte snatched the crown from the Pope to crown himself Napoleon I, Emperor of the French.

"Now," she mourned, "we shall have to wait many years until the King returns from over the water, but that glorious day I shall not live to see. Yours, my dear children, will be the joy of crying *'Vive le Roi'* while your sons pin the white cockade to their hats to serve the King as did your father and his ancestors."

Until the Revolution engulfed France the Comte de Coucy had been a soldier, but he refused to emigrate across the Rhine with many of his fellow officers. He believed that, by remaining in France, he could serve the King and Queen better than by joining the Prince de Condé's army at Coblentz, nor did he expect to be molested in the quiet village of Merçuay where the de Coucys lived.

The Comte's confidence that his family would be safe suffered a severe blow when the long arms of the sansculottes reached out to throttle the de Coucys in their savage embrace. Under the terrible law of the suspect, when every man lived in fear of his neighbour or turned against his own brother, the family was arrested and imprisoned. Such were the obscene absurdities of the Revolution that even Eugénie, a baby of two and a half, was suspect and an enemy of the people.

In her fetid prison Madame de Coucy was in despair as daily the child, deprived of proper food and fresh air, grew thinner and paler, her mother's anguish increasing with her fears that Eugénie would not survive until her nurse, Rosalie, came to the rescue. To help the mistress and her children to whom she was devoted, Rosalie loudly professed the revolutionary sentiments which enabled her to gain access to the de Coucys' prison. In a desperate attempt to save Eugénie's life she offered to take the child, now a mere featherweight in her arms, to the local Committee of Public Safety to beg for her release.

Eugénie had so often heard the story of her rescue that she no longer knew if she herself remembered seeing a room filled with men, their long greasy hair crowned with foxskin caps, their shoulders swept by the brushes. From men as ferocious in their dealings as in their appearance little mercy might be expected but, by a fortunate chance, the brother of the tyrant Maximilien Robespierre was visiting the Committee. Robespierre le Jeune melted at sight of the child, taking her in his arms to kiss her, but to his amusement she pushed away the bristly chin which tickled her.

"So, *ma mignonne*, you don't like kisses? Wait a few years and you'll welcome them eagerly enough. In the meantime here's a bonbon to sweeten you."

Frowning, Eugénie rejected the sweet as she had rejected the kiss; in prison no bonbons had come her way. So mercurial were the revolutionaries in their treatment of aristocrats that Rosalie was terrified lest the child should have aroused Robespierre's wrath but, when it erupted, it was directed at the Committee morosely watching the scene.

"By arresting this baby of two and a half," he stormed, "you make yourselves a laughing stock and the government ridiculous. Take her, citizeness—" he handed the child back to Rosalie—"and bring her up to be a good republican. I will sign the order for her release."

Snatching up the order and Eugénie, Rosalie rushed away, to keep the child in her care until the nation revolted against the Reign of Terror and in their turn the terrorists mounted the guillotine to which they had sent so many thousands, but for Robespierre le Jeune Rosalie could not help feeling a little regret; he had shown himself to possess some human instincts!

Now at last the prison doors opened to release their victims, but for the de Coucys freedom was bitter-sweet; the Comte de Coucy did not long survive the privations of his imprisonment, His widow's first journey was to take his body for burial at Lentilles, his family's home, but she refused when her brother-in-law, the Chevalier de Coucy, begged her to remain with him and his wife; she had decided to settle at Vitry-le-François.

"Even during the Revolution Vitry was an oasis of calm," she told the Chevalier, "so that I do not anticipate any persecution by the authorities for my sympathies, but there is an even more important reason for choosing to make my home at Vitry, an excellent convent where Eugénie can enjoy the education which befits a de Coucy. Unfortunate that Christine is now too old to go to school."

In a small house in the Rue de Frignicourt Madame de Coucy brought up her daughters to share her ardent attachment to her religion and her King but, as Eugénie grew up, she was less concerned with Louis XVIII's problematical Restoration than with her own future, summed up in the one word, marriage. When Christine married the Vicomte de la Guérivière and went to live in Bar-le-Duc, her lonely sister waited expectantly to be told that her mother had chosen a husband for her, naturally from the narrow circle of the old nobility. Eugénie knew that the choice was limited, so many young men were abroad, living penuriously as émigrés, while others, despite their fidelity to the Bourbons, had joined the army, unable to resist sharing the glory that Napoleon Bonaparte was winning for France.

One of them was Eugène de Villers, the object of Eugénie's adoration ever since the de Coucys befriended the boy orphaned of both parents by the guillotine. The Comte de Coucy had encouraged Eugène, whose fervent wish it was to join the army, telling him, "You may be surprised that I, who had the honour of serving the King, do not oppose your joining the army of a republic but no one, royalist or republican, can fail to rejoice at the splendid victories won for France. Remember always, Eugène, that by whatever name a government is known it is for France you will be fighting and your allegiance is to her."

The red-letter days in Eugénie's life were those of Eugène de Villers's leave at Vitry, even though all his conversation was devoted to long recitals of bloody battles, hard-fought campaigns and the object of his own hero-worship, General Oudinot. Had Eugène given the matter any thought he would have said that he saw nothing odd in Eugénie's attentiveness; it was natural for a de Coucy to be interested in deeds of heroism. He failed to realise that it was not the narration but the narrator who held her attention.

"I suppose, Eugénie, *you* would be surprised that Oudinot, whose courtesy and chivalry are by-words—he's known as the Bayard of the army—is not of noble birth, in fact I believe his father to be a brewer at Bar-le-Duc."

Pleased with the rare opportunity of teasing Eugène—so well matched, Eugène and Eugénie!—she protested, "Why should I regard chivalry as the privilege of one class alone? I see no reason why the son of a brewer should not be as chivalrous as the son of a duke!"

"Such revolutionary sentiments from you! As it happens you are right." Eugène earnestly emphasized his point. "Bonaparte, the Emperor, knows that men crave to improve their standing in the world, that's why he's created Marshals of the Empire, to fire every soldier's ambition. He says that men even of the lowest rank carry a Marshal's baton in their knapsacks, and if you think that doesn't make them fight better you're wrong. Take Oudinot. He joined the army as a simple grenadier at the age of seventeen; now he's a general, a count of the Empire and, mark my words, he'll go higher yet.''

Carefully Eugénie, who had not the faintest interest in the heights to which General Oudinot's career might take him, stifled a yawn as she moved her chair a little closer to Eugène's.

"You're contradicting yourself, Eugène. First of all you say your Oudinot is not of noble birth and now you say that he's a count."

"Don't be so childish! Imperial nobility! It's not the same as ours—however many barons, counts and even princes Bonaparte creates they won't be aristocrats for several hundred years."

"You are severe, Monsieur le Vicomte!"

"Well, perhaps I am, a little," Eugène conceded before brushing the subject aside to continue his litany of praise of Oudinot and what the enemy called his "infernal column" of grenadiers, but Eugénie, absorbed in admiration of Eugène's broad shoulders set off by his uniform, had ceased to listen. If only *he* would look at *her* in admiration, but he seemed oblivious of the fact that she was now a girl old enough, well, almost old enough, to be married. Eugénie underrated the charm of a sweet face and the steadfast expression of her blue eyes. She could only hope that Eugène would realise that her devotion to him outweighed what she mistakenly regarded as her lack of beauty.

To bring him round to the subject closest to her heart, she bravely interrupted his flow of words.

"Your General Oudinot, is he married?"

"Yes—no—I've no idea, anyway it's of no importance. In a soldier's life marriage is purely incidental."

Ruefully Eugénie realised that he had failed to take the bait as, ignoring her intervention, he continued eagerly.

"Do you know there's scarcely an inch of Oudinot's body without a wound scar?"

Eugénie thought it becoming to lower her eyelids and stiffen a little in her chair, which finally succeeded in making Eugène aware of her.

"I beg your pardon for making so improper a remark but, when I talk about Oudinot, I get carried away."

As if she did not know it! At last incredibly Eugène seemed to have exhausted his subject. He rose, stretched himself and sighed happily. "Only two days' more leave before I rejoin the regiment. I must pay a few farewell calls, so *à bientôt*, Eugénie."

Humming *"Malbrouck s'en-va-t'en guerre,"* he left the salon without a backward glance and Eugénie in despair how to make him conscious of her existence other than as a sounding board. What if she disguised herself as a man and joined the army? How glorious to save Eugène's life in battle, but the fascinating prospect had to be sadly rejected. In spite of her military ancestry Eugénie knew she was far too small and slender to be a war-scarred heroine.

Eugénie was mistaken if she believed that her mother was not aware of her affection for Eugène de Villers. Madame de Coucy could not help knowing it but, fond though she herself was of him and admitting that his impeccable lineage, his parents martyred in the royal cause, made him all she could wish as a husband for her daughter, his lack of fortune made him ineligible. The Comtesse wanted a better fate for Eugénie than to live in penury on a junior officer's pay or to follow the drum like so many young women. Eugénie was still young enough to wait and in these extraordinary times a man might easily win both fame *and* fortune with his sword, but until such time, it were better that she did not fix her hopes on Eugène de Villers, especially as Madame de Coucy was in the dark as to his feelings.

Eugène's departure left a blank in Eugénie's life which a few trivial tasks or visiting her mother's friends could not fill. Her chief occupation was listening for the postman's horn, but when Eugène's infrequent letters came they were always a disappointment. After a perfunctory enquiry about Madame de Coucy's health the remainder of the page was devoted to his hero whose hour had come at last. Eugène waxed lyrical to describe how Oudinot was largely responsible for the French victory over the Austrians at Wagram. Although wounded in the arm and unable to ride, he had taken over command of the Corps of Marshal Lannes, Duc de Montebello, mortally wounded in the action at Essling in May.

Immediately after the battle General Oudinot received his Marshal's baton, a distinction Eugène indignantly declared to be long overdue while conceding that the delay might be attributed to the new Marshal's frequent absences from the field to recover from his wounds.

Eugénie looked in vain for one word about herself. As if she cared a button whether one more soldier had found a Marshal's baton in his knapsack although she doubted whether generals carried knapsacks! She dismissed Marshal Oudinot from her mind.

Eugénie had almost given up hope of any break in the monotony of her existence when a letter arrived from Christine, saying that she had been invited to a reception to be given by Marshal Oudinot to celebrate his marshalate and his elevation to the dukedom of Reggio. He had most kindly included Madame de Coucy and Eugénie in his invitation.

While waiting for her mother to decide whether she would accept the invitation, to hide her impatience Eugénie asked, "Where is Reggio, *maman*? Surely it is not in France?"

"I believe it is in Italy," was the cold reply. "Apparently all the ducal titles Bonaparte bestows on his marshals are Italian."

"Surely as a Lorrainer Marshal Oudinot might have been made Duc de Bar." She giggled. "I confess that Duc de Bar-le-Duc would be silly though."

Her mother frowned. She herself took no cognizance of the Imperial nobility with whom she scorned any social contact. Certainly she had no intention of accepting this invitation for herself but she was reluctant to deprive Eugénie of so rare a treat. It might, moreover, give her thoughts another direction than Eugène de Villers, but Madame de Coucy was too sanguine. Excited though Eugénie was at the prospect of a really grown-up reception her overriding wish to be allowed to go was to be able to write about meeting Marshal Oudinot to Eugène which might, she hoped, bring him in the future to regard her as worthy of slightly more of his attention.

--◦◦{‖}◦◦--

Madame de Coucy was a little touched by the unspoken appeal in Eugénie's eyes, but she sighed that it was beyond her power to make her daughter's life more lively. With Christine as chaperone the child could come to no harm, however distasteful her mother felt it to let her make what was her debut in Bonapartist society.

"I shall not myself accept this invitation," the Comtesse said briskly, "but I have decided that you may do so. Rosalie shall escort you to Bar and thereafter you will, of course, be in Christine's charge."

Eugénie was delighted by her mother's decision. On their rare visits to Christine she enjoyed touring the historic old city under her brother-in-law's guidance. Her favourite excursion was to climb to the old town where from the ancient clock tower there was a magnificent view to the wooded country beyond the city's confines.

Always, when they sat down to catch their breath after the steep ascent, Monsieur de la Guérivière had something new to tell her about Bar-le-Duc. From him she learned that James Stuart, called the Old Pretender, would climb up from the Lower Town for a breath of fresh air during the years he lived in exile in Bar. Eugénie's romantic imagination was stirred to know that it was from this city that, disguised as a servant, he set out to regain his kingdom, the unfortunate expedition the English called "the '15." Never did Monsieur de la Guérivière fail to bemoan the example set by the English when they cut off the head of their King, Charles I.

Invariably the little outing ended by a visit to the cathedral of St. Etienne, where the two knelt together to pray for the martyred kings, Charles and Louis, and also for the two unhappy princes, James and Charles, who had failed to restore the Stuart line to the English throne.

As he rose from his knees, in a whisper Monsieur de la Guérivière would add, "And let us pray that we shall be more fortunate than they and live to see our rightful monarch restored."

On her present visit to Bar there were no excursions to make as Monsieur de la Guérivière was absent from the city

on business. Eugénie, therefore, was able to give herself over
entirely to eager anticipation of the Marshal's reception.

In deference to her mother's opinions Eugénie was determined not to be impressed by the luxury of the Hôtel
Oudinot, the extent and beauty of the grounds and the company assembled yet, as she surveyed her fellow guests, she
was uncomfortably conscious of the contrast between her
simple white muslin gown, the wreath of greenery in her
hair and the elegance of the ladies' dresses and richness of
their jewels. As she strolled through the salons at Christine's
side she reminded herself that, whatever the appearance of
these Bonapartists, their birth was almost certainly inferior to
hers, a decision which enabled her to hold her head high,
unaware of how quaintly the air of consequence she assumed
sat on a young girl. In any event, Eugénie was here to see
Marshal Oudinot, but she scanned every face they passed
without discovering anyone remotely resembling the idea
she had formed of Eugène's hero.

"Where is the Marshal?" she whispered to Christine.

"Over there on the sofa," her sister whispered back.
"Most unfortunately he recently suffered an accident to his
leg and he is only able to walk a few steps."

Eagerly Eugénie followed the direction of Christine's
eyes, scarcely able to control her disappointment at the sight
of a man in a plain brown coat lying with his leg propped
up. That man of slender build and expression mild rather
than martial, was he the great general of whom Eugène never
spoke but in raptures? Where was the giant of ferocious
aspect and bristling side whiskers, where the gorgeous uniform, where the glittering decorations, where the clanking
sabre? In spite of herself Eugénie was obliged to concede that
the Marshal would scarcely wear a sabre when lying on a
sofa, but how could she tell Eugène that she found Marshal
Oudinot's appearance insignificant, that in the flesh he bore
not the faintest resemblance to the image he had conjured
up?

Indignantly Eugénie edged closer to the sofa to be again
dissatisfied, not that the Marshal called for music, but that he

did so in an ordinary voice, not in the thunderous accents of one accustomed to command. As the band struck up the guests drifted indoors to take part in the dancing while Eugénie, knowing no one, stood disconsolately beside her sister, wistfully surveying the dancers of whom she longed to be one, unaware that the Marshal was watching her.

With a jerk of his head Oudinot summoned an aide-de-camp.

"You see that pretty young girl in white muslin standing next to Madame de la Guérivière. She is Mademoiselle de Coucy. Go and ask her to dance."

Obediently Captain Lachaise threaded his way through the crowd to bow to Christine and seek her permission to lead Eugénie into the set now forming. Overjoyed at finding a partner for the rare luxury of dancing, soon even Eugène de Villers was forgotten while Marshal Oudinot might not have existed. The dance was a brisk one called "*Le Grand'père*," no longer fashionable in Paris, but still popular in Bar. As Eugénie and her partner twirled and advanced, circled and reversed, Captain Lachaise gasped, "I can't imagine why this dance is called '*Grand'père*.' *My* grandfather certainly could not keep up with the tempo."

Eugénie merely smiled, too full of enjoyment to utter a single word. What greater happiness could there be than to give herself over to the rhythm of the music with a handsome young officer? If only she could dance like this at Vitry, but her mother's friends were all so old—and to Eugénie so dull!

When the excitement of her entry into Barrois society ended Eugénie returned to the endless empty days at Vitry, only slightly enlivened by the news that Bonaparte's new Empress, the Archduchess Marie Louise, would pass through the town on her way from Vienna to Paris.

"Could anything be more cruel than making the poor Empress agree to the divorce because she is no longer capable of bearing children?"

Madame de Coucy, careless that her criticisms of Napoleon might be carried to the secret police, roundly expressed her disapproval of his divorce from Josephine, her hostility to the Emperor increasing as he established himself ever more securely on the throne of France and as master of Europe.

"How cowardly of Bonaparte to attack her in a woman's most vulnerable point!"

"Then why, *maman*, as you disapprove of Bonaparte so much do you bestir yourself to see the new Empress? Goodness knows, enough members of the Imperial family pass through Vitry without your taking the smallest interest except to pull the shutters close."

"I beg you will not speak of those upstarts as the Imperial family!" Only to Josephine, an aristocrat by birth, did Madame de Coucy concede her title. "You forget, Eugénie, that the Archduchess Marie Louise is the niece of our martyred Queen and a daughter of the oldest reigning house in Europe. From the depths of my heart I pity the poor girl, sacrificed in marriage to a man she is known to hold in aversion."

With Eugène de Villers always uppermost in Eugénie's thoughts, she wondered if the Archduchess had left her heart behind in Austria. From a spirit of contrariness Eugénie had decided not to take any notice of Marie Louise's entry into Vitry, but she could not help feeling a spurt of excitement when the sound of galloping horses drew her to a window just in time to glimpse the couriers, their jackets covered in dust and their horses flecked with foam, riding into the Place d'Armes and hear them shout, "The Empress is at your gates!"

Minutes later a cortège rolled by at so breakneck a speed that all that was visible of the Empress was the skirt of her amaranth dress embroidered in gold.

"Do you know who were the ladies accompanying the Empress?" Eugénie asked her mother idly.

"One must have been her sister-in-law, Caroline Bonaparte, who calls herself Queen of Naples." Madame de Coucy's unaristocratic sniff was distinctly audible. "The other no doubt was her Lady of Honour, the Duchesse de Montebello."

—◆〖〗◆—

Eugénie hid her amusement that, in spite of her avowed anti-Napoleonic feelings, her mother seemed to know so much about the Imperial entourage.

"What exactly is a Lady of Honour? She must be someone important to ride in the same carriage as a Queen and Empress."

The question aroused sad memories in Madame de Coucy, who remembered the Princesse de Lamballe, Lady of Honour to Marie Antoinette, in all her youth and beauty, and her tragic end, her severed head paraded on a pike and her body subjected to unspeakable obscenities.

"But what does a Lady of Honour *do?*" Eugénie persisted.

"Her duties and responsibilities are endless—she has sole charge of the Queen's household or, in this case, the Empress's. She arranges the rota of ladies and gentlemen in waiting, whom the Empress should receive and how much and to what charities she should contribute. She is the most important person near the Empress and has great influence."

"Then I should not care to be a Lady of Honour." Eugénie tossed her head. "I want to be free to come and go as I wish."

"My dear child, you will be free to come and go only as your husband permits."

"But I haven't got a husband," muttered Eugénie petulantly; she lived in a constant state of anxiety that her most intimate friends at the convent might marry before she herself did.

Whenever they were out of earshot of the nuns, the girls' talk was all of marriage and the final months of their schooldays seemed interminable but inevitably the last day came. Before saying their farewells Eugénie and her two closest friends, the two Paulines, Pauline de Cloys and Pauline de Montendre, strolled under the lime trees of the convent garden.

A marriage had already been arranged for Big Pauline, Pauline de Cloys, who listened with a superior smile to the earnest discussion of the other two.

"Who knows if we shall ever meet again?" said Eugénie

sadly. "Little Pauline will return to Abbeville in the north while Big Pauline—lucky Pauline—is to live in Paris, while for me there is no change of scene; I shall remain at Vitry."

Overcome by the thought of their separation, the girls walked on in silence until Little Pauline came to a sudden stop.

"Promise me, Eugénie, promise me that you will send me news of your betrothal with a golden ring—you can send the details later."

Slightly chagrined that it was Little Pauline who first thought of this romantic notion, Eugénie determined to improve on it.

"Yes, I will, but if your betrothed or mine is decorated with the Legion of Honour I think we should add a star to the ring."

"Two stars for a baron!" riposted Little Pauline.

"Then three for a count!"

"But what for a duke?"

The three girls laughed merrily at the ridiculous idea of so brilliant a marriage for either of the two who were not yet bespoken.

"Oh, for a duke nothing will do but a spray of diamonds."

Eugénie had secretly long been worried if she would ever be able to send Little Pauline even a golden ring. Although Madame de Coucy kept her own counsel her daughter knew that her mother's straitened circumstances were making it difficult to provide her with an adequate dowry. Perhaps, Eugénie thought mournfully, the marriage, for which she herself felt the time had long since come, might be so delayed that in desperation she would be obliged to accept an offer from the first person who made it, even from someone she disliked.

When she ventured to suggest this to her mother, Madame de Coucy was displeased.

"Naturally, Eugénie," she said repressively, "I should never force you to marry anyone you positively disliked but, when the moment comes to arrange a marriage for you, you will of course be guided by your family's advice. In a matter so serious as her marriage a girl must always be guided by the advice of her elders."

It was not in Eugénie's nature to sulk, nor did girls of her age and class argue with their parents, but she found it hard to be patient. Her hopes rose when Madame de Coucy announced her intention of selling her property at Merçuay, confirming her daughter's suspicion that the sale was necessary to increase her portion.

"You know how long I have hesitated to sever my links with the home where I spent so happy a childhood and the early years of my married life." In spite of her resolution Madame de Coucy sighed. "But, as we are now so definitely settled at Vitry, it is obvious that I shall never again occupy the château."

Whatever her mother's reason for selling Merçuay, the prospect of a journey was exciting to Eugénie, who had never travelled farther from home than Bar-le-Duc but, when the trunks were corded and a chaise hired, she was seized by a strange presentiment—they were not going to Merçuay!

"What nonsense is this? Of course we are going! All our preparations are made and I can conceive of nothing which should stand in our way."

Eugénie was silent but her firm belief that they would not go was confirmed when a letter from Monsieur de la Guérivière caused Madame de Coucy to ponder for a long time. She did not disclose the contents to her daughter nor did Eugénie ask; if her mother wished her to know she would tell her, but when the Comtesse sent a servant to Lentilles to request the Chevalier de Coucy to come to Vitry without delay, she guessed that the letter contained something of importance because, ever since the Comte de Coucy's death, his widow had relied on his brother's advice when faced with a problem she felt unable to solve alone.

Eugénie was not present at the conference between her mother and her uncle but, as the upshot of their deliberations was the postponement of the journey to Merçuay, Madame de Coucy was obliged to take her daughter into her confidence.

"I should tell you, Eugénie, that the letter I received from my son-in-law enclosed an invitation to a soirée to be given by Marshal Oudinot which he is most insistent we should accept."

She paused, looking to the Chevalier to know whether she should continue; when he nodded approval, she went on.

"I may be at fault in telling you this, but you are a sensible girl and nearly eighteen. Your uncle and Monsieur de la Guérivière are both of the opinion, with which I am inclined to agree, that we should accept this invitation as they believe that the Marshal may have something in mind as he asked my son-in-law a number of questions about you."

Eugénie flushed with excitement. "Something in mind" could only mean some project of marriage, with one of the young officers on the Marshal's staff perhaps, even with the aide-de-camp with whom she had danced, but the Chevalier thought it advisable to warn her kindly, "Of course we may all be mistaken and this invitation is merely courtesy on the Marshal's part to Christine and her husband who has official dealings with Oudinot."

This reasoning did not impress Eugénie. If mere politeness was the motive for the Marshal's invitation then why was he so insistent that she and her mother accept it? She preferred her own interpretation, but she did not voice it, sure that her mother and uncle would dampen her enthusiasm, no doubt because they did not wish her to be disappointed.

As usual when the de Coucys visited Bar, Christine sent her calèche to fetch her mother and sister as they were too poor to keep their own carriage, but Eugénie paid scant attention to the road they were travelling, in any case familiar to her. She was wholly absorbed in the important question of what she should wear at the soirée, unable to decide between the blonde or the muslin of her two evening dresses, sighing that there had been neither time nor money for a new one to be made. Abruptly she was shaken out of her thoughts when one of the horses stumbled, overturning the caléche. While the coachman struggled to calm his frightened beasts the de

Coucys managed to scramble out to find that fortunately they had suffered no great harm; Madame de Coucy had sprained her wrist and Eugénie's eye was badly bruised, painful and unsightly, but the injury was not serious.

"Why, oh, why," wailed Eugénie as she picked herself up off the ground, "did I say we were not going to Merçuay? By now we would have been safely on our way."

"Nonsense, child, don't get hysterical!" Madame de Coucy's reproof was the sharper because she herself was so shaken by the accident but, when at last they arrived at the Rue du Bourg, she submitted to Christine's insistence that she call a doctor.

"I was dining with the Marshal," the doctor told Madame de Coucy as he bound up her wrist, "when Madame de la Guérivière sent for me. He was extremely distressed to hear of your mishap."

The Comtesse inclined her head. Mere politeness on the Marshal's part, she thought, but she regarded his courtesy as officious when Oudinot immediately cancelled his soirée. To her surprise he called in person not once but repeatedly to enquire after Eugénie's progress, continuing his visits even when her eye had regained its normal colour and the doctor pronounced her completely recovered.

Madame de Coucy was at a loss what construction to put on these attentions to so young a girl as Eugénie by so prestigious a figure as Marshal Oudinot, Duc de Reggio, banishing as absurd the unwelcome suspicion that the "something in mind" he had for her might be for himself. Now, with Monsieur de la Guérivière's abrupt question, "Eugénie, will you marry Marshal Oudinot?," she knew her surmise to have been correct, but it was Christine who voiced her own incredulity.

"Surely you are jesting, *mon ami*," she broke the silence to say to her husband. "The Marshal's acquaintance with our dear Eugénie is of the slightest; he cannot be serious in wishing to marry her."

"Believe me it is no jest," Monsieur de la Guérivière replied emphatically. "If you will permit me to repeat the substance of my conversation with him you must agree with me that Oudinot is both perfectly serious and impatient to receive Eugénie's answer to his proposal."

When his recital ended Monsieur de la Guérivière waited in some anxiety to hear his mother-in-law's reaction but, as she maintained her silence, he was obliged to direct his next speech to her albeit with some hesitation.

"You may, Madame la Comtesse, consider my point of view too material," he said, "even perhaps unduly favourable to Marshal Oudinot, but you must agree, madame, that the prospect offered Eugénie is dazzling and one quite beyond her expectations. While sharing your devotion to our legitimate sovereign and your principles, nevertheless I recognize that the present régime gives every appearance of permanence nor can we ignore the trend of society, deplorable though it may seem to us. The days are gone, perhaps for ever, when a man's birth counted for more than his deeds but do not, I beg you, take this opinion as treachery to our caste. Simply my position forces me to adopt a point of view more worldly than yours. Although not our equal by birth, yet Marshal Oudinot has shown himself a good Frenchman, an honourable man of outstanding courage which has taken him to the greatest heights. Should we not regard these qualities as recommending him even to a de Coucy?"

With some constraint Madame de Coucy murmured that she had been pleasantly surprised by the Marshal's gentlemanly appearance and manners; she had anticipated someone much more uncouth. Whatever her own feelings about his plebeian origins, she was certain that, were Eugénie to accept his offer, she would never forget that she was born a de Coucy nor all she owed to the name and great traditions of her ancestors.

The de la Guérivières, anxiously awaiting the decision Madame de Coucy would make for her daughter, were aware that she had brought Eugénie up to regard Napoleon Bonaparte as a usurper. Would she veto out of hand an alliance with one of his Marshals which would take her into the enemy's camp and force her into allegiance to the man her mother detested, or would Madame de Coucy accept her son-in-law's argument and do violence to her cherished beliefs? To their extreme astonishment Madame de Coucy waived her right to decide Eugénie's future.

"In the extraordinary circumstances of this offer you naturally look to me for guidance, which is only proper," she said slowly, seeking her daughter's direction in the darkness, "but, although conscious of the responsibility I am putting on your very young shoulders, I have reached the conclusion that I should neither advise nor influence you in any way. One thing only I would ask of you, that, as Marshal Oudinot has so frankly outlined the advantages and disadvantages of marriage with him, whatever your decision may be you will not be so discourteous as to keep him awaiting your answer too long."

Monsieur de la Guérivière could not help his amusement that Madame de Coucy seemed to attach as much importance to the politeness which she regarded as an essential element in the aristocratic code of conduct as to her daughter's future.

Eugénie gave no sign that she had heard her mother's speech, her mind a jumble of words—"a golden ring," "a ring with a star," "for a duke nothing but a spray of diamonds." Marriage was the sum total of her ambition but *this* marriage, this cold, calculated offer so remote from her romantic dreams? How arrogant was Marshal Oudinot's insistence on his wealth, his social position, his establishments and his need of a wife, but of Eugénie herself nothing but her suitability to fill the role he designed for her, no hint that he wanted her and her alone—and how peremptory was his demand for an early answer, treating her like a column of his grenadiers waiting to manoeuvre at his command!

What was the Marshal's motive in making her an offer of marriage? Was it her impeccable lineage? How often had she heard her mother and her friends sneer at Bonaparte's policy of fusing the old aristocracy of birth with his new aristocracy of the sword by promoting marriages between the higher ranks of his army and young girls of the old nobility. Was she herself merely an instrument of this policy? Eugénie was ready to acknowledge that Marshal Oudinot had won honours even exceeding those earned by her own ancient and distinguished family, but what had she to offer him save her youth and the noble birth he lacked?

Her friend, Adèle Boulon de Chavanges, had married a man many years older than herself known as the most foul-mouthed old revolutionary in the Imperial entourage, yet the news had trickled back to Vitry that she was enjoying great success at the Tuileries, peacocking as the Maréchale Augereau, Duchesse de Castiglione. Between the two Marshals Eugénie was ready to concede that any comparison could only be in Oudinot's favour, but what did she know of him? Madame de Coucy had assured her that she would never be forced into marrying anyone she positively disliked, but her acquaintance with the Marshal was too slight for her either to like or dislike him. All very well for her mother to say that love came after marriage, but where was the certainty?

Never yet had Eugénie been obliged to make any decision of importance without reference to her mother, so why should Madame de Coucy saddle her with the burden of determining her whole future, failing to give her the smallest hint of what she should decide, but even Madame de Coucy's wishes mattered less to Eugénie than Eugène de Villers's; months must pass before she could hear from him and she must not keep the Marshal waiting!

Had Eugène's been the offer of marriage, how eager would have been her response, but she was desolately aware of deceiving herself if she believed that he wanted her any more than she wanted Marshal Oudinot, yet while a vestige of hope remained—for might not Eugène change his mind about her?—she could not marry the Marshal.

Eugénie opened her mouth to tell her family what she had decided but, to her horror, the words that tumbled out were, "Tell Marshal Oudinot that I accept his offer."

The opening and closing of the door told her listeners that she had fled from the room, leaving them as astonished by her answer as she herself.

--◦◦❦ ❧◦◦--

$-\cdot\!\!\twoheadrightarrow\!\!\{\,2\,\}\!\!\twoheadleftarrow\!\!\cdot-$

". . . And at the point of his sword the Seigneur de Fayel forced his wife to eat the heart of Raoul de Coucy, whereupon the Lady of Fayel took a vow never to eat again and slowly faded away from starvation."

Eugénie's childish imagination had been captured by the story of her ancestor, Raoul de Coucy, the soldier poet who, as he lay dying during the Third Crusade, begged that the heart which had beaten only for his Saviour and the Lady whose guerdon he wore upon his sleeve might be taken back to France for her to cherish.

Fancying herself a lady of high chivalry, Eugénie would refuse to eat until scolded by Rosalie—dear Rosalie, who saw nothing romantic in the *Châtelain de Coucy*—only saying sourly that Sieur Raoul's heart must have been pretty noisome after its long journey from the Holy Land to Fayel.

At this crisis in her life it was to the Lady of Fayel and Raoul de Coucy that Eugénie's thoughts returned, hopeful of emulating their courage and constancy but, aghast at her impulsive acceptance of Marshal Oudinot's offer, she gained no comfort from them. Why had she uttered the words, so contrary to her intentions but irrevocable? No de Coucy ever went back on his or her word!

Throughout the night she continued to seek what mysterious influence, over which she had seemed to have no control, had prompted her decision, but by morning she was no nearer finding an answer, still less of discovering in herself any spark of feeling for Marshal Oudinot.

Wisely Madame de Coucy left her alone. When Eugénie came downstairs she was pale but resolutely composed but, after one swift glance at her daughter, her mother began to speak of indifferent matters; she would go to Merçuay later on; should Eugénie now not wish to accompany her she was sure she might count on the Chevalier de Coucy's escort. Eugénie guessed that, now her marriage was settled and the size of her dowry of no interest to the Marshal, her mother would perhaps reconsider parting with her old home as the sacrifice might no longer be necessary.

Too proud to ask whether Monsieur de la Guérivière had already sent the estafette to Plombières, Eugénie held a little aloof from her mother and sister as she alternated between dread of the Marshal's return to Bar and anxiety to have done with the embarrassment of meeting him as her future husband. Foolish little things worried her—how she should address him and what she should wear—but the greatest anxiety she felt was meeting the man with whom she was barely acquainted but to whom, she supposed, she was now betrothed. Brought up in the strictest propriety, she had never been alone with any man except Eugène de Villers, but then she was too young for it to matter.

When at last Pils came to the Rue du Bourg to announce that the Marshal had returned to Bar and that he would present himself within the hour, the moment came all too soon for Eugénie, who clung to her mother in panic, the rigid control she had kept over herself in her presence crumbled away.

"Eugénie, you are being childish," Madame de Coucy reproved her. "Monsieur de la Guérivière naturally informed the Marshal of your acceptance of his offer but he rightly expects to hear you confirm that answer from your own lips. Diffidence and modesty I expect from you, but cowardice and irresolution have no place in a de Coucy."

Her mother's rebuke served to increase Eugénie's distress but escape was impossible as the sound of carriage wheels was heard outside the house. Madame de Coucy gave Eugénie a warning glance as she left the salon when the servant scratched on the door to announce the Marshal, who entered with a lithe and eager step to take Eugénie's hand, lightly kissing her fingers.

"Mademoiselle de Coucy, in consenting to become my wife you have made me very happy. May I now hear from you yourself the decision I have already heard from your brother-in-law?"

Paralysed with nervousness, Eugénie stood silent as a statue, desperately summoning the Lady of Fayel to her aid until at last she managed to stammer, "I consent."

The bald words seemed to satisfy the Marshal as, still with her hand in his, he led her to a sofa, sitting down beside her while he outlined what the future held for her.

"Until now you have been a daughter in your mother's house with few duties and responsibilities but, when you marry me, this will change; you will have charge of my household at Bar and my country house at Jeand'heurs, nor will that be the end of your obligations. In return for the benefits the Emperor confers on his Marshals he requires us to keep the state befitting our rank and fortune. In Paris I have a small house in the Rue de Bourgogne where we will stay when we attend the Tuileries. You will naturally be invited to join the Empress's *cercle* and, whenever the Emperor himself or a member of the Imperial family visits Bar-le-Duc, it will be your duty to entertain them. While I am at home I shall, of course, give you my support but, as you already know, I am obliged to absent myself for long periods at a time."

Eugénie felt a touch of malice in the Marshal's words as if he took pleasure in frightening her about the future since he was well aware how quiet her life had been and how remote from these pomps. Possibly he sensed her feeling because he now turned to another subject.

"It may not yet have occurred to you that, given the difference in our ages, you will still be a young woman when I am an old man, that is if I survive, because even a Marshal's life is full of hazard."

This, at least, Eugénie knew because Eugène de Villers had been at pains to dwell on the magnetic attraction Marshal Oudinot possessed for the enemy's fire.

"We soldiers, Eugénie—I have no use for ceremony—always go into battle confident of victory." He edged closer to her. "You need only to take a leaf out of my grenadiers' book to overcome all obstacles, to be not my infernal but my celestial column."

Oudinot felt he had now said enough and that the time had come to show himself a man of action rather than of words. Taking Eugénie in his arms he kissed her repeatedly, holding her in a tight embrace until she succeeded in breaking away.

"Come, come, Eugénie, don't be a goose!" he adjured her. "To be timid and retiring is natural and proper in a young girl but out of place in one about to be married. Are you afraid of me? A soldier's wife must never show fear, especially one of your birth and upbringing. Look at me! Away from the enemy I am the most harmless creature alive."

But Eugénie's eyes remained downcast as she faltered, "I am sorry—it is too soon—I am not yet accustomed to the idea of marrying you, Monsieur le Maréchal, of being your wife. To me you are still a stranger."

A little touched by Eugénie's pathetic apology, the Marshal conceded, "Perhaps I am too impatient, should have given you longer to enable you to know me better, but the service of the Emperor leaves us, his soldiers, little time for courtship. I admit my fault—you are even more inexperienced than I had imagined, yet it is your sweet innocence which attracted me. Once we are married I assure you that this will change but, although my fervent desire is to marry you without delay, I am obliged to leave you.''

To himself rather than to Eugénie he muttered, "When that idiot, Louis Bonaparte, took it into his head to act like a Dutchman born instead of being merely the Emperor's lieutenant subservient to his commands, at least he had the good sense to quit the Dutch throne, which forced the Emperor to annex the Netherlands and send French troops to keep order, the army I have the honour to command.''

The Marshal was speaking of matters of which Eugénie was totally ignorant; at her convent she had been thoroughly grounded in the achievements of the Bourbon kings, but of the Emperor Napoleon she knew nothing save the bitterness he had engendered in her family and their friends.

Idly playing with Eugénie's fingers, the Marshal continued, "I am required to remain in the Netherlands until the Emperor and Empress make their proposed tour of the country, for which as yet no date has been fixed, but of one thing you may rest assured, that as soon as I am permitted to return, I shall do so with the utmost speed.''

He made no further attempt to embrace Eugénie, shortly afterwards taking his leave. She could not suspect how great was the restraint he was putting on himself although at his now daily visits she began to wonder whether he were not teasing her when he talked about her appearances at Court, how everyone at the Tuileries would be curious to see the new Maréchale, but also that she would discover the jealousy existing among the Marshals whose wives naturally echoed their husbands. Since Oudinot himself was on good terms with the Ducs d'Auerstadt and Albuféra, Eugénie would most probably make friends with the Maréchales Davout and Suchet while no doubt her friend, Maréchale Augereau, Duchesse de Castiglione, would guide her in the strange surroundings, but Oudinot warned:

"Now that the Emperor has married the Archduchess Marie Louise the old nobility has ousted us, whom *your* caste call parvenus, but as a de Coucy no doubt they'll take you to their hearts. Etiquette is now so rigid that at times we of the

--◄ ►--

old brigade wonder whether we are at Versailles in the time of Louis XIV rather than at the Tuileries at the Court of Napoleon I. Have no fears that anyone will outshine you; I shall see that your dress and diamonds are equal to the best."

The Marshal was mistaken if he hoped to impress Eugénie with his generosity. Her mind was fixed only on the day of his departure for Holland but still he lingered awaiting his orders. His frequent visits to the house in the Rue du Bourg had not gone unnoticed in Bar, where speculation was running high as to his intentions, already the subject of much gossip since the cancellation of his soirée. To scotch the rumours flying about he proposed to give a large dinner party when he would announce his betrothal, telling Madame de Coucy that he had no desire to conceal his happy situation.

She acquiesced politely but Eugénie, shrinking from meeting the curious faces of his friends, begged her mother not to insist on her going, only to meet a stern refusal.

"I am out of patience with you, Eugénie. Remember that you yourself will shortly be presiding at the Marshal's table so you must learn to take your place at it. As for being nervous at meeting his friends! You have only to remember at all times that you are a de Coucy and if Marshal Oudinot honours you by making you his wife, you honour him by taking him as your husband."

This haughty pronouncement confirmed Eugénie's suspicion that her mother still found difficulty in reconciling herself to her daughter's marriage to a brewer's son. Happily for both de Coucys the dinner passed off better than either had expected, Madame de Coucy obliged to admit that the Marshal was an accomplished host, while Eugénie was relieved that he treated her with formal courtesy; but a far greater ordeal loomed ahead of her.

As the date for his departure from Bar was now fixed the Marshal was anxious that, before he left, Eugénie should visit his country estate of Jeand'heurs, which he had lately acquired with the handsome endowments accompanying his dukedom and marshalate. The ancient abbey of Jeand'heurs, once the property of the Premonstratian Order, had suffered many vicissitudes until the Revolution, when the monks were dispersed and the buildings sold as national property.

As soon as he bought Jeand'heurs the Marshal set about restoring and embellishing his estate, set delightfully in the splendid wooded country some seven miles out of Bar-le-Duc. He demolished the abbey church, too ruinous for preservation, rebuilt the imposing staircase of what was now a château and furnished the great salons with the finest productions of the Paris cabinetmakers, but it was the park, some five miles in circumference, which was Jeand'heurs' chief glory. Here Oudinot created a French garden, made rides through the beech woods and built a tower, dedicated to the grenadiers who had served under his orders. Near the château itself he set up a trophy of his Italian campaign, a cannon called the Mincio to commemorate Napoleon's passage of that river in 1800.

"I shall have the Mincio fired to celebrate our wedding," the Marshal told Eugénie gleefully. "It is always fired to celebrate some great event, and what could be more important than our marriage?"

Eugénie merely nodded, shying away as she always did whenever Oudinot spoke of the day she dreaded so much. She was blind to the magnificence of the château, indifferent even to the beauties of the park, thinking only of the unwelcome prospect of spending whole days with her betrothed whom until now she had seen only for short periods at a time. Her fears were realised when the Marshal, with an indefinite absence ahead of him, felt justified in relaxing the tight rein he had been keeping on himself.

Suggesting to Madame de Coucy that she would find it too fatiguing to accompany him and Eugénie on a tour of his domain, he dispensed with her chaperonage to wander alone about the woods with her daughter who, after two days of these solitary walks, was so wretched that she begged her mother to take her away.

In Madame de Coucy's presence the Marshal's conversation was only of the improvements he intended to carry out at Jeand'heurs, enlarging the stables, arranging galleries to house his collection of arms and armour and busts of all the Marshals and a library for his books, but it did not take much for the Comtesse to guess that, alone with Eugénie, he might be less circumspect in his propositions and behaviour. Because she blamed herself that she had left her daughter so unprepared for an intimate relationship with a man, although that was the way in which she herself had been brought up and respect for tradition was one of her guiding principles, she upbraided Eugénie severely.

"What is this nonsense? How can I tell the Marshal, who has only a few days longer to spend in France, that you wish to leave him, to leave Jeand'heurs of which he is so proud and where every attention is paid to your comfort?"

Eugénie found it impossible to explain that it was not the grandeur of Jeand'heurs, but the Marshal's ardour which was responsible for her misery, that when they were alone he lost no opportunity of making violent love to her. She could only repeat her entreaty to return to Bar which finally, although with the greatest reluctance, Madame de Coucy was obliged to permit.

Oudinot made no demur when the Comtesse informed him of Eugénie's wish to leave Jeand'heurs, but it was obvious that he was deeply offended which encouraged her, anxious to put as much distance between them as possible, to hope that her immaturity would cause him to regret his choice, even perhaps to cry off!

Having gained her point in leaving Jeand'heurs, Eugénie dared not protest when her mother insisted that instead of returning to Vitry they remain at Bar until the Marshal left for Holland. Madame de Coucy had no intention of telling her daughter that, however little she herself cared for the alliance, a rupture now must seriously damage Eugénie's prospects of another marriage. As the Marshal gave no sign of life Madame de Coucy's anxiety increased but, the day before he was due to leave Bar, he called at the Rue du Bourg. The Comtesse had time only to whisper urgently, "All I beg of you, Eugénie, is to think carefully before you take any step which you may regret for the rest of your life."

Merely bowing to the Marshal as he entered the salon,

she whisked herself away. Without greeting Eugénie, he addressed her coldly, his face set in stern lines.

"Mademoiselle de Coucy, I find you frigid and unresponsive, unable apparently to realise that you are no longer a child but a young woman about to be married—if you do not understand what marriage entails then I must request Madame de Coucy to enlighten you. From my affianced bride I have the right to expect some sign of affection—not only do you show me none but, whenever I approach you, I am repulsed so that at times I have felt in you a positive dislike."

Eugénie was fully conscious of meriting the Marshal's reproaches but, her tongue tied by the restrictions of her upbringing, she managed only to stammer, "Monsieur le Maréchal . . ." before he cut her short by mimicking her tone.

"Will you continue to call me Monsieur le Maréchal or even perhaps Monseigneur le Duc de Reggio when I get into bed with you? Proud as I am of my marshalate and my ducal title, from you I look for a less formal address. In case you do not know it, my name is Charles."

Shrewdly Oudinot had probed the most sensitive part of her armour, her dread of "what marriage entailed." What she had experienced at Jeand'heurs was enough for her to fear what else might lie in store, of which she had only the haziest notion. Before her lay two alternatives, either to break her word and confess that she could not now marry the Marshal, a course incompatible with the de Coucy code of honour, or steel herself to the inevitable.

Perhaps as angry with himself as with Eugénie, the Marshal was essentially too kind-hearted not to relent when he looked at her stricken face. Speaking now with greater gentleness, he said, "I see now that I have been too rough with you, for which I am sorry. Why should I expect you to realise that soldiers live on borrowed time? You must learn to tolerate my bluntness, to appreciate that my life has been spent largely in the camp and on the field, while you have been shielded, perhaps too much, from the world, too carefully brought up. I must have been at fault, Eugénie, in failing to make you aware of my tender regard for you, that nothing is further from my mind than to hurt you in any way. I promise that I shall be as patient with you as I hope you will be with me so long as you remember that a woman is necessary to me, and for too long I have been without one. Well, is it to be peace or war?''

When Oudinot chose to exercise it, he had an irresistible charm. Even a girl so inexperienced as Eugénie began dimly to apprehend that this was no cardboard figure of a hero, not even the hero of Eugène de Villers's worship, but a man of flesh and blood, ready and eager to entrust her with his domestic happiness. Here and now she must show the same resolution as the Lady of Fayel, make it plain that in chivalry a brewer's son did not exceed a de Coucy. Words were still beyond her but the Marshal, watching her face closely, seemed satisfied by the change in her expression.

"I see that you have made your decision—it is a wise one which I assure you you will have no cause to regret. Only I beg you that, during my absence, you make an effort to understand something of a man's nature. I have given you reason, as we both know, to realise my impatience for our marriage but, in the Emperor's service, our wishes wait on his. As soon as His Majesty gives me leave I shall return to Lorraine as fast as horses will bring me.''

This reprieve, promising perhaps a long absence, enabled Eugénie to steel herself for the Marshal's embrace but, wisely, he merely kissed her hand before turning away rapidly as if not trusting himself to linger.

"Au revoir, my Eugénie. You send away a man much happier than the one who came here.''

A moment later the Marshal was gone.

Throughout the summer Oudinot remained in the Netherlands, curbing his impatience to return as the visit of the Emperor and Empress suffered one delay after another; not until October did they finally arrive.

"I have no doubt,'' Napoleon told the Marshal when he had reviewed his troops at Utrecht, "that our excellent reception by the Dutch people is due to your impeccable discipline and the admirable arrangements you have made. You may take it that I am pleased."

Oudinot seized this moment of the Emperor's good humour to broach his plan to marry, to be gratified by Napoleon's instant approval.

"Go and marry Mademoiselle de Coucy and make me some fine soldiers for my armies—you have only to follow my example." Fondly he took the Empress's hand. "You may bring your Duchesse de Reggio to the Tuileries where the Empress and I will be happy to receive her."

Napoleon seemed in no hurry to leave Holland, touring the canals, inspecting the ports, giving audiences and, as always, finding time for the theatrical performances in which he delighted, rounding off his visit with a grand ball at Amsterdam for the Dutch dignitaries while the Marshal chafed at the delay in obtaining his order of release.

In his brief moments of leisure Oudinot faithfully recorded all the Emperor's activities in his letters to Eugénie, which she dutifully answered in tepid little notes devoid of any warmth or colour. As the months went by without bringing him back to Bar, gradually her fears had diminished only to revive with the news of his imminent return. No sooner had the Imperial cortège crossed the Dutch-German border than Oudinot hastily made his preparations to leave, but it was not until Christmas Eve, 1811, that he arrived at Bar almost as breathless as if he were leading his grenadiers in a hot engagement.

Madame de Coucy was distressed that, so far from overcoming her nervousness, Eugénie seemed even more apprehensive. Obviously some plain words were necessary.

"My dear child, to all women marriage presents a great challenge," the Comtesse told her. "Some accept that challenge to lead useful, happy married lives, but those women who allow thoughts of self to override all other considerations are rarely happy themselves and neither are their husbands."

--◄██►--

Choosing her words with even greater care, Madame de Coucy continued, "Do not imagine, dear Eugénie, that you are alone in fearing all that is required in marriage. I assure you that there is only one bad moment to overcome, but thereafter you will be quite at ease and tranquil if, in the forefront of your mind, you keep the knowledge that marriage leads to the greatest blessing that *le bon Dieu* bestows on women, a child of your own to love and cherish."

Eugénie bowed her head submissively but her mother's lesson would have impressed her less had she not at last received a letter from Eugène de Villers. British victories in the Peninsular had increased the difficulties of communication with the French army so that only at this late date did Eugène acknowledge Eugénie's announcement of her betrothal.

"What stupendous good fortune, dear Eugénie," he wrote, "to marry Marshal Oudinot, to be constantly with him, sharing his glory. I still do not fully understand how your betrothal came about, but I wish you all the happiness you deserve and which no one merits more than he. If ever I come on leave my first visit will be to the Maréchale Oudinot, Duchesse de Reggio, the little sister of whom I am so proud."

All Eugène had then to write was his hope that Eugénie would speak of him to the Marshal, on whose staff he longed to be. Merely as an afterthought did he mention the British victories at Fuentes d'Onoro and Albuera but only to assert his confidence that before long the French would turn the tables on the English Lord Wellington.

After folding up Eugène's letter, for a long time Eugénie gazed forlornly out of the window, seeing nothing but a future in which he would have no part. Had she needed confirmation that all he wanted of her was to serve his interests she had it now so that, when the Marshal presented himself at Vitry, she welcomed him more warmly than she would have done before receiving Eugène's letter. When he told her that he would like their marriage to take place on January 19 she made no demur; since it had to be, the date was a matter of indifference to her.

"The question now is not one of my own anxiety," the Marshal said heavily, "but, as you should by now have realised, I am not my own master. Mounting tension between the Emperor and the Czar is a threat to peace. The army is already massing in the east and His Majesty has informed me that I am to command the Second Corps now stationed in Westphalia."

Eugénie, her mind occupied with a problem remote from war or peace, looked blank, which made Oudinot a little impatient.

"I see that I must explain to you how this probable war has come about—undoubtedly the fault is Alexander's. After our defeat of the Russians at Friedland in '07 he met Napoleon at Tilsit—the setting was romantic, if you have a turn for such things, a pavilion on a raft moored midstream on the River Niemen which divides Prussia from Russia. When the sovereigns emerged after two hours it was not as victor and vanquished but as firm friends. Napoleon had obviously felt the full force of Alexander's charm while the Czar was as clearly bewitched by the Emperor who, when he chooses, exerts powers of seduction as irresistible as his military genius."

Eugénie roused herself from her own thoughts to ask, "Why, if the Czar and the Emperor were so friendly, should there now be war with Russia?"

The Marshal sighed.

"Friendship does not always endure. When the two men met again in the following year at Erfurt, of which I had the honour to be Governor and where the Emperor presented me to the Czar in most flattering terms, the almost passionate sympathy between them, though apparently still as warm as at Tilsit, had cooled as the sovereigns' ambitions and policies were seen to diverge. While the war in Spain continues Napoleon needs Alexander's neutrality, but the Czar refused to commit himself so that where the Emperor had hoped for steel he found only lather. Since Erfurt the rift has widened still further because of Alexander's obstinacy so that war can now scarcely be avoided."

A brooding look fell over the Marshal's face and he was silent. Eugénie was desperately summoning up her courage to speak when in a more cheerful tone and with a smile Oudinot resumed, "Whatever may happen, the Emperor is indulgent enough to permit my marriage before I join my command. All that remains to do before I make you my wife is to take the short journey to Paris to obtain his signature on our marriage contract. What makes you look so confused, Eugénie? I hoped, indeed I was assured, that we had resolved all our difficulties, that you were not still afraid of me."

"No, no, it is not that," she stammered untruthfully. "It is something else . . ."

"Well, tell me—I am here to smooth away all your problems."

Ever since her betrothal Eugénie had been haunted by the need to take the Marshal into her confidence, but she had never felt sufficiently at ease with him to broach the subject—it must be now or never—further delay was impossible.

"I have a—a—confession to make . . ."

Oudinot, in excellent humour, assumed a severe expression as his eyebrows shot up.

"Oho, a confession! Something terrible, I have no doubt. During my absence in the Netherlands you betrayed me, is that it?"

"Of course not! How could you think so? Please do not tease me, it is something quite different. You see, when I was at my convent, I made a promise . . ."

Feeling increasingly foolish, Eugénie revealed her pact with Pauline de Montendre. "But I have no money to buy a diamond spray and nor has *maman*."

"So, my clever little Eugénie secures a duke for herself and expects him to pay her debts of honour." The Marshal roared with laughter. "Well, it has been known that I myself have incurred such debts and the rule in gambling is if you play you must pay."

--••=i( )i=••--

When Eugénie ventured to look at him she saw that the seriousness of his words was belied by the twinkle in his eyes.

"Very well." He heaved a mock sigh. "I suppose I am now compelled to assume responsibility for your obligations so, when I am in Paris, I will go to Nitot, the Emperor's jeweller, to buy a modest spray of diamonds for you to send to your friend, nor should I be surprised if I did not find something for Eugénie as well but, I beg, make no such rash promises in the future or you will bankrupt me."

The Marshal was as good as his word. On his return from Paris with the Emperor's signature on the marriage contract he brought a charming little spray for Eugénie to send to Pauline de Montendre, nor was that all. From behind his back he produced a velvet case on which lay a diamond parure so glitteringly magnificent that Eugénie could only gaze at it in astonishment, completely overcome.

"And in return?"

Eugénie was obliged to submit to a crushing embrace. During the Marshal's absence she had reasoned with herself about her dislike of physical contact with him and believed that she had achieved some serenity. It had been comparatively easy to accept the kisses of a shadowy presence but in his arms all her security vanished. For once he seemed content enough because she had made a tremendous effort of will, or perhaps he was so pleased with his own excitement in offering his gifts that he failed to observe her rigidity.

But there was something more to come. From a pocket Oudinot drew a bracelet which puzzled her by its haphazard variety of stones.

"I hope that when I am away you will wear this always and think of me—I will explain. The cameo stands for $C$, jasper for $H$, amethyst for $A$, ruby for $R$, lapis lazuli for $L$, emerald for $E$ and sapphire for $S$, the whole forming the name Charles. Nitot tells me that these gewgaws are all the rage in Paris."

Eugénie thought the bracelet hideous, consoling herself that she need wear it only when Charles was present. Ac-

companying his words by running kisses lightly up her arm
as he clasped the bracelet round her wrist, he muttered gleefully that January 19 could not come too soon for him.

Although the Marshal would have preferred the wedding
to take place at Bar he had yielded, gracefully enough, to
Madame de Coucy's insistence that it should be at Vitry, the
civil ceremony at the Mairie at eleven o'clock, followed by
the nuptial mass at midnight, preceded by a reception and a
supper for a few relatives and intimate friends.

Marshal Oudinot's interpretation of a quiet wedding
startled the de Coucys because, when he arrived at Vitry on
January 19, 1812, he was accompanied by an entourage
which to Eugénie seemed to number the entire officer corps
of the French army, but which in fact was merely his personal staff. Her role as the Maréchale Oudinot began when
one by one the Marshal presented his aides-de-camp but she
was too confused by so many strange names and faces to retain more than a blurred impression of them all. Only Lachaise she recognized as the young officer with whom she
had danced at Bar two years before.

When everyone had been presented, Oudinot drew
Eugénie aside.

"I have brought with me some gifts which I should like
you to present on my behalf to the men who are in some sort
my children and for whom I hope you will come to feel the
same affection which I am certain they will feel for you."

Timidly Eugénie took the gifts, for one a colonel's ai-
grette in diamonds, for another an emerald and diamond
ring, for General de Lorencez, the chief of staff, the badge of
the Legion of Honour encircled in brilliants—no one was
forgotten. For each as he took his gift and respectfully kissed
Eugénie's hand she managed to raise a tremulous smile. One
gift only the Marshal said he would himself present, an exquisite diamond ring for Madame de Coucy.

"It is a poor exchange for the gift of her daughter to me,
but I trust she will wear it as a sign of my gratitude and esteem for her."

"Nothing, Monsieur le Maréchal—Charles—could give

me greater pleasure than this charming gesture to my dear
mother," but Eugénie's lip trembled as she remembered that
in the new world to which she was now being introduced, a
world of new faces, new attitudes and new loyalties, she
would lack her mother's guidance and help.

The day wore on, seeming interminable to Eugénie
until, when Christine reminded her that it was time to
change her dress, she was granted a brief respite from the
noise and chatter. With her sister beside her she mounted to
her own room where the coiffeur, who had arranged her hair
in the morning, was waiting to adjust her veil of family lace
within a wreath of orange blossom crowned by the diamond
tiara she had found on her dressing table, another of the
Marshal's princely gifts. No one could have been more gener-
ous, but Eugénie looked at the diamonds with lacklustre
eyes.

Christine, guessing something of her younger sister's
feelings, sent Rosalie away and drew Eugénie into her arms.

"Do you remember, dearest Eugénie," she asked tenderly, "how shocked you were to learn that Monsieur de la
Guérivière was eighteen years older than I, yet you have seen
for yourself how happy is our marriage, how loving and con-
siderate is my husband. Believe me, I have no regrets and I
am just as sure that you will have none in marrying a man
older than yourself. After all, in marriage difference in age
counts less than difference in background and ideas. My husband is 'one of us,' sharing our beliefs and aspirations."

Conscious of having said the wrong thing, Christine bit
her lip. What community of beliefs and aspirations could
there be between her sister and Marshal Oudinot, whose origins, upbringing and loyalties were poles apart from
Eugénie's? Lest her sister should be thinking the same thing,
Christine hurried on.

"One thing you *can* do when you are married—try to
curb our dear mother's outspokenness about her opinions,
which have frequently gravely embarrassed Monsieur de la
Guérivière. You know that he is as good a royalist as we are,
but he is also the most loyal of men. On his return from emi-

gration he had only two alternatives, to take a post in the administration or to starve. His sense of honour would be deeply offended if he accepted his daily bread from one hand of the Emperor while biting the other."

Eugénie, feeling a great deal of sympathy with her brother-in-law since she found herself in the same position, murmured that she would do her best as she sighed for Monsieur de la Guérivière, who had once been a soldier and was now tied to an office desk. Eugène, she was sure, would never be able to tolerate a sedentary life. She caught herself up abruptly. In a couple of hours she would marry Marshal Oudinot and never again must she think of another man.

Fearing that anything further she might say would be indiscreet, Christine silently hooked Eugénie into her white satin gown before kissing her affectionately and leaving the room. When at last Eugénie slowly descended the stairs it was to hear her sister, who stood in no awe of Marshal Oudinot, upbraid him for his simple undress uniform.

"Fie, fie, Monsieur le Maréchal, just think how Marshal Murat would put you to shame."

This sally provoked general laughter among the guests who all knew of Murat's penchant for extravagant dress, of the enormous white heron's plume he sported in his shako and his fantastic uniforms which, the Emperor said scornfully, resembled the dress of a ringmaster in a circus rather than that of a Marshal of the Empire.

Oudinot merely grinned, the boyish grin which at times made Eugénie like him quite well, and slipped away, his absence unnoticed as everyone's attention was centred on the bride until a loud knock was heard on the door and a servant announced:

"Monseigneur le Maréchal Oudinot, Duc de Reggio, Grand Cross of the Legion of Honour, Knight of the Order of the Iron Crown."

The guests broke into spontaneous applause as Oudinot strode into the salon in a Marshal's full dress, the seams of his dark blue coat and upstanding collar heavily embroidered with gold oak and laurel leaves, his slender waist swathed in

--◆❧◆--

the many folds of his silken sash, the broad red ribbon of the Legion of Honour slashing his white nankeen waistcoat, on his breast its star and the cross of the Iron Crown. One white-gloved hand rested on the pommel of the diamond-encrusted sword presented to him by the city of Amsterdam, while beneath the other arm he carried his bicorne, edged with snowy white ostrich feathers.

Overwhelmed by his magnificence, visible sign of the honours the Marshal had won, Eugénie humbly took her place beside him at the supper table, likening herself in her white dress to the novice who has yet to prove herself.

But for the aides-de-camp supper would have been intolerable. Eugénie was grateful that their laughter and toasts made her forget how soon she must take her irrevocable vows. Even when they all left the house to drive to the Mairie she was still at a loss to know why she had consented to marry Marshal Oudinot.

The civil ceremony was brief and to the devout and royalist de Coucys both republican and distasteful, but not the mass at the church of Notre Dame in the Place d'Armes, where Nicolas-Charles Oudinot and Marie-Charlotte-Eugénie-Julienne de Coucy knelt side by side to be joined in marriage before men and God.

As soon as the mass ended the Marshal rose briskly to his feet to announce his intention of driving to Bar, brushing aside Madame de Coucy's protest about the bitterness of the weather.

"Pah, with four horses it will take no more than a couple of hours."

The Comtesse could only acquiesce; her daughter's welfare was no longer her responsibility, but parting from her mother proved almost too much for Eugénie, who clung to her in such desperation that Madame de Coucy was obliged to remonstrate with her in a whisper, "Dear child, we are not being separated for long as I shall join you at Bar very shortly—and it is unkind to the Marshal to show such grief at leaving me. From now on your affections are first of all for him, your home is with him. I shall never love you less ten-

-------◆〖〗◆-------

derly, nor will you, I know, feel less loving to me, but you must not distress your husband by letting him suspect that you have any regrets in going with him."

Eugénie knew how wise were her mother's words but she could make no answer, the words stuck in her throat. All she could do was to give Madame de Coucy one beseeching glance before stepping into the waiting carriage, thankful that Christine was accompanying her and the Marshal to Bar and still more grateful that her sister kept up a continuous gay flow of chatter, relieving her of the necessity of talking to her bridegroom.

She must have dozed because, when the carriage came to a halt, she was momentarily at a loss to know where she was before she realised that they were depositing Christine in the Rue du Bourg. Then the carriage drove on to the Hôtel Oudinot over roads covered with a powdering of snow.

The white satin dress was laid aside, the diamonds carefully replaced in their cases. Moments later Eugénie Oudinot was alone with her husband.

## 3

The weeks following her wedding were the most wretched
Eugénie had ever known; everything contributed to increasing her misery. After the modesty of her own home the grandeur of the Hôtel Oudinot was oppressive, the continuous
round of entertaining a strain to one whose life had hitherto
been limited to a small intimate circle. She had to remember
to curb her tongue, to speak not of Bonaparte, the usurper,
but of the Emperor and His Majesty, but worst of all were the
nights when to his love-making the Marshal brought the
same fire as in battle, leaving his young bride exhausted and
sick with revulsion.

As the days advanced, preparation for his new command
obliged Oudinot to confer with his chief of staff far into the
night when the door leading to Eugénie's bedroom stayed
closed, but she remained wakeful, dreading that it might still
open, sustained only by the knowledge that within a very
short time her husband must leave Bar.

Only when the Marshal was securely shut up in his
study did Eugénie revive. Then the aides-de-camp on duty

unbuckled their swords, exchanged their heavy full dress for undress uniforms to dance with the young women invited to dinner. If any one of them had a presentiment that from the forthcoming campaign he would not return he shrugged it off, intent on making the most of the present, yet still anxious to be gone to the war, the reason for his existence, the only life he had ever known. Each nursed the secret hope that a marshal's baton or at the least the coveted epaulettes of a colonel lay in his *sabretache*, or the star of the Legion of Honour or a growled word of approbation and a tweaking of the ear from the Emperor.

Gradually, as the aides' faces become familiar, Eugénie learnt to attach a name to them. To Lachaise she was grateful for the dance which had given her so much pleasure. Most of the others, she was surprised to find, were scions of noble houses, supposing with a touch of scorn that the Marshal liked to surround himself with aristocrats, herself among them. De Bourcet, jolly and plump, always rushed to the pianoforte to play for the dancing; the youngest, de Thermes, scarcely more than a boy, was bashful as a girl; de Cramayel was always joking, de Lamarre coolly polite, de Crillon artist rather than soldier in his bearing. From the rest two stood out; Charles Jacqueminot, arrogantly conscious of his good looks, paid particular attention to Eugénie, trusting that she would further his ambitions by speaking well of him to the Marshal. The other was a hussar, Michel Letellier, a little older than his colleagues, taller by a head and handsome as a Greek god. Only Eugénie, whose own wretchedness made her sensitive, perceived the strain of melancholy underlying Letellier's gaiety.

On the evenings when they danced Eugénie sat alone, wistfully watching the dancers as her foot tapped out the rhythm of the music. The Maréchale Oudinot, Duchesse de Reggio, might be only twenty, but her rank and consequence obliged her to remain a passive spectator of the dancing she adored. She was not aware that Letellier watched her covertly until one evening he came up to her laughing.

"Why do you always sit alone, Madame la Maréchale,

while we are all dancing? Will you not permit me to lead you on to the floor?"

Eugénie could not resist so gaily charming an invitation, forgetting everything but that in Letellier she had found the perfect partner whose steps were in such harmony with her own. The sound of a door opening and closing broke the spell. Charles must have come in—and gone out! Feeling a little guilty, she excused herself to Letellier to slip down to the study to ask timidly:

"Was it you who entered the salon, Charles? Why did you not stay? Can you not spare even a few minutes to relax and enjoy yourself?"

As the Marshal did not look up from his maps, nervously she repeated her question, only to recoil when he at last turned round to show her the sternest face she had yet seen.

"Eugénie, *I* do not dance, for which there are two reasons. My wounds make it difficult and, more important, I consider it unbecoming in a man of my age and rank to jump about with a lot of young people, with my subordinates. The Emperor thinks as I do. At Erfurt the Czar Alexander danced, but not Napoleon. Forty is forty, he said."

Eugénie hung her head to hide her discontent. Naturally she understood about Charles's wounds, but how miserably aware she was of his youthful vigour. Why must *she* not dance because the Emperor did not? Her resentment prompted her to pluck up enough courage to murmur, "But, before the Emperor married Marie Louise, I heard that he took dancing lessons . . ."

"I am not the Emperor," was the cold reply. "A man, let us say in middle life, should not behave like a schoolboy. Dance if you wish, that is if you wish to dance with a man other than your husband, with Letellier, for instance."

There was an edge to Oudinot's voice and his grim expression did not relax. Was it possible that he was jealous? But of what had he to be jealous? That Letellier could make her laugh while he himself did not even try?

"No, Charles," she said a little wearily. "I do not care to

dance with anyone in particular and with no one at all if you disapprove."

As she made her way disconsolately to her own room, the sound of music was wafted up the stairs. For the first time she had found what it meant to be married to a man so much older than herself.

Soon, as Charles spent more and more time conferring with his staff, to her secret joy she realised that the longed-for end was in sight. In a very short time now he would leave for Westphalia where the Grande Armée was massing, by its presence either to bring the Czar to heel or else to launch a massive campaign against the Russians. In a well-meant effort to console Eugénie for the absence of her bridegroom, the aides-de-camp told her that never before had they seen the Marshal, always so eager to go to war, so reluctant to leave home.

"See what you have done to the Marshal, Madame la Maréchale," Letellier teased. "We shall be obliged to ask him to promote you to the staff so that you can come campaigning with us."

"When I was very young, Captain Letellier," Eugénie answered sedately, "I longed to become a soldier, but now I should prefer to stay quietly at home."

"Then, madame, we shall have to persuade the Emperor to wage a short campaign so that we can bring the Marshal home to you as soon as possible."

Only with an effort was Eugénie able to return his smile, conscious of how shocked he and the rest of the staff would be to know that she longed for her husband to go away even, though she stifled the wicked thought, never to return. If only during his absence he would permit her to visit her mother at Vitry and why should he not? Since his establishments continued to run with the same military efficiency as before her marriage her presence at Bar and Jeand'heurs was superfluous. At times she felt that, so long as a woman presided at the head of his table, it mattered little to him who she was and she was certain that in his bed he would far rather have found someone more responsive. Eugénie had to scold herself into remembering that, for better or worse, she was now the Maréchale Oudinot, Duchesse de Reggio, a rank the world might envy but which to her was repugnant since Charles went with it.

When a few days later the Marshal announced that he had a happy surprise for her she assumed that he was about to make her a parting gift of yet another parure of jewels, but the surprise was an unpleasant one.

"As I am reluctant to be parted so soon from my little bride I have decided that you will accompany me on my journey eastwards for as long as I am permitted to keep you with me. The Emperor's irrevocable order is that, immediately the campaign opens, wives must be sent home; nothing and nobody is allowed to distract the armies from their task. Whether or no we fight is still problematical so that as yet I cannot tell how long your stay with me will be."

Nothing could have been more unwelcome to Eugénie than her husband's decision which shattered all her hopes of his lengthy absence.

"Then you have no idea how long I must remain with you?"

"*Must*, Eugénie? How long *must* you stay with me? That does not sound very loving; I had expected some sign of pleasure from you."

Frightened of having revealed her real feelings, Eugénie stammered that she had expressed herself badly: she had wanted to know how much she should pack.

"Oh, if that is all—you should take some of your best gowns because on our way I shall certainly be obliged to do some entertaining."

More entertaining! More curious eyes to whose scrutiny she must submit, but on what grounds could she protest? That she was timid? Of that Charles was already well aware. That she could not feel at ease with new faces, still less with him, that three weeks was too short a time to turn a virtual stranger into a husband even though, as she constantly reminded herself, a husband by her own choice. This was

---··◄◖ ◗►··---

something she must at all costs conceal from him, with the optimism of youth hoping that in time she would be able to reconcile herself to the inevitability of her marriage.

Marshal Oudinot was not deceived by Eugénie's disingenuousness; on the contrary it amused him. He had neither expected nor wanted the response to his ardour of a woman more experienced. His penchant for young girls had dictated his choice of a wife and overcoming Eugénie's resistance was one more battle he enjoyed waging, confident of final victory, although he would allow her no indulgence until he achieved it.

"I know what is at the back of your mind," he teased her. "You are afraid of my finding consolation for your absence elsewhere, but you may rest assured that I shall not take a leaf out of the book of the Marshals in Spain."

Lest Charles should make practical demonstration of his fidelity Eugénie asked hurriedly why he disapproved of his fellow Marshals fighting in Spain.

"My little innocent! What a child you still are, though now you're a married woman I think it will soon be time for you to grow up. It is not in my nature to speak ill of others, but I must tell you that the conduct of some of the Marshals in Spain is a scandal. They make the mistake of believing that, far from the Emperor's presence, they may do as they please, forgetting both that his eyes are everywhere and that he is a prude. He, of course, may do as he pleases although he insists, especially since his marriage to Marie Louise, that everyone else act with propriety, at least in public. In Spain Soult and Victor drag their whores with them even when they are campaigning, two sisters from Seville. I hear they are very beautiful and travel in magnificent style. The troops snigger at 'les Maréchales' as they call them although the Duchesse de Dalmatie and the Duchesse de Bellune are safe at home in France."

Oudinot himself sneered as he added, "Anyway, Victor will shortly be joining us so his 'Maréchale' will be left lamenting because even he would not dare to bring her with him to this campaign. The worst of it is that the senior officers follow the example set by the Marshals. Each has his mistress riding with him escorted by a cavalry trooper—no way to make war! Now I've shocked you, Eugénie, haven't I?''

She was indeed shocked, which was what Charles had mischievously intended, but his own mood changed as he continued:

"Look at Masséna, under whom I fought in Switzerland, who once was a general almost as brilliant as the Emperor himself, but what is he now? An aged and broken man, relieved of his command in Portugal which has been given to Marmont, and all for the sake of a woman about whom he is besotted, although everyone believed him a devoted husband. In general the men tolerate their officers' mistresses— the rank and file have their camp followers and *cantinières*— but Masséna's tart is another matter. He insults his uniform by dressing her as an officer, adding insult to injury by decorating her with the insignia of the Legion of Honour, dishonouring that great distinction men have fought and died to win.''

Charles's indignation gave way to mirth as he chuckled.

"Masséna was fool enough to invite all the other Marshals in Spain to a dinner presided over by his whore. I hear Ney told him what he thought of him—trust *Le Rougeaud* to open his mouth wide! Even though Masséna is my senior I should have done the same. When Ney is on a horse his only rival is Murat but once his foot is on the ground he invariably puts it in his mouth.''

Although repelled by Charles's revelations about the close circle of Marshals which he himself had entered only three years before, Eugénie knew that, having married into the Grande Armée, she must learn to take it as it was, but she refused to believe that all the Marshals were tarred with the same brush, failing to understand that, between a man's conduct in war and his private life, there might be an enormous gulf.

The Marshal rallied her on her shocked expression.

"Come, come, Eugénie, we're not all such bad fellows.

Some of us may be a little lax, but I assure you that even the Spanish Marshals know how to sit tight in the saddle. True," he sighed, "we have suffered some reverses, but that is the hazard of war. I am confident that the situation will soon change and we will chase the English out of the Peninsula."

That was what Eugène had said, and he was fighting in Spain. Surely, if she remembered him only as the friend of her childhood, it could not be wrong to think of him, but soon Eugénie was caught up in her preparations for departure and there was time to think of nothing else.

While the Emperor remained in Paris, giving as yet no indication of when he would join the army, the Oudinots set out from Bar in the dreary February weather of 1812. Eugénie had expected that she and Charles would travel alone but to her surprise she saw a number of carriages drawn up in the courtyard.

"I suppose," he laughed, in excellent spirits now that once again he was going to war, "you thought I sat at a camp fire in bivouac, sharing their rations with the men? On the field, yes, but not in quarters. You have only to look round this carriage to see in what state a Marshal of the Empire travels. The Emperor's coachmaker made this travelling carriage for me, but it is by no means as luxurious as His Majesty's."

Looking about her, Eugénie was sure that nothing could exceed the luxury of the elegant upholstery, the ingenious bookcase convertible into a writing desk, the canteen of solid silver cutlery and her own and Charles's magnificent toilet cases. At that moment he called her attention to the first carriage in line drawing away and she saw Letellier waving gaily from the window. Eager to explain the routine of his march, Charles reminded her that Letellier and Jacqueminot were his first and second aides-de-camp.

"Their duty is to go ahead of us to arrange the change of horses at the posting houses. As my chief of staff de Lorencez travels with me, accompanied by his bride who stays with him as long as you remain with me and will return with you to Bar. My servants and the remainder of my staff make up the rest of the party but, when at Münster we pick up my escort, there will be considerably more of us."

Eugénie's eyes grew wide with surprise.

"How do you think I am to eat if my cooks do not travel with me? I see that I shall have to teach you about campaigning. I have a great deal to teach you, have I not, little Eugénie?"

Resenting the implied reproach, she looked away, blaming his impatience rather than her own shortcomings, but soon everything was forgotten except the novelty of the scenes through which they passed, drawing from her exclamations of wonder and delight even though in the thin mist and drizzle there was little to admire in the mournful countryside.

The Marshal lay back in his corner, his legs stretched out in front of him, listening with amusement to Eugénie's artless comments.

"The world is a big place, isn't it?"

Turning to face him, Eugénie was emboldened to answer, "Yes, indeed, Monsieur le Maréchal, the world may be a big place but, although you have travelled across Europe time and time again, you know very well that I have never been farther from home than Bar-le-Duc." Encouraged by Charles's smile, she added, "Although in this weather I prefer to see the world from the shelter of this comfortable carriage."

"Not I, Eugénie. Nothing would displease me more than to spend the whole of our journey cooped up here."

Eugénie sighed. What wrong thing had she said now? She awaited Charles's reproof, telling her of his eagerness to arrive at their final destination, to join his Corps and prepare for battle, but that was not his reply.

"My wish," he said, "would be to halt somewhere for the night."

Hastily Eugénie turned back to gaze out the window. Why, whenever they were alone, did Charles appear to have only one thought in his mind? Happily for her peace, they were rarely alone since at every halt what seemed an endless stream of officers came to pay their respects to Marshal Oudinot.

"How gay they all are," Eugénie remarked pensively, "that they are going off to war."

"Why should we not be gay? We are all impatient to earn more of the glory which has always awaited us at the end of our march, the glory which for nearly twenty-five years has spread its lustre over the French army wherever it has fought."

At last Charles began to doze, leaving Eugénie to puzzle about men's enthusiasm for going to war. What would they do if there were no war, if the Emperor and the Czar reached an understanding to keep the peace? Then, all the hundreds of thousands of men marching eastwards from France would turn about to home and hearth and the joyous welcome of wives and mothers. How often had she heard Charles hum *"Malbrouck s'en-va-t'en guerre,"* apparently forgetting that the song ended with Malbrouck's body brought home on a litter. She shied away from her reaction should Charles's body be brought home thus. She would grieve for anyone killed in war, but would it be as a wife for a husband?

Only occasionally when on their route the Oudinots met the advance guard of aides-de-camp did Eugénie feel lighthearted as Letellier who, as always, watched her closely, detached himself from the group of young men to stroll lazily over to her to whisper in her ear the latest droll story going the rounds which brought a smile to her serious face. Then, once again he and Jacqueminot departed for the next stage, leaving Eugénie curiously forlorn.

When they had been travelling for six days there came a longer pause at Münster, where Eugénie was dismayed to learn that the Marshal was to give a reception to the officers of his Second Corps, some twelve hundred, all anxious to be presented to his Maréchale. A determined effort of will and a summons to the Lady of Fayel alone carried her through the day to find to her consternation that a fresh trial was in store; the local nobility was as desirous of meeting the young Marschallin as the French officers to greet the Maréchale. Among

--◄❦►--

so many strangers, each anxious to pay her a compliment, Eugénie lost all sense of her own identity, frequently looking round to see who was addressed as Madame la Maréchale Oudinot, Duchesse de Reggio, before she was shocked into realising that it was she herself.

Although even she was losing her enthusiasm for the long daily drives she was glad to be on the move again as each stage forward was a stage nearer to leaving her husband. Now their route lay over the dull German plain but, since the Marshal was busy poring over his maps or conferring with members of his staff who joined them in the carriage, she was not obliged to make painstaking conversation with him, fend off his broad remarks or submit to his lengthy embraces.

Soon she learned the trick of questioning him about the places through which they passed, all familiar to him from his many campaigns in Germany. At Hanover the Marshal was particularly pleased to inform her that the province had been captured from its Elector, the King of England, but at Magdeburg he was less triumphant.

"How well I remember," he mused, "that at Tilsit Queen Luise of Prussia begged the Emperor to allow her country to retain Magdeburg which we captured after Jena in '06. She was a most beautiful woman and Napoleon, with unusual gallantry, presented her with a rose. With a look so beseeching that I doubt if *I* could have resisted it, she implored him to let Magdeburg come with it."

"And the Emperor promised to give it back to her?"

Oudinot pretended to be scandalized.

"Eugénie, Eugénie, I'll never make a general of you! Of course we could not return the city to the Prussians— Magdeburg is of great strategic importance."

Although unable to argue with Charles, Eugénie failed to see why Magdeburg was so important to Queen Luise; it was a dismal place, but she was sorry for the poor Queen who, instead of the city for which she longed, received only a rose which would soon wither and die.

On the approach to Berlin the Oudinots were obliged to

thread their way through long columns of men in full marching order who cheered at the sight of the Marshal's carriage.
He was obviously pleased with this evidence that he was as
popular with the rank and file of his Corps as with the officers, but his good humour vanished when one of the many
estafettes constantly dashing up and down the road thrust
his head through the open carriage window to gasp, "By
order of His Imperial Majesty the Emperor," before saluting
and wheeling his horse towards the direction from which he
had come.

As Oudinot scanned the dispatch his face grew sombre.

"Terrible mistake, tactical error," he muttered to himself,
shaking his head as he repeated the words until Eugénie
dared to ask what was wrong.

"I am deeply concerned," he answered, so irritated that
for once he had to unburden himself to someone, whomever
it might be. "In ordering me to make a triumphal entry into
Berlin at the head of my Corps the Emperor is making a
grave mistake. He should know better than I just how reluctant an ally of France the King of Prussia is."

Working himself into a fury which alarmed Eugénie by
its violence, he stormed, "Does Napoleon think that the
Prussians have forgotten the bitter humiliation of their defeat
at Jena in '06 or that Frederick William has forgiven Napoleon's icy contempt at Tilsit where he treated the King as a
trophy of conquest rather than as a fellow sovereign, made
worse by the affection shown to Alexander? Does the Emperor really delude himself that Frederick William willingly
deserted his dearest friend, the Czar, to become the ally of a
man and a nation he loathes? My intention was to enter Berlin quietly not to arouse more of the King's anger than he
feels at the presence of a French army in his capital. Now the
Emperor decrees otherwise."

Angrily the Marshal tapped the order in his hand.

"An order is an order but . . ."

The stream of language he let out shocked Eugénie so
much that she covered her ears with her hands. How far she
still was from understanding him! If he had much to teach

her, she had still much to learn about him; she had known
something of the Marshal, now she was making the acquaintance of the grenadier.

His burst of anger had relieved the Marshal's feelings
but his face was still dark as he continued passionately,
"Why does the Emperor persist in his refusal to realise the
importance of conciliating Frederick William to the hilt?
When we march against Russia in the spring Prussia will be
the rear link in our communications, and the devil knows
how far they will be stretched. If things should go ill with us,
although that is inconceivable, then the King could cut our
communications and our homeward links. I suppose as usual
it will fall to me to pacify him."

Charles threw himself back on the carriage cushions
with such violence that Eugénie was shaken up, but he had
forgotten all about her. His expression showed how far from
pleasant were his thoughts but she dared not intrude on
them. She was thankful when at last they reached Berlin,
where they took up their residence in the Sacken palace
which the King had put at the Marshal's disposal. However
bitter Frederick William's animosity to Napoleon, to Oudinot
he showed great personal kindness, remembering his chivalrous conduct in Prussia.

Most of the time Eugénie was obliged to remain out of
sight as, in crossing the River Elbe, she had already gone
beyond the limits imposed by the Emperor on the wives of
officers. Glad though she was to be spared the jolting of the
carriage, she found that Charles, however busy, never
seemed to tire. As much as she longed for rest and sleep she
did not know how to deny him, her only support that the
moment of their parting could not now be far away.

Had it not been for the constant menace of the nights,
Eugénie's time was not unpleasantly spent because Letellier
always managed to call to "pay his respects to the
Maréchale." Jacqueminot came frequently too, but he did not
make her laugh as did Letellier, whom she missed when he
was sent forward. She did not, however, lack for company as

Charles was eager to introduce his bride to the senior officers passing through Berlin on their way to the east.

Marshal Victor, Duc de Bellune, Eugénie disliked on sight, both for his arrogance and for what Charles had told her of his discreditable conduct in Spain. Sensing the antagonism between the two men she surprised herself by a spurt of loyalty to her husband when she learned that Victor was not popular with the troops of the reserve Ninth Corps he commanded while she had seen for herself in what esteem Oudinot was held by officers and men alike.

Although Oudinot himself liked Marshal Ney little better than he liked Victor, Eugénie was delighted to meet the hero of a hundred brilliant cavalry charges. Michel Ney, Duc d'Elchingen, was no courtier. Instead of kissing Eugénie's hand, he shook it warmly, keeping it in his massive paw, his speech as forthright as his manners.

"Ha, you old dog," he addressed Oudinot, "you found yourself a very pretty young girl, but a very small one." Eyeing Eugénie's slender figure, he asked, "Don't they come any bigger in Lorraine? But perhaps you've not taken care of that yet."

Eugénie took no offence because she did not understand Ney's sly question but Charles glared at *Le Rougeaud*, who winked at her.

"Marshal Ney," Charles told her icily, "will command the Third Corps in the forthcoming campaign. I hope, Eugénie, that you will remember the names of the Corps commanders so that, when hostilities begin, you will be able to follow the bulletins intelligently."

Nodding dismissal, he walked across the room to open the door for her, but Eugénie went with some regret. She liked Ney's childlike simplicity and would have been happy to talk to him but, as she wished him Godspeed, she wondered what had made Charles so cross. Dawn was already breaking when at last he joined her, having conferred with Ney throughout the night. For once he turned away from her to fall into an exhausted sleep, sighing and again sighing as

---

--◄⊰ ⊱►--

if weighed down by great care, but in the morning he was calm and cool as usual.

Eugénie was permitted to leave her seclusion for the great event of their stay in Berlin, the King's inspection of Oudinot's Corps. From the windows of the French embassy she watched the troops march on to the parade ground, dazzled by the colour and variety of the hussars, cuirassiers, dragoons and lancers, resplendent in wasp-waisted and befrogged tunics, gold-laced dolmans edged with fur slung negligently over one shoulder, brass helmets trailing long black horsehair plumes, colbacks, *schapskas* topped with tall white aigrettes, all in contrast to the sober dark blue of the artillery and the distinctive facings of the infantry, unending columns although this was but one corps of the Grande Armée.

The parade lasted for hours but Eugénie felt no fatigue as she watched it, fascinated by its diversity and magnitude. A feeling she had never before experienced stirred within her, admiration for the great man who had created this magnificent machine, the Emperor Napoleon whose name her mother never mentioned except with a sneer. Surely, if Madame de Coucy, despite her royalist allegiance, had been able to witness this unique spectacle, could she have failed to feel proud of being a part of this Empire, even to share her daughter's sudden realisation that fate reserved nothing better for a Frenchwoman than to live under the reign of the Emperor Napoleon?

When Charles rode down the ranks of his men beside Frederick William for the first time she saw her husband as Eugène de Villers had described him to her, his bearing such that he seemed to be the King's equal if not his superior! Eugénie was forced to admit that it was no negligible thing to be the wife of one of the paladins of the Empire—if only she were able to reconcile herself to the man!

In the Sacken palace that evening as the Marshal unbuckled his sword and struggled to unhook the tight collar of his tunic, she haltingly expressed her pride and admiration of the parade, but he shrugged off her tribute; he did not care for praise. His duty was to turn out a body of men well trained, well equipped and full of fight, and duty was the God he worshipped.

"We did our best," he said heavily, "though I still refuse to believe that Frederick William loves us, but I am satisfied with the discipline of my Corps which will undoubtedly give a good account of itself."

Yet, while the Marshal continued to seem out of spirits, his pessimism was not shared by his generals.

"What a pity," sighed General de Lorencez, "that the Emperor speaks of a three weeks' campaign; there's little satisfaction in a mere walkover."

Far worse, for soldiers thirsting for more glory, should the negotiations still proceeding between the Emperor and the Czar prove successful and there be no campaign at all! But this opinion the General kept to himself since it was obvious that the Marshal neither shared it nor concurred with his chief of staff's sanguine estimate of the campaign which still hung in the balance.

Even Eugénie realised that Oudinot regarded the invasion of Russia as something infinitely hazardous, if not totally misguided but, with the news that Napoleon had rejected the Czar's ultimatum and was preparing to leave Paris for the east, the Marshal regained his cheerfulness which was shared by Eugénie for his departure was the signal for her order of release.

On the morning of May 2 the carriages waited in the courtyard of the Sacken palace to carry Marshal Oudinot and General de Lorencez eastwards and Eugénie and Nicolette de Lorencez homeward to France. So relieved was Eugénie at parting from her husband that she even attempted a response to his last embrace before, next moment, he jumped into his carriage and—"*Fouette cocher! Malbrouck s'en-va-t'en guerre!*"

With very different feelings the two young women watched the carriages out of sight until even the dust had settled before they, too, mounted their carriage and gave the coachman orders to set off. Nicolette de Lorencez, wildly in love with her husband, could not restrain her tears, making

Eugénie feel guilty that she had no regrets, only thankfulness, in leaving the Marshal. Distressed by her young companion's grief, she made an effort to cheer her up by reminding her of a scrape in which they had both been involved,
how they had been unable to control their laughter when a
comical general of the old school, his hair powdered and tied
back in a queue, minced into the room to pay his respects to
Madame la Maréchale and Madame la Générale. Naturally offended by their mirth, he took himself off in a huff.

Eugénie succeeded in bringing a smile to Nicolette's
face, even rousing her to recall that her husband had chided
her for not having more *tenue,* while the Marshal threatened
to send Eugénie home if she did not know how to behave
like a Marshal's lady.

"And we both looked so contrite that the men had difficulty in controlling their own laughter. Then General de
Lorencez said we were only silly young girls and they would
have to forgive us—after all our combined ages added up to
considerably less than either of theirs."

Eugénie had seen Charles's lips twitch when she whispered that between them she and Nicolette could count no
more than thirty-six years.

"I ought to confine you to barracks," Charles had
growled in his parade-ground voice, "but I'm afraid I can't
do without you. I shall have to punish you in my own way."

What that way had been Eugénie had rather not recall.
The moment of which Madame de Coucy had spoken seemed
to be of interminable duration. While Nicolette, although a
bride of no longer standing, was already pregnant and slept
for most of the day, Eugénie was alone with her thoughts.
Was Charles disappointed that she had not fulfilled the hopes
he surely had, which any man must have, or did her uncon-
trollable shrinking from him make him regret marrying so
immature and ignorant a young girl? Was the story Charles
had told her about Marshal Marmont intended as an oblique
reproach?

Although not particularly intimate with Oudinot, Marmont, still flushed with the excitement of being made Mar-

shal, repeated to his colleague the substance of a conversation he had with the Emperor about his "domestic unhappiness" during Napoleon's prolonged stay at Schönbrunn after the great victory over the Austrians at Wagram.

"You will never have a child by Madame Marmont," the Emperor had said curtly, "but you cannot wish a name like yours to die out. If you divorce her, you will be free to choose a wife among the most distinguished families, one who will give you heirs to your rank and honours."

"Of course," Charles had added, "it was only a trial balloon to test Marmont's reactions because, as we later found out, the Emperor had already decided to divorce Josephine since she was not capable of giving him the heir for whom he longed."

Now it occurred to Eugénie that perhaps Charles had married into an aristocratic family not only to leave an heir to his own fortune and honours but to blazon the arms of an ancient line on his own recent coat of arms. Glancing at the girl sleeping beside her, she envied the sweet air of content Nicolette wore even in repose. Should her husband be killed she would have the consolation of his child but what would be Eugénie's own future if her separation from Charles should prove eternal? At the age of twenty she would be the widowed Maréchale, burdened with the responsibility of his two mansions, lonelier because she had known them only filled with gay young men. Her short experience of marriage would not tempt her to marry for a second time, not even Eugène de Villers if he now wanted her. Cowardly though she knew it to be, because Nicolette had her own anxieties, Eugénie could not help confessing some of her fears during their long days together.

"But, dear Duchesse," the child attempted to reassure her, assuming a pretty protective air, "you know that, although the Marshal has suffered so many wounds, he has always made a wonderful recovery. My husband says that all the men the Marshal has commanded believe that a special providence watches over him."

Touched by Nicolette's earnestness, Eugénie kissed her affectionately, after a short pause beginning to speak of the contrast between this and their outward journey. Now there were no unwelcome receptions to attend, no troops to be reviewed and the roads, though dusty, more easily passable. Where the trees had been bare and leafless, they were bursting into a green spring.

When the two young women reached Mayence Eugénie was particularly chagrined to find that they had been travelling on a parallel route to the Emperor who had left Paris on May 9. She would have been so happy to see him but, while she had taken the road by which she had come to Berlin, he had travelled by a southerly route to Dresden where he had set up court with the Empress, his entry into the city greeted by the ringing of bells, salvoes of artillery, lighted flambeaux and all possible pomp and ceremony.

While the Emperor held court at Dresden for his father-in-law, the Emperor of Austria, a host of minor German princes and finally the King of Prussia, Eugénie was on the last lap of her homeward journey. She felt a little prick of satisfaction that the official report had been at pains to stress the excellent reception Napoleon had accorded Frederick William. Charles had been mistaken in believing the Emperor to be unaware of the importance of conciliating the King of Prussia!

As the carriage approached Bar-le-Duc the two young women were on familiar ground, their excitement at being home again growing as they drove through the city where Nicolette was set down at her own house while Eugénie proceeded alone to the Hôtel Oudinot. With no duties to occupy her, she found the house melancholy like all empty houses. She wandered through the rooms, yawning her way until a few days after her arrival she received a letter from the Marshal dated from Marienwerder. To find the place on one of his maps Eugénie went to his study, so charged with his personality that she could almost fancy the scent of his tobacco lingering on the air.

Once, greatly daring, she had remonstrated with him

about his passion for his pipe, only to hear him growl, "In this room I am the Grenadier Oudinot, the title in which I take the greatest pride, and a grenadier smokes a pipe. In your salons, Eugénie, I will play the Marshal but not here; this study is my bivouac."

Seating herself at his desk, Eugénie held a one-sided conversation with the man of whom she thought always as the Marshal, never as her husband.

"Now that I've seen you as a soldier, as a commander, in all your glory as a Marshal of the Empire, I am more than ever at a loss to understand why you married me. Because I am a de Coucy? There is no shortage of girls of the old nobility who would make you a better wife than I, but is that not largely your own fault? Do you ever try to understand my problems, to make any allowances for me? You treat me like a doll to be played with for an hour, then tossed aside."

Eugénie was ready to concede that the Marshal had charm, although for her he had none. Ought one not to love one's husband, she asked herself, just because he was one's husband? Perhaps she had not tried hard enough because she respected, even admired, but could not love Charles.

Once or twice, to break the monotony of roaming restlessly about the house, she drove out to Jeand'heurs, but there seemed little point in opening up the château to stay there alone, especially as one by one the male servants were leaving, conscripted for the Russian front. They came ceremoniously to take leave of her, always with the same parting words.

"Rest assured, Madame la Maréchale, that if we meet Monseigneur we will tell him that you were well and happy."

Happy? Scarcely! Avidly Eugénie studied the *Moniteur*, brought by couriers to Bar four times a week, alternating as she read between longing for wiser counsels to prevail to stave off war and despair that it was inevitable. The first official reports told her little more than that the Grande Armée was pressing eastwards across the Prussian and Polish plains and that at Insterburg the Emperor had reviewed Charles's

--◦◦{ }◦◦--

Second Corps. At least she now had news of her husband, whose letters arrived as slowly as those from Spain. Months had gone by since she had received word from Eugène de Villers, but for him she spared only a passing thought; Charles alone mattered to her now.

No further bulletins were issued while Napoleon lingered at Gumbinnen, convinced that the threat of his massive force of nearly 700,000 men now approaching the Russian frontier would bring a détente, but the Czar's only reaction was his assurance to the French ambassador that the Russians would not fire the first shot though, should they be attacked, they knew how to defend themselves.

On the empty days with no *Moniteur* Eugénie paced the house like a caged lion until the next issue of the newspaper arrived to report that on June 24 the French advance guard, including Marshal Oudinot's Corps, had crossed the River Niemen near Kovno. It was war! Her disappointment was so bitter that she hardly cared to continue reading that the Emperor, mounted on a horse named Friedland, had himself crossed the Niemen where he and the Czar had sworn eternal friendship but the river bore not even a spar from the ark of peace, sunk with all hands since Prussia and Austria were now reluctant allies of the French in the invasion of Russia.

Napoleon, gaily playing with his whip as he tunelessly hummed *"Malbrouck s'en-va-t'en-guerre,"* was in excellent humour in contrast to his mood of the previous day. When reconnoitring the ground on the Prussian side of the river a hare started between his horse's legs, causing the animal to rear and dislodge its rider. The Emperor got to his feet unaided to read on the faces of his entourage the same dismay they saw on his. Whose the voice that cried, "It is a bad omen! A Roman would turn back!"? Was it the voice of a man or the prompting of Napoleon's inner consciousness? For the rest of the day he was silent and sombre but, as on the morrow he rode on to Vilna, hastily evacuated by the Czar, he was animated by the long tale of his resounding victories, confident of winning one more, the great victory all Europe expected of him.

---

Yet, during the fortnight he remained in Vilna, his uneasiness returned, showing itself in hesitation and indecision as the Russian army avoided an engagement but, while the enemy refused to stand and fight, the elements took the offensive. A freak summer storm blew up, terrible in its ferocity, the temperature dropped alarmingly, snow and hail covering the city in darkness at noonday. The storm ceased as abruptly as it began, leaving ten thousand horses lying dead and not a few men. As if this calamitous loss of horses were not enough, the cavalry, already short of forage, lost a further five thousand animals from colic after eating green rye.

Napoleon was imperturbable; replacements would certainly be found on the way but, as he pursued the Russians, still eluding him, the Grande Armée marched through a desert, cattle and horses driven before the fleeing inhabitants. Without transport to draw them, forges with their smiths had been left in the rear, no nails or iron to make them were found in the empty villages and the horses were perforce obliged to proceed unshod.

Happily for Eugénie's state of mind news of this misfortune for the cavalry was not published. Madame de Coucy's arrival at Bar to keep her daughter company was a welcome relief from her oppressive solitude, but not her reproaches for Eugénie's melancholy and idleness.

"I realise, my dear child, your anxiety for the Marshal, but so passive a state as yours achieves nothing," she scolded. "You need to bestir yourself, to occupy your time with something useful. What a pity . . ."

She did not finish her sentence but Eugénie was conscious of what her mother had intended to say, that it was a pity that no child was on the way to give her thoughts a happier direction, a regret she herself had increasingly come to share.

Whenever she visited Nicolette and observed the progress of her pregnancy, Eugénie was convinced that, were she herself in the same condition, she would be content, even to the point of showing something more than mere submission to Charles. Although it was painful to witness Nicolette's

happiness she could not keep away from her, her envy growing with her mounting obsession to bear a child. Even in the
short months of her married life Eugénie had come to realise
that loving was more important than being loved. While certain that she would never be able to love Charles, he alone
could fulfil her desire for a son or daughter to cherish but,
until she saw him again—and when would that be?—her
longing must remain unsatisfied.

When one of Charles's rare letters arrived at last it was
brief, saying little more than that he was in good health and
she was constantly in his thoughts but, although he was now
all-important to her it was the occasional note from Letellier
which Eugénie read and reread. Was it because he confirmed
that all was well with the Marshal? Eugénie avoided asking
herself why she wished that Letellier had given some news of
himself rather than waste precious paper apologising for his
handwriting because his only table was his saddlebag.

"Now that you have news of the Marshal," Madame de
Coucy told her daughter, "I trust that you will make an effort
to curb your restlessness. He would, I am sure, be displeased
to know that your time is spent only in bemoaning his absence."

What would Madame de Coucy's reaction be if she knew
*why* Eugénie bemoaned her husband's absence? Would she
approve or disapprove, or did she believe that her daughter
had become so attached to the Marshal that she could not
bear to be away from him? It did not matter. Her habit of fil-
ial obedience was too strong to flout her mother's urging.
Dutifully she set about carrying out Charles's instructions,
drawn up as precisely as a battle order, for the alterations
and improvements to be made to his houses, yet still her
primary occupation was to search on his maps for the places
figuring in the bulletins.

Hard though she tried, she could make little of them other
than that there was dissension among the Russian generals
and the Russian army continued to avoid a battle. The news
from Spain, though more specific, was far from encouraging
since only British victories were reported—at Ciudad Ro-

drigo, Badajoz and, latest of all, Marshal Marmont's defeat by Wellington at Salamanca. How right Oudinot had been when he told Eugénie he would never make a strategist of her; she did not grasp that the serious turn the war was taking for the French in Spain had its repercussions in the Russian campaign.

Then a cryptic note from Charles, written from Vilkomir, a place so small that Eugénie failed to find it on the map, again threw her into despair although he said only that the enemy's shot would have none of him, his bones were too solid. Charles must not, must *not* die until she had achieved what was now her sole and overriding desire.

Madame de Coucy finally lost patience with Eugénie as she stormed about the house, railing against Bonaparte, against Czar Alexander, against war and the stupidity of men who made war.

"I am surprised at you, Eugénie—your behaviour is most unlike yourself. No good can come of giving way to temper—you will merely make yourself ill," her mother reproved her. "Unfortunately I promised to spend a few days at Lentilles with the family but I hope that, when I return, it will be to find you in a more sensible frame of mind."

So long as Madame de Coucy remained at Bar Eugénie made an effort to control herself, but no sooner had her mother left than her depression and fears returned until the arrival of a package from Berlin offered a welcome diversion. During their stay Charles had sat for a bust intended to take its place in his gallery of distinguished commanders at Jeand'heurs.

Eugénie refused all offers of help in opening the packing case, tearing off the many layers of paper which protected the bust until at last it was revealed, only for a moment later a scream from her bringing servants rushing to the salon.

"What is the matter, Madame la Maréchale? Is there bad news from Monseigneur?"

Eugénie could only point to the bust where one shoulder had detached itself from the neck as she wailed, "It is a bad omen! Something terrible must have happened to the Marshal. Little news has come from him lately and this must be the reason."

Useless for her people to try to soothe her by telling her that the damage was only to a piece of plaster soon mended. Too overwrought to heed them or even to remain passively at Bar, she set off impulsively to Lentilles, seeking comfort and reassurance from her family. When the de Coucys had recovered from their surprise at her unexpected arrival and had chided her gently for her fantasy, her mother and aunt returned placidly to their sewing while the Chevalier de Coucy resumed his reading of the *Moniteur*. For Eugénie's benefit he read aloud:

" 'The Emperor had reached Smolensk, the largest city on the road to Moscow, by forced marches, the city where the Russian army at last decided to stand, to meet defeat at His Majesty's hands. The Russians were forced to abandon Smolensk which our army found in flames when they entered the city. Losses on both sides were heavy.' "

Madame de Coucy and her sister-in-law paid little attention to the report while even Eugénie listened with only half an ear until the Chevalier read on, unable to stop himself.

" 'On August 17 at the moment when the Duc de Reggio was about to cull the fruits of victory, he was shot in the shoulder by a ball. Although the wound is serious there is hope. The Marshal was carried to the rear and is being taken to Vilna.' "

As soon as she heard the name "the Duc de Reggio" Eugénie knew all her foreboding justified. She fell into a faint, recovering consciousness to hear her uncle shouting in her ear, "He is only wounded, *wounded*, that is all!"

For Eugénie, convinced that Charles was dead, it was enough! Slowly and emphatically the Chevalier read the report again until she was obliged to recognize that Charles was still alive, or at least he had been when the bulletin was issued.

Struggling up from the sofa on which she had been laid she cried, "I will go to Vilna! *Maman*, my uncle, do not try to prevent me! If Charles is still living he needs me . . ."

--◦❈ ❧◦--

". . . but not as much as I need him" was her silent thought but one she could not voice. If he were only wounded in the shoulder . . .

"My child," Madame de Coucy's voice was very gentle, "you cannot take so arduous and hazardous a journey alone."

"She shall not go alone; her uncle shall escort her."

Distraught as she was, Eugénie yet threw her aunt a grateful glance while the Chevalier immediately declared himself ready to accompany his niece but Eugénie, at the mercy of her obsession, barely thanked him for his kindness and courage in agreeing to journey with her into the wake of an army engaged in a momentous campaign. She could think only of the damaged bust and her imperative desire to find her husband alive.

To prepare for an immediate departure Eugénie returned to Bar, where she was relieved to find a letter from the Marshal, gazing at it for a long time, fearful of opening it until Madame de Coucy insisted on her doing so.

"My Eugénie," the Marshal had written, "if you hear of my wound from other sources, do not be alarmed for it is not, I hope, dangerous. However, it forces me to leave the army for the rear. I shall not be able to write to you again because of the failure of communications."

That was all. Of the engagement in which he was wounded the Marshal said nothing, nor of the bloodiness of the battle, nor the dysentery rife in the army caused by the oppressive heat which increased his own fatigue and inflamed his wound, nothing of the tender efforts of his staff to make him more comfortable by cutting branches from the surrounding woods to place round his tent to give him some illusion of refreshing coolness.

Even if Charles had written of these things Eugénie would not have cared; nothing mattered to her but her immediate departure for Vilna but her mother, who took a more optimistic view, tried to dissuade her from undertaking a journey so long and so perilous.

"Are you not exaggerating the danger, Eugénie?" she

asked. "The Marshal writes you in his own hand and minimises the gravity of his wound. Wait a day or so when you might have better news which would obviate the necessity of your going to him."

Eugénie's "I will brave all the Cossacks in Russia to reach Charles" surprised her mother who, remembering her timidity at Jeand'heurs before her marriage, had not suspected her of such passion.

While Madame de Coucy stared at her daughter, it was the Chevalier de Coucy, who had accompanied them to Bar, who observed a note which Eugénie had overlooked, attached to the Marshal's letter. Why, when she took the note from her uncle and glanced at the signature, did she feel a slight disappointment? The note was from General de Lorencez, who wrote at the Marshal's bidding to tell her not to undertake the long journey to join him, but the General himself had scrawled, "Believe me, follow the dictates of your heart," perhaps a little wistful that Nicolette would not accompany her.

In triumph Eugénie read the note to her mother and uncle, who found themselves unable to make any further protest since General de Lorencez had cut the ground from under their feet. If he believed that the Marshal would welcome Eugénie's presence they could not prevent her going to him. Now all was bustle and hurry as arrangements were hastily set in train for the long journey, which left Eugénie no leisure to indulge her shame at her hypocrisy.

## 4

In her haste to be on her way Eugénie was irritable with her family, heedless of the fact that her uncle might need a little time to arrange his affairs or to pay attention to the friendly argument between the Chevalier de Coucy and Monsieur de la Guérivière.

"With all respect, sir," her brother-in-law gently reminded the Chevalier, "I am younger than you and better able to support the rigours of the journey. It is I who should accompany Eugénie."

"I agree that you are younger." The Chevalier smiled. "But you have a young wife and family in addition to your work and your career while I have no such responsibilities."

Monsieur de la Guérivière's murmur that he would seek leave from his post was waved aside by the Chevalier who insisted that, as head of the family, it was his duty to care for and protect every one of its members; it was he who must escort Eugénie. Nevertheless, with more encouraging news from Russia, he urged her to postpone her departure at least until the next bulletin was published. Should the rumours of

peace proposals prove correct then undoubtedly Marshal Oudinot would be sent home, rendering his niece's journey un-
necessary, but Eugénie continued adamant in her refusal.
With or without her uncle she was resolute in her determination to go to Vilna.

The check she met came not from her family but from
something she had forgotten until she instructed her coachman to prepare her travelling carriage.

"But, Madame la Maréchale," the man reminded her,
"you lent your carriage to Madame de Lorencez to go to
Paris."

Now she remembered that, when Nicolette told her that
her own travelling carriage was quite worn out and that, during her husband's absence in Russia, she did not feel she
could order a new one as she would be doing no travelling
except to go to Paris for the birth of her child, Eugénie had
immediately offered her the use of her carriage.

Chafing at the delay, Eugénie was forced to wait for
three interminable days while her coachman was sent to
Paris to return with the carriage. For the first time since she
heard of Charles's wound she laughed when Madame de
Coucy urged her to take the magnificent sables which had
formed part of his wedding gift.

"In this weather, *maman?* I should frizzle to death—and
long before winter sets in we will have returned home."

Then she shrugged her shoulders. Why argue about so
trivial a matter when she cared about nothing except to be on
her way?

The excellent state of the roads made progress good
enough to satisfy anyone but Eugénie, for whom the carriage
wheels did not turn fast enough, although at one moment
they seemed to say "Charles is better" only at the next
"Charles is worse." Constantly she urged the coachman to
make better speed until her uncle was obliged to remonstrate
with her.

"Is it not reasonable to remember that bad news always
travels fast? That we have received no news of any kind
suggests that my nephew may already have reached a state of

convalescence and we should therefore regard the absence of anything to the contrary as good news."

Neither moderation nor good sense had any effect on Eugénie, alternating between optimism and despair, although in her more reasonable moments she felt guilty in permitting her family to believe that love of her husband had prompted her to go to him, while her motive was purely selfish.

There was still no news of the Marshal at Mayence, but the travellers were warmly welcomed by old Marshal Kellermann, whose courtesy and powdered wig belonged to another age. He begged them to rest awhile at his nearby estate of Johannisberg, but Eugénie would not stay although her uncle would willingly have lingered for old men's talk of bygone days.

When at Berlin Eugénie found a letter in Charles's own handwriting she felt justified in her haste.

"Much firmer than his earlier letter," the Chevalier approved. "I see the Marshal is taking the journey to Vilna in slow stages and supporting it very well, but how does it come about that he knew you to be in Berlin or indeed that you had left Bar?"

"Because, my dear uncle," Eugénie replied triumphantly, "while waiting for my carriage to return from Paris I wrote to inform the Minister of War of my departure, but I took good care that he did not receive my letter before we left in case he forbade me to go. No doubt he sent one of the Imperial couriers—they travel faster than anyone else—to warn the French ambassador in Berlin not to allow me to proceed and probably he in his turn was able to reach Charles somewhere on his way."

"Then, my dear niece, now that some part of your anxiety is relieved, do you not think we should take a brief rest here? You would not wish to arrive at Vilna in a state of exhaustion. You know that the worst part of our journey lies ahead—and the carriage is in urgent need of repair."

This was the only argument to which Eugénie paid any heed. Rest she was in too febrile a state to take, but she was obliged to concede the folly of risking a complete breakdown of her carriage, so she consented to remain for a few days in Berlin. When the friends she had made earlier in the year came to visit her she was amazed to see that they were loaded with provisions of every kind but, when she protested that on their way they would find everything they needed, wiser heads were shaken.

"An army of seven hundred thousand men has gone before you," they told her. "Please believe us when we say that it would be foolish to depend for supplies on what you may find on the road because without a doubt you will find very little."

One visitor who proffered advice not food was Marshal Augereau, Duc de Castiglione, whose appearance was exactly what Eugénie had once imagined Charles's would be, but she marvelled that her friend, Adèle Boulon de Chavanges, should have married so coarse a man. Neither in manner nor in language had Augereau ceased to be the soldier of the revolutionary armies of '92 but, however rough he was, his heart was kind.

Taking the Chevalier a little apart, he told him that the battle of Smolensk was not the decisive victory the Emperor craved, even though it had achieved the freedom of Lithuania from the Russian yoke and restored the old kingdom of Poland.

"The b—r thought the Czar would sue for peace as soon as his army lost a battle, but Alexander knows his own country better than *Le Tondu*. Alexander says winter will win his war for him but our Emperor expects to have dealt with him finally long before it sets in."

In a still lower voice Augereau warned the Chevalier of the dangers lying ahead, particularly on the next stage of their journey.

"Do not at all costs travel at night with your little lady after you have passed through Kustrin, citizen."

Although shocked by the epithet the Marshal had used for the Emperor and wincing at the revolutionary address to himself, the Chevalier listened attentively as Augereau added:

"Once beyond the Oder you'll find your road lumbered up with all the b—y ragtag and bobtail which follows in the wake of an army, thieves, marauders and worse, the b—rs. Remember, citizen, travel only by daylight and even then stop for nothing and nobody."

The Chevalier thanked the Marshal courteously for his warning which he found sufficiently alarming to reason once again with Eugénie about the hazard of pressing eastwards, but without making the smallest impression on her, so early next day they again mounted the carriage bound for Danzig, Königsberg, Kovno—and Vilna! All too soon they realised the truth of Augereau's admonitions.

The horses, poor beasts, but the best available at the posting houses, sank up to their hocks in sand, slowing down their progress intolerably so that darkness overtook them in the thick forest bordering the Vistula, lit only by the glaring eyes of wolves who howled at the passing carriage. At Marienwerder, where the inhabitants remembered Oudinot's chivalrous conduct when he occupied the town, they were royally received but at the next stage they were even more fortunate because they met young de Thermes, who earnestly assured Eugénie that her husband's convalescence was proceeding normally.

"You know, Madame la Maréchale, we who are privileged to fight under the Marshal's orders are always amazed at his rapid recovery from his wounds. When you reach Vilna the Marshal will welcome you on his own two feet and with both his arms." De Thermes blushed at the image he had conjured up. "I wish, madame, that I might have the honour of escorting you even if only to the next stage, but my orders are formal; I must return to France without delay."

With a final salute de Thermes galloped off before Eugénie or her uncle could question him about the progress of the war, but soon they were heartily regretting that he had not accompanied them, so wicked a pace set by the postillions that Eugénie was convinced the carriage would over-turn.

"Uncle, I am sure they intend to take us to some lonely spot to rob us, even kill us, and we shall never reach Vilna!"

"Do not give way to ridiculous fancies, Eugénie." The Chevalier spoke with greater asperity because the postillions had paid not the slightest attention to his remonstrances at their wild speed. Although he would not admit it, he shared his niece's anxiety. "I warned you that we should take the route recommended to us, but you insisted on having your own way."

"But, Uncle, it was because this was the shorter."

As the carriage bounced up and down they were both obliged to cling to the straps to avoid being thrown on the floor but at last they lurched to a sudden halt. Although expecting a pistol to be brandished in her face, Eugénie courageously thrust her head out the window, only to see the men staggering to the inn where they had drawn up.

"It's all right, Uncle, they're only drunk!"

"I cannot see that is a cause for satisfaction—they could have overturned us just the same."

In their mutual relief at parting with the postillions their brief disagreement was forgotten; Eugénie was ashamed of arguing with her uncle who for her sake had sacrificed his safety and comfort. The least she could do was to make a show of cheerfulness even if she felt none.

Now, with the greater part of their journey behind them, they left the endless Prussian sandy waste, the dirty little inns and revolting food to come in sight of the sea at Königsberg. At any other time Eugénie would have been excited as she had never yet beheld the sea, but she was dismayed when General Loison, commandant of the city, told her that Charles had left Vilna.

"Not in Vilna? He is returning to France then. Shall I meet him en route?"

"No, Madame la Maréchale." General Loison shook his head. "Should Marshal Oudinot be moving at all it will not be in this direction. On September 7 the Emperor won a great victory over the Russians at the Moskowa, a mere seventy miles from Moscow to which he is now marching."

For some days the travellers had been without any news of the Grande Armée but now General Loison read them the 17th Bulletin with its triumphant conclusion that victory at the Moskowa was never in doubt. The truth, as told by the couriers speeding with news of the victory to the capitals of Europe, was somewhat different but the General did not feel obliged to impart it to his guests.

Five times in the sixty days of the campaign the Russian army had slipped from Napoleon's grasp as the Grande Armée, progressively reduced in numbers, marched slowly and doggedly on through the scorched earth of Russia, a country empty and devastated as the Russians left nothing of any use to their enemy. The heat, which caused many deaths through exhaustion, made the march tiring and depressing but when heat gave way to cold drizzle and a violent wind the change in the weather was not welcome, presaging autumn.

The spirits of the French army rose when, in the defence of Moscow, the Russian army stood in the Emperor's path. The bulletin had stressed the Emperor's perfect health while the truth was that he was suffering from a feverish cold and migraine but, as usual on the eve of a battle, he rode along the ranks of his Grande Armée. In the Russian lines the flicker of innumerable torches and the shifting flames of bonfires lit up the night while the chanting of the priests as they. paraded the holy Black Virgin of Smolensk to inspire the moujiks to the defence of Holy Russia added to the weirdness of the scene.

In the French lines the activity was of a different kind as the Old Guard cleaned and polished their weapons, brushing their uniforms to appear as immaculate as if on parade to guard their Emperor who, mounting his horse as the sun rose, exclaimed jubilantly, "This is the sun of Austerlitz!"

But the battle of the Moskowa, a conflict lasting fifteen hours, even bloodier than Smolensk, could not stand comparison with that great victory in Austria. In the hellish terrain of the plateau of Borodino desperate men engaged in hand-to-hand fighting under a hail of grapeshot. Still the Emperor, although entreated to send in the guard, refused to commit his last reserve yet, at the end of that interminable day, the Grande Armée had covered itself with glory, even though, like the enemy, they had lost some 40,000 men, including the staggering total of eighty-nine generals. Once again under cover of darkness the Russians slipped away, robbing Napoleon of the fruits of victory.

Moscow lay seventy miles away. Only in Moscow was peace to be found. With the French army entrenched in his capital surely Alexander would be forced to sue for peace but the Czar, in whose life religion was now the paramount force, had no such intention, convinced of his divine mission to destroy the man, once his dearest friend, whom he now called the infernal being who was the curse of the human race. For that infernal being there was no alternative but to push on to Moscow.

When she had heard General Loison's opinion of the probable whereabouts of her husband Eugénie burst out, "Wherever my husband may be now I shall find him! We have not travelled six or seven hundred miles in order to turn tail and go home. Were it only for an hour I shall see my husband!"

General Loison sighed as he reminded her that the Emperor's orders were formal; no officers' wives were to cross the Vistula and already she was two hundred miles farther on, almost at the Niemen. Any wives who remained in Vilna were being sent back immediately to Königsberg. Eugénie made it plain that this information did not impress her in the least so, again sighing, General Loison tried another line of argument.

"It is my duty to warn you, Madame la Maréchale, that the forward march of the Grande Armée has left the roads in a terrible condition with almost total disruption in the means of transport."

Faced with Eugénie's determination to proceed, finally the General was obliged to admit defeat but his warning proved as valid as Marshal Augereau's. Progress became intolerably slow as now the carriage wheels sank not into sand but mud made glutinous by incessant rain. Such lodging as they found for the night was miserable and Eugénie felt a pang of conscience on her servants' account but even more acutely at her uncle's weariness although he did his best to hide it from her.

"Dear Uncle, I am sure you are not fit to continue this interminable journey." Gently she took his hand. "Can I not persuade you to turn back?"

"My dear niece," the Chevalier reproved her, "your father was not the only de Coucy with a high sense of duty. I undertook to escort you to Vilna, nor shall I leave you until I have delivered you safely to Marshal Oudinot, whom I am convinced we shall find in the city. I cannot believe that General Loison was correct in saying that the Marshal had left Vilna."

The travellers were overjoyed to find the Chevalier's conviction confirmed when at the next stage they met a lady who had just left Vilna and was able to reassure them that the Marshal's convalescence was proceeding normally but, being still unable to ride, he could not return to his command.

So Charles was still in Vilna and Eugénie on her way to him! Nothing else mattered but it was forced on her notice that everywhere postmasters were hostile and suspicious, horses ever scarcer, food harder to come by, so that the travellers blessed the Berliners' foresight although little now remained of the provisions they had brought. The villages through which they passed were ruined, the ragged inhabitants gaping dully at the carriage. Silently the Chevalier pointed out black circles of fires at abandoned bivouacs and crops trodden into the earth by the passage through the fields of thousands of men and horses.

Eugénie could not escape realising that war was not all the heroism and chivalry of her romantic imagination but something infinitely more sinister, especially when here and there on the wayside she noticed the little mounds marked by rude crosses of branches, the graves of men fallen on the march. They served to strengthen her determination that Charles should not find such a grave in this alien land without leaving a son to revere his name and inherit his honours. She would take her husband home with her, leaving the Emperor and his Grande Armée to manage their war as best they could without Marshal Oudinot. Eugénie had yet to learn that the wishes of a young woman could not dictate the destiny of nations.

At Kovno Eugénie's spirits rose when she found Colonel Jacqueminot on the lookout for her. To speed them on the last fifty miles of their journey he had requisitioned artillery horses, a great improvement on those at the posting houses, but still this last stage seemed longer than all the rest. Endlessly she questioned him about her husband.

"Will he . . . will he send me away?" she asked fearfully.

"Nothing is farther from the Marshal's intentions." Jacqueminot laughed. "For the last week he has been on the *qui vive* but, I am obliged to warn you, it does not depend on the Marshal alone—the Emperor has the final word."

Eugénie brushed the Emperor aside, but he was not so easily dismissed. Although the rain had ceased and with it the mud, once again the wheels were sinking into sand, obliging the travellers to leave the carriage to proceed on foot to lighten the load. As the Chevalier stumbled along, Jacqueminot supported Eugénie, to her amazement suddenly breaking into bitter laughter.

"Forgive me, Madame la Maréchale, for what must seem to you to be ill-conceived laughter. I cannot but think how bizarre is your presence in these deserts, all because of a devouring ambition which has driven us to the end of the world, disrupting our lives and paralysing our future. Whither will it lead us? We are all at the end of our tether."

Never had Eugénie heard anyone speak in such terms of Napoleon, such an expression of hostility from a brave man and one whom she herself had seen go so gaily off to war, but Jacqueminot looked for no response from her as he continued his lament.

---◆◆❯◆---

"Already the Emperor has been overtaken by innumerable misfortunes. Yes, he is marching towards Moscow, is perhaps already in the city, but what will he find there? The army is increasingly threatened by the Russians who refuse to stand and fight but harass our advancing columns. I begin to wonder, we all of us begin to wonder," his voice was now a whisper, "who, if any of us, will ever see France again."

Was it possible that a man of Jacqueminot's rank and service could indulge in so vehement an outburst? What terrible things had happened in Russia that an officer of the Grande Armée should turn against his beloved Emperor? Eugénie kept silence as they shuffled through the sand until they were able to remount the carriage. Now Jacqueminot, perhaps regretting his protest, spoke in a normal voice as he asked Eugénie's permission to leave her.

"I must go ahead to warn the Marshal to expect you at any moment. You are quite safe without me."

Mounting his horse he disappeared in a cloud of dust as Eugénie watched him open-mouthed until she gave a sudden cry.

"Look, Uncle, there is Vilna!"

Before them lay the domes and spires of the city, the end of their long pilgrimage. The Chevalier turned a beaming face to his niece.

"As soon as we have seen the Marshal we must go to give thanks to Almighty God for our safe arrival. I shall not fail to tell my nephew with what fortitude you have endured the hazards of this journey and that he has every right to be proud of his young Maréchale." The Chevalier stooped to kiss Eugénie's forehead. Moved and ashamed, she took his hand and kissed it affectionately.

"My dear, dear uncle, it is you who have shown the greatest courage—but for your care and patience we should never have arrived."

They were not yet at the end of their journey. Between them and the city was a short incline, a mere wooded knoll which later they learned was called Ponary, where evidence of the army's passage was even more distressing, dead and

putrefying horses and the wreckage of artillery trains. To
make the descent easier for the horses the travellers again left
the carriage. Suddenly Eugénie let go of her uncle's arm;
with keener sight than his she had recognized one of the two
horsemen approaching at a gallop.

"Michel!" she cried, then blushed furiously as she realised that, instead of the formal "Captain Letellier," she had
addressed him by his Christian name. Quickly she glanced at
her uncle, fearing that he might be shocked by her familiarity
to one of the Marshal's aides-de-camp, but the Chevalier had
not apparently noticed anything untoward.

"Since Jacqueminot returned, the Marshal has been
counting the minutes," Letellier called out as he held in his
restive horse. Was it imagination on Eugénie's part or had
she heard a faint whisper carried away by the wind, "And so
have I!" But already he had wheeled his mount, shouting as
he galloped off, "I will ride on to announce your arrival. I
have left a man on the box to guide you to the Marshal's
lodging."

Overwrought and her eyes full of tears, Eugénie saw
nothing of the city as they rattled over cobbled streets to
draw up at the porte cochère of a mansion where Charles, a
broad smile on his face and his arm in a sling, stood awaiting
them. With his free hand he wrestled with the carriage door
but it was Letellier who opened it to hand Eugénie down.
Did he press her hand slightly as he helped her to descend?
Such thoughts must not be allowed to obtrude at a moment
like this; she had braved all the hazards of this lengthy journey for one purpose alone, yet it still required an effort to
submit to Charles's warm embrace. A moment later, the Marshal loosened his grasp to take the Chevalier's hand, saying
with the courtesy which distinguished him, "For all you
have accomplished in bringing my wife to me words are in-
sufficient to thank you, Monsieur le Chevalier. I beg you to
believe how sensible I am of the sacrifice you made in leaving your own family and the comfort of your home, but believe also in my eternal gratitude."

In a hubbub of conversation, of question and answer,

the weary but excited travellers entered the house, Eugénie dutifully clinging to Charles's sound arm as they mounted the staircase to a joyous welcome from all his personal staff. So merry were they that she felt she must have dreamt Jacqueminot's outburst, but in a very short time she was made to recognize the Emperor's omnipresence when an attaché from the Duc de Bassano's staff was announced.

"Please forgive my intrusion, Monsieur le Maréchal," he said formally, "but his Excellency the Minister of Foreign Affairs wishes me to confirm the arrival of the Duchesse de Reggio as this information must immediately be conveyed to His Majesty the Emperor and a courier is on the point of leaving for Moscow."

"Well, as you may see for yourself, Madame la Duchesse de Reggio has just arrived," was Charles's gay answer. "Tomorrow we will call on the Duc de Bassano so that he, too, can see her with his own eyes."

When the attaché had bowed himself out of the room Charles laughed at Eugénie's fears.

"Don't look so anxious, *ma bonne*. The distance from here to Moscow, or wherever the Emperor may now be, is so great and the roads so bad that the courier will be a long time on his way. Should the Emperor send an order for you to leave Vilna it cannot reach us for some time and, by then, who knows?"

Eugénie was not convinced. Surely the Emperor had far more important matters on his mind than poor Eugénie Oudinot, who wanted only to nurse her husband back to health? But this hypocritical speech caused Charles to frown.

"You must not criticize the Emperor, Eugénie. His word is law."

She stole a glance at Jacqueminot, but his face remained impassive. What would be Charles's reaction if he knew of his aide-de-camp's condemnation of the Emperor, but to her astonishment she saw embarrassment on the faces of some of the other young men. Was it possible that they shared Jacqueminot's feelings? To them all it was a relief when dinner was announced and Eugénie took her place at the head of the

Marshal's table, lingering as long as she could over the meal but, as soon as coffee had been drunk, Oudinot rose to conduct her uncle to his room, nodding dismissal to his staff. Last to leave was Letellier, wearing a look so dejected that she longed to bring the smile back to his face, only to remind herself sternly that at this of all moments his depression or gaiety was no concern of hers; she was here for one purpose and one only.

Though worn out with her journey and the emotions of the last few weeks, Eugénie was painfully conscious that her most severe trial lay before her but, if she must play her part well, she must believe it to be no part. When the door opened to admit her husband, his one arm held out to her, she went to him blindly like a sleepwalker, her fingers working delicately up the sleeve of his wounded arm until they reached his shoulder.

"What are you doing, Eugénie?" the Marshal asked as avidly he covered her hand with kisses.

"I am making sure that your arm is still firmly attached to your shoulder," and to his great amusement she told him of the broken bust.

"My foolish little Maréchale! If one were to credit every sign and portent nothing would ever be done. Did you not realise that it was the bust which suffered in my place? Now, if it had arrived intact . . ."

Eugénie disengaged her hand to put her finger on Charles's lips to draw him into her arms.

Much later he murmured, "I had begun to fear, Eugénie, that you regretted our marriage, that I was perhaps not the man for whom you had hoped, that in some way I had failed you. The great change I now find in you makes me very happy."

Heartily ashamed of the deception, although the lie came readily to her lips: "I was a young recruit, Charles, but now I am a seasoned soldier who has learnt his drill, received his baptism of fire and may even be well on the way to earning promotion."

Charles gave one of his loud bellows of laughter.

--··◄█ █►··--

"Am I then to take it that you think you have reached the point where I shall dress you up in grenadier's uniform to accompany me when I return to my command? I am not taking a leaf out of the Spanish Marshals' book!"

"But did you not tell me that Maréchale Suchet was with her husband in Spain?"

Charles drew away from her to say morosely, "The war in Spain is very different from this war in Russia; undeniably there it is difficult and dangerous but the army in the Peninsula has one great advantage we do not. They are next door to France while here we are nearly a thousand miles from the French frontier . . ."

"And our communications are stretched," Eugénie broke in.

"How did you know that, my little strategist?"

"You told me, when we were in Berlin. Then I did not understand what you meant but now I think I do."

"So you are determined to impress me with your military science? I must admit that you have learned your lesson well, but why are we wasting time, Eugénie, there were other lessons for you to learn."

Despite her artless efforts to postpone the moment she dreaded, Eugénie could no longer do so but, if the Lady of Fayel could conquer her abhorrence of eating Raoul de Coucy's heart, she must be as stoical in the face of her own ordeal, Charles's gratified murmurs in her ear the reward for her efforts.

After the rigours of her journey she could at least enjoy the comfort of Charles's lodging and being once again the centre of attention to his young men. In superb October weather with only a nip of frost in the air at night the Marshal toured the large and populous city with her, pointing out the many handsome churches and public buildings and the palace now occupied by the Duc de Bassano, on whom together they paid their promised call.

Eugénie marvelled that Charles seemed to have forgotten what had brought the French to Vilna, but it was forced on her own notice when in their excursions they met soldiers sent back from the front to nurse their wounds, less painful than the terrible homesickness they suffered in this alien land, a sight familiar to the Marshal but new to Eugénie.

"Can nothing be done for these men?" she asked pitifully.

"There are too many of them, the hospitals are over-crowded and the inhabitants more hostile than one could wish."

He changed the subject, but Eugénie could not so easily dismiss it from her mind, although another anxiety took its place. Charles spent an increasing amount of time with the Duc de Bassano, but he parried all her questions until finally she begged him not to treat her like a child; she *must* know what was afoot.

"Do not we all!" he growled. "All that I know, and Bassano knows no more, is that the Emperor found Moscow in flames. After spending a month in the city he and the army have now left it."

"Then the Emperor is retreating?"

"No one has used the word retreat. The sum of my knowledge is that the army has withdrawn from Moscow, perhaps with the intention of taking up winter quarters."

As this news, impossible to conceal for long, became generally known, the cloak of serenity dropped from the faces around her, a look of resignation replacing the carefree aspect of the young men who had left Bar-le-Duc so enthusi-astically eight months ago. In Eugénie's presence they made a show of high spirits but even Letellier, normally so gay and full of fun, was subdued, while Jacqueminot was increas-ingly withdrawn and silent. In spite of their depression Eugénie was always more comfortable with her near contem-poraries than with her husband but she had learned to con-ceal from Charles how much she enjoyed their company and their graceful homage. Now, however much she longed to cheer them all, in his presence she dared not, only make parade of her devotion to him, even playing the flirt although his ardour needed no provoking from her. His recovery was making rapid progress, too rapid to please Eugénie so long as

the question mark which hung over her head remained un-
answered.

By the increasing gravity of Charles's expression and the
sighs which at times escaped from him during the night she
realised that he was planning to return to his command, her
suspicions confirmed by the sudden activity of his staff.
When she came upon Pils arranging Charles's maps in order
and laying them in a trunk it was obvious that his departure
from Vilna was imminent.

Now the tables were turned as not Charles but Eugénie
sought every occasion to arouse a desire which alone could
fulfil her own. Hating what she did, nevertheless she was in
the grip of an obsession which forced her to overcome her
repugnance. All would be worthwhile if only, when Charles
went away, she had the certitude of the child for whom she
longed.

Then it was the last dinner, the last evening with the
staff, whose determined efforts to be gay only saddened
Eugénie, the last night. At dawn the carriages rolled noisily
into the courtyard as she wondered dully at the difference in
sound of a carriage departing from one arriving. The last
embrace, then Charles was gone, leaving Eugénie desperately counting and recounting the days, but her arduous
journey, her painful submission had been vain, as barren as
she herself.

Eugénie plumbed the depths of misery, her illness of
mind rather than of body as she raged that she had married a
bigamist; Charles was married to her by the rites of church
and state, but by inclination and desire he was also wedded
fast to war; he had left her to follow his greater love, his
departure the knell of her hopes.

In more reasonable moments she realised the puerility of
her complaint at his quixotry in returning to his command
when the newly created Marshal Gouvion St. Cyr, who had
taken over his Corps, was himself wounded. Oudinot had
conceived it to be no more than his duty not to await the Emperor's orders but, for the sake of the army and his own conscience, to resume his command.

Lacking any news of her husband or the Emperor's movements, depressed that the fine autumn weather had turned to damp and fog, Eugénie would have sunk into total apathy had not her uncle insisted that she occupy her idleness usefully. Despite the early snow lying on the ground he made her take a daily outing, but the benefit was lost when one day the horses shied at a corpse in their path. Shuddering at her first sight of death, Eugénie made the sign of the cross, whispering an anguished prayer for the repose of the dead soldier's soul.

The Chevalier's efforts to rouse her from her lethargy were seconded by the Duc de Bassano, who begged her to exert herself to keep up the spirits of the Polish ladies in Vilna.

"Nothing exceeds their patriotism," the Duc told her earnestly. "They have sacrificed all their personal possessions, jewels, cashmeres, anything of value, to help their husbands raise regiments to fight alongside the Emperor, but they count it no sacrifice if it leads to freedom for Poland from the Russian yoke."

Eugénie was herself surprised that she enjoyed meeting the Polish ladies, all chic and elegant, all greatly encouraged by the presence among them of a Marshal's lady whose own unhappiness made her sensitive to the brooding anxiety underlying their gaiety. They made much of her, cajoling her for news but, having none herself, she could give them none. Eugénie rebelled, however, when the Duc de Bassano asked her to attend a review of the Neapolitan Guard marching to join their King, Marshal Murat.

"You *must* do so," her uncle reproved her, "firstly because the Duc de Bassano wishes it, and secondly because it would certainly be the Marshal's desire that by your presence you should cheer the troops; I need scarcely remind you how hard a campaign lies ahead of them."

Unwilling to confess that she was haunted by the corpse she had seen, Eugénie was obliged to comply, to learn a few days later that for the Neapolitans their passage through

Vilna was a one-way journey. Born and reared in the sun-shine of Italy, they were unable to withstand the increasing cold, perishing to a man.

Now every drop in the temperature coincided with bad news. Although the Duc de Bassano was a dedicated Bona-partist and the Chevalier de Coucy an ardent royalist, the Duc seemed to find comfort and support in the older man's calm good sense. Early one morning while Eugénie and her uncle were still at breakfast, Bassano came in person to reveal under pledge of secrecy news from Paris which had petrified him with horror. A General Malet, already under house ar-rest, had succeeded in making his escape and with several fellow conspirators had seized several prominent members of the government, and, alleging that the Emperor had been killed, proclaimed the republic.

"That anyone should even for a moment have credited Malet," the Duc sighed bitterly, "is inconceivable did it not show how nervous is the state of Paris. The attempted coup was nipped in the bud and Malet has been shot, but what will be the Emperor's reaction when he learns of this out-rage?"

His listeners had no answer for him. If a half-mad gen-eral with a handful of conspirators could so hoodwink the government, even for a few hours, then the outlook was black indeed.

"I am at my wits' end," Bassano continued, "to know what reassuring news to send to Paris which is clearly in a state of great effervescence, but it is just as vital to allow no hint of the conspiracy to be known here. Any sign of panic in Vilna would seep out along the lines of communication which must, at all costs, be kept intact."

The Duc de Bassano turned to Eugénie.

"Madame la Maréchale, you are the senior French lady present in Vilna; your conduct will be closely watched. I rely on you to see that the Polish ladies do not become discour-aged. Let them dance, if they can find anyone to partner them, because, in spite of our reverses, they have not lost faith in us. I realise the great responsibility I am asking you, young as you are, to assume, but I am confident that you will fail neither me, Oudinot nor the Emperor."

When the Chevalier returned from escorting the Duc to his carriage, he took Eugénie's hand in his.

"My dear niece, I know how quiet and retired a life you led before your marriage and I know also that your chief concern is with Marshal Oudinot's safety, but I am equally sure that, were he aware of the situation here in Vilna, he would expect you to show neither anxiety nor fear."

"I will do my best, Uncle," was the humble answer, but Eugénie was moved more by respect for the Chevalier than by what Charles's wish might be.

The temperature showed no sign of relaxing its fall; it now stood at twelve degrees. In a rare letter from Christine they learned that bitter winter gripped the whole of Europe; in Bar a wolf, maddened by hunger, had bitten a number of people, many of whom had died of hydrophobia. In Paris itself wolves were prowling in the streets, such was the cold in France. What hope then for Russia?

When the Duc de Bassano paid Eugénie and the Chevalier his next visit it was to tell them that the Emperor now knew of the Malet conspiracy, which had suggested an immediate return to France, but on second thoughts Napoleon decided to remain with the army.

"So he is still with his troops?" enquired the Chevalier.

"As far as I know yes, because the only news we receive is from stragglers who have made their way here. Communications are irrevocably broken."

"That must mean that you have also no news of my husband?"

"I have news of no one."

"Should I take my niece away, perhaps to Warsaw?" But her uncle's question was interrupted by Eugénie.

"Without news of Charles I refuse to leave Vilna and on no account will I go to Warsaw. Surely you remember, Uncle, that, before he left, Charles carefully mapped out the route we should take if we should be forced to go, although he did not think that possible. We were to travel the way we came, by Kovno and Königsberg to Berlin."

The Duc de Bassano nodded agreement.

"Whatever the Maréchale's reasons for remaining in Vilna my considered opinion is that she is right to do so. If we should be forced to evacuate the city we shall have ample warning." He turned to Eugénie. "Even had you expressed the desire to leave I should have begged you to stay because of the disastrous effect on morale your departure would have."

Eugénie's decision to remain in Vilna was in no way influenced by the Duc de Bassano's plea but by one consideration only. If Charles were still alive he must return through Vilna, where she was determined that he should find her waiting for him. During the weeks of his absence she had thought deeply about her attitude to him and had come to feel both remorse and shame. No one but herself was to blame for what all too soon she had known to be a mistake, but for her there was as little escape from the obligations of marriage as for the Grande Armée to evade the pursuing Cossacks and the even more bitter enemy, the infernal cold.

Eugénie now saw her obsession to bear a child as pure selfishness. Since there was no hope of one and perhaps never would be she felt her punishment to be just but, if she made a sincere effort to be a more loving wife to her husband, perhaps God would relent towards her, forgive her weakness and grant her the indulgence of becoming a mother. Despite the piercing cold into which she rarely penetrated, she slipped out of the house to the nearby church of St. Anne, there to pray, a little for herself but still more for Charles.

In a rough shack of beams hastily knocked together but glorified by the name of "palace" since it was the Emperor's bivouac, Napoleon, guarded by a solitary grenadier, dozed fitfully, the benison of deep sleep denied him by the sombre thoughts chasing through his tired brain.

Since his ominous fall at the Niemen he had been haunted by the warning voice which cried, "A Roman would have turned back!" He had not done so, could not do so, but his determination to proceed had led him to stare not into the triumph he had expected, but into the sour face of disaster.

Every bulletin stressed his perfect health but he alone knew how frequently the agonizing pain of enuresis sapped his energy, making him sluggish and apathetic, out of temper and ever more conscious that he no longer wore the boots of Lodi, Arcola, Austerlitz, Jena and Wagram. He had put on weight, his hair had thinned and, although he was only forty-three, had he not ordered his architects to build him a palace for a man growing old?

The edge of his desire for conquest had blunted during the years of peace following his marriage to an Austrian Archduchess, peace which had lulled him into a sense of security he now knew to be false, acutely aware of the tenuous nature of his victories at Smolensk and the Moskowa, aware also that war in Spain, the chink in his armour, the running sore in his body politic, had robbed the Grande Armée of its most experienced troops. Almost he snorted. So Wellington now occupied Madrid? It would not be for long! Just as soon as he freed himself from the Russian tangle into which he was knotted, he would teach that "sepoy general" who was the greater commander! Had he not, he Napoleon, Emperor of the French, defied the Czar's allies of space and time, to lead his Grande Armée fifteen hundred miles across Europe into Moscow, the very heart of Holy Russia?

From the heights above the city, his heart swelling with pride, he had gazed on the golden onion domes, barbaric steeples and towers burnished brighter by the setting sun, confident that, when the great Russian nobles saw the French masters of their capital, they would force Alexander to renounce further war.

To the Old Guard had fallen the honour of leading the French troops into Moscow behind their band playing *"La Victoire est à Nous,"* while he took up his residence in the Kremlin but his stay there was short. As night fell the sun seemed to have returned with greater splendour but the radiance was of a thousand fires lit by the Russians, who rather than let their capital fall intact into enemy hands, had made it a funeral pyre. For days the fires burned unchecked as the Muscovites had removed all the fire engines; when at last the flames died down ten thousand houses, more than five hundred palaces and churches were reduced to ashes.

For a month he had lingered in burning Moscow, each day his hope of negotiating peace with the Czar dying a little while his soldiery drank and pillaged, tearing shawls and sables from the shoulders of the few women remaining in the city, the rings from their fingers, the diamonds from their ears, a surfeit of loot but no substitute for the absence of flour to make bread or meat to roast.

By the middle of October, with no sign of the Russian army, which had withdrawn before the French, or word from the Czar, it was stalemate and obvious that Moscow could not be held during the winter. Before it set in there was ample time to reach Vitebsk, there to take up winter quarters and renew the war in the spring. So, on October 18, a futile month after entering Moscow, he gave orders to evacuate the city, leaving Marshal Mortier to cover the departure of the Grande Armée.

A frown crossed his face. He knew himself accused of indifference to the fate of his soldiers but his instructions to Mortier to pay every attention to the sick and wounded belied the charge.

"Sacrifice your baggage, sacrifice everything to bring them out of Moscow. The waggons must be for them, even your own saddles if need be," he had ordered the Marshal, anything preferable to allowing his men to fall into Russian hands.

He had seen how they dealt with their own wounded, pitilessly firing their improvised hospitals or shooting the hapless men out of hand, nor did they treat their dead with greater respect; the road from Moscow was strewn with piles of dead which the retreating Russian army had no time to bury. Thank God, he treated the Russian wounded differently but he trembled for the French prisoners, frequently bought by the peasants from the Cossacks for the pleasure of shooting them!

Pah! War was a barbarous profession! Wherein lay its art? Simply in being stronger than the enemy at a given moment. His army, still invincible, was stronger than the Russian army. Not the Russians but the four elements were responsible for the disaster which had overtaken him—the scorched earth of the interminable Russian plains, the fires of Moscow, the waters of the English Channel which preserved his bitterest enemy from invasion and the final obstacle, the icy air of the River Beresina. He shivered a little.

Yet, when the Grande Armée, numbering some 100,000 combatants and thousands of camp followers, marched out of Moscow the auspices were good. The commissariat had failed but the autumn weather was superb with only a few degrees of frost and a radiant sun. Now, three weeks later, that army was reduced to 36,000 men and as far as eye could see the countryside was blanketed in deep snow. In truth from the sublime to the ridiculous was only a step!

Napoleon groaned; the misery of his poor soldiers broke his heart, already weighed down by anxiety for Marshal Ney, whom he had created Prince of the Moskowa after the battle. Somewhere in that snowy waste Ney was fighting a Russian contingent but where was he?

"I would give the three hundred millions in gold that I have in the cellars of the Tuileries to save him," he had cried.

It was not necessary; the indomitable Ney had fought his way through to join the main army, that army marching doggedly on, harassed by marauding Cossacks and an enemy even more terrifying. In defence of Holy Russia the women, merciless and revengeful as the Furies, seized pitchforks and any lethal weapon they could find to attack the weary men as they fell by the wayside overcome by cold and hunger.

In the midst of his Old Guard he, the Emperor, had tramped short stages on foot, passing men by the roadside holding out to him a precious piece of firewood or, dying, still raising a feeble cry of *"Vive l'Empereur!"*

And the army had staggered on to Smolensk, where a partial thaw made a blackish slough of streets of burned-out houses and the acrid smell of smoke still lingered on the air.

The Grande Armée was now a mere rabble; only the guard marched with haversacks and rifles. The remainder no longer had strength to hold their weapons in their numbed hands, their path strewn with abandoned cannon, impedimenta of all kinds, even the booty dragged from Moscow. Discipline had vanished; everyone marched for himself alone, twitching his face to prevent nose and ears from frostbite. On roads like glass and with no ice crampons horses fell and could not rise, like the men who lay down to sleep never to wake. Horsemeat alive or dead was their sole subsistence, although somehow food was always found for him. Thank God he was not reduced to the horror he had seen—a woman, a colonel's wife he had been told, although heaven alone knew how she had come to join the rabble—tearing into a living horse to get at its warm liver.

Away in the north Oudinot's and Victor's Corps which

had joined forces were intact but even in this crisis the two Marshals could not overcome their personal antipathy to co-ordinate their efforts; their counter-attack failed.

From the plateau on which his shack rested the Emperor looked out on the two bridges crossing the Beresina, partially burnt by the Russians and impassable. Beyond the river lay Vilna, well stocked with food and ammunition but, with the obstacle in front of the army, Vilna seemed as distant as Paris.

The door of the shack burst open, rousing the Emperor from his nightmare to cry, "How shall we get through? How shall we get through?"

"Sire, Marshal Oudinot has a plan!"

At any other time young de Lamarre would have been overawed to find himself in the presence of Napoleon, but his message was too urgent for personal feelings to prevail. The Marshal proposed to make a feint at Studianska upriver where there was a ford to deceive the Russians watching from the farther bank into believing that this was to be the main crossing of the river.

Immediately in full possession of his faculties, the Emperor listened attentively, muttering, "I have played the Emperor long enough. It is time to play the General."

With a recrudescence of his fabulous energy he made his preparations. His papers had long since been burnt. Now he ordered all the eagles, the standards of the army, to be brought to him to be destroyed, adding his own clothing to the fire so the enemy could not display it as a trophy of war.

While de Lamarre sped back to Marshal Oudinot with the Emperor's approval of his plan Napoleon rallied his genius to save the remnants of his army.

In the total absence of news of the Emperor and the army even the bravest Polish ladies began to lose heart while Eugénie was a prey to fears which, in spite of herself, she could not banish. She now never ventured out of the house, not because of the cold but lest in her absence some message came from Charles. Every time horsemen or carriages passed through the street she rushed to the window, only to turn disconsolately away when they failed to stop at the house. The Duc de Bassano shared the universal anxious ignorance, particularly at a loss to understand why units from Spain, reinforcements for the Grande Armée, were still marching forward. Where would they find the main body of the army? No one could hazard a guess.

Eugénie and her uncle were sitting silently at breakfast, both too dispirited to attempt conversation. The fate of the Neapolitan Guard present in her mind, she wondered if Eugène de Villers might be serving in one of the Spanish contingents, praying that he was not, yet when the door was suddenly flung open, her first thought was that it must be Eugène who by chance had discovered her presence in Vilna.

She screamed with fright, clutching the Chevalier's arm, at the ruffianly figure who entered only to be reassured as, beneath the grime and several weeks' growth of beard, she recognized Letellier's features. His abrupt appearance, clearly in the last stages of exhaustion, his clothes in rags, could mean one thing only—a terrible disaster must have overtaken Charles!

Eugénie rushed towards Letellier, who led her to a chair, holding both her hands in his, icy to her touch, as he muttered in a voice raw with cold and fatigue, "I bring you news of your husband, Madame la Maréchale."

"He is dead!"

"No, no, the Marshal is alive, but wounded. I assure you that the wound is not mortal—he is even now on his way to Vilna."

Letellier released Eugénie's hands to search among his rags until he found a scrap of paper in Charles's handwriting but she trembled too much to hold the letter. Gently her uncle took it from her to read the few written lines but she heard only the phrase "return to France."

"Come, Captain Letellier, let us go to meet him!"

He shook his head; his orders were strict. Under no circumstances was she to leave Vilna.

---

"That we shall see! Wounded and exposed to this horrific cold, my husband needs all the help I can take him. Uncle, *you* will not prevent my going?"

Before the Chevalier could answer, Letellier broke in.

"Knowing that this would be your wish, the Marshal's order was that, even if I am obliged to lock you in, I am not to permit you to leave."

To all Eugénie's pleading Letellier remained adamant, at the same time doing his best to minimise the gravity of the Marshal's wound, until he could no longer withstand her peremptory demands for the truth.

"The Marshal," he began slowly, "was on his horse when he was struck in the thigh by a case shot. Unable to detach his foot from the stirrup he was dragged along on the ground until the terrified animal's bridle was seized and it was brought to a halt and we were able to lift the Marshal up. No, Madame la Maréchale," he answered Eugénie's unspoken question, "it was not I but Lachaise who stopped the poor brute."

"And then . . . ?"

Letellier stirred uncomfortably in his chair, failing to answer until Eugénie repeated her question.

"Since this is your wish . . ." He made a gesture of resignation. "But I repeat that, though serious, the wound is not mortal. When we carried the Marshal to the rear he was conscious although unable to speak. The Emperor, who was near at hand, sent his own doctors to tend the Marshal but it was the chief surgeon of our Corps who tried to extract the ball. . . ."

"How?" demanded Eugénie inexorably.

"If you insist on hearing—like the hero he is the Marshal refused to be tied down, his only concession allowing Pils to give him a piece of cloth on which to bite while the surgeon probed the wound."

Letellier did not reveal that the surgeon had been unsuccessful in extracting the ball, merely adding the reassurance, "The Marshal is now on his way to you, weakened neither physically nor morally."

The Chevalier, watching his niece closely, perceiving

how near she was to breaking point, intervened to give her time to compose herself, forestalling any further questions from her to demand of Letellier, "Where then is the army? Where is the Emperor? For many days we have lacked news and everyone in Vilna is in the greatest state of alarm."

Even Eugénie, despite her deep anxiety for her husband, was amazed by Letellier's sudden outburst.

"The Emperor? What have we to do with him who are the victims of this mad gigantic undertaking, of the boundless ambition and terrible egotism which has cost France four hundred thousand men, sons, fathers and husbands! You ask me, sir, for news of the army. What army? There is no longer an army. It has ceased to exist."

Tears started to Eugénie's eyes as she remembered with what insolent pride the soldiers of Oudinot's Corps had swung along when he reviewed them in Berlin.

"You see me?" Letellier continued bitterly. "I am one of the strongest, still one of the best clothed, one of the few, the happy few who by some miracle has—so far—escaped the general disaster."

Horrified by Letellier's tirade, uncle and niece gazed at each other, then more closely at him. Tragedy had etched deep lines on his handsome face, deathly pale beneath the grime; his uniform was threadbare, his boots tied together with string, but he was now oblivious of his listeners as, with mounting emotion, he continued to recite the death of the Grande Armée.

"When we left Vilna at the end of October the Marshal rejoined his command at Vitebsk. Together with Marshal Victor's Corps we were detached from the main body of the army to cut off the Russians advancing from St. Petersburg, so we did not march along that fatal road to Moscow. We were still an organized body of men, well clothed and well fed, though reduced in numbers, so that, on rejoining the army retreating from Moscow, we were horrified by the ragged and frozen remnants shambling through snow and ice."

Letellier repressed a shudder as he recalled that phantasmagoric sight, the mere skeletons of men, their gaunt faces grey with fatigue, marching out of step, huddled in whatever they could find to protect them from the cold, women's cloaks, pieces of carpet, greatcoats burned into gaping holes, all differences of rank effaced by the common misery, a gang of convicts rather than the proud soldiers of the Grande Armée.

Letellier gulped down his emotion.

"We did what we could to help them with food and clothing but disorder is the most contagious of diseases. Instead of taking heart from us, those pitiful scarecrows demoralized our men—and we had reached the Beresina."

For the first time Eugénie and the Chevalier heard the name of that river of ill omen.

"It was the Marshal who saved the situation, madame. To give the sappers time to mend the broken bridges over the river he made a feint which deceived the enemy and so the Emperor and the Old Guard were able to cross." His voice sank to a whisper. "And some of the army."

Letellier fell silent. How could he bring into this warm comfortable room the horrors he had witnessed, the nightmare that would dog him so long as he lived—the disorganized rabble crowding the frail bridges which finally collapsed under their weight, their screaming bodies planks for others to walk over, the thousands who died attempting to ford the river, men, their women and children, frozen in the icy water, drowned or cut to pieces by jagged edges of floating ice. Words could not describe the abomination of that crossing nor the perpetual menace of the Cossacks swooping down on the defenceless survivors. They had all grown old in this terrible war!

Aware suddenly of the silence Letellier succeeded in returning to the present.

"The Marshal crossed the river safely, and we with him. It was then that he was wounded. After the doctors had attended to him we withdrew to a village, some forty of us, officers and men, only to find ourselves surrounded by a troop of Russians, Hussars and Cossacks."

To reassure Eugénie, who stared at him with a stricken face, Letellier managed a smile while some strength returned to his voice as proudly he told her that her husband had called for his Grand Cordon of the Legion of Honour; if he were to be taken prisoner it would be as a Marshal of France, not a bandit!

"Although helpless and in pain the Marshal was magnificent, madame, directing our defence so boldly that the enemy was duped into believing that we numbered more than the eighteen to which we were reduced, but he was again wounded although this time the wound was indeed slight."

The smile vanished from Letellier's face as he fell into a mood of bitter despair, rocking to and fro in his threnody for the Grande Armée.

"But now, O God, what is to happen to us? Even if those men who were able to cross that hellish river resist the lethal cold and gripping hunger which in that desert waste finds only dead horses to appease it, even if this debris once rejoicing in the name of the Grande Armée reaches Vilna, what can we do with the Russians at our heels?"

His eyes narrowed as his voice rose in anger.

"Not the enemy but hunger and cold, the infernal cold worse than hunger, have beaten us because every time we turned and fought the Russians gave way."

Though anguished with pity for Letellier, Eugénie was yet obliged to bring him back to the present.

"But where have you left the Marshal?"

"On the road to Vilna, madame. With him are his doctor, his aides-de-camp and, of course, Pils. He has an escort because the Cossacks are everywhere, swooping down when one thinks oneself safe, so you see, Madame la Maréchale, that we dare not let you run the risk of attempting to join the Marshal."

"But is the risk not greater for a wounded and helpless man?" The Chevalier posed the question.

"No, sir, because to defend him he has the escort the Maréchale would lack. I beg you to believe me that the Marshal's life is not in danger and the safety of his journey is assured."

Exhaustion had reduced Letellier's voice to a whisper

but, even during his impassioned tirade, his eyes constantly strayed to the breakfast table. At last he asked faintly if he might have something to eat.

"Good God! You are famished and I allowed you to go on talking!"

Calling for hot coffee and more bread, Eugénie busied herself with serving food to Letellier. Only when a little colour returned to his cheeks did she venture to question him about other members of the Marshal's staff, especially General de Lorencez and Colonel Jacqueminot. So far as he knew the General was safe but Jacqueminot . . .

"Oh, he's a hero! The Emperor wanted a Russian to interrogate so Jacqueminot rode hell for leather after the Cossacks, scooped up a non-commissioned officer, threw him across his saddle and swam with him across the river. After the Emperor's congratulations he's bound to get a promotion—if he survives," he added drily as he rose saying that he must go to give the Duc de Bassano an eye-witness account of the crossing of the Beresina, nor would he be persuaded to stay even to change his clothes.

Alone, the Chevalier and Eugénie looked at each other in horror until he said, "First Jacqueminot, now Letellier! In God's name what has happened to Bonaparte? At a time like this there can be neither royalists nor imperialists, only Frenchmen. May the Almighty grant that the Grande Armée come safely through its ordeal."

With one accord Eugénie and her uncle fell on their knees to pray. Ridiculous though she knew it to be, she felt herself in some way responsible, not for the disaster which had overtaken the army, but her husband. Solely for her own ends she had followed him to Vilna and she would be well punished if his desperate wounds made it impossible for him to fulfil her selfish desire.

Eugénie's remorse increased with the cold but still Charles did not come, until she felt she could no longer bear the strain of waiting. Then an aide-de-camp announced his imminent arrival. It was time! Neglecting to put on her furs, Eugénie rushed to the porte cochère where a weird apparition had come to a halt. Long icicles dripped from the carriage roof, from the lamps, from the harness of the horses whose breath froze as it met the air. On the box there seemed frozen statues rather than men but, with the aid of the indoor servants, they succeeded in lifting the Marshal out of the carriage. Stiff with cold and bent double with pain yet Oudinot indomitably insisted on mounting the stairs unaided, only to collapse when he had crawled to the warmth of the stove. When he had been got into bed and his dressings changed, the doctor whispered to Eugénie that the wound would not heal until the foreign bodies which had penetrated it with the impact of the ball were ejected—shreds of his shirt, his flannels, breeches and astrakhan pelisse.

When the doctor had left, Eugénie sat alone at her husband's bedside. Gazing at the ashen face on the pillow her only feeling was one of pity, not now for herself but for him. Charles was no longer a stranger to her although remote from her own experience were the ordeals he had endured. She could only hazard a guess at his state of mind as from time to time a groan, quickly repressed, escaped him. With a gesture which surprised herself she laid her cool hand on his fevered forehead when he briefly opened his eyes and smiled faintly at her. A sudden hope filled her heart that perhaps this marriage into which she had entered under so strange a compulsion might yet turn out better than she had expected, but this was no time for indulgence of her own feelings. Charles's recovery must take precedence.

Gradually a little life came back to the Marshal, but far greater than the pain from his wounds was the anguish caused him by the army's calamitous retreat.

Although in his presence none of his entourage dared blame the Emperor for the disaster, somehow he was conscious of the bitter murmurs behind his back. Single-minded himself, Oudinot did not realise that his young men were suffering a sense of guilt that they had survived while thousands had perished, as well as the haunting fear that their escape was illusory and that many of them would never return to France, yet the Marshal was not such a martinet as to deny them succour. As stragglers came to the house they were invited to sit down to eat, raising a cheer at the sight of

Eugénie's table laid with fine linen, silver and loaded platters, which moved her to tears. To do them honour she presided over their meals, averting her eyes as, despite their valiant efforts to control their appetites, they fell upon the food. Only when hunger was assuaged did they rival one another in recounting their misfortunes, their laughter touched with hysteria, but laughter did not last long.

Hard on the Marshal's heels the tragic remnants of the Grande Armée poured into Vilna, men without leaders and leaders without men, none more heartbreaking than the wounded for whom no place could be found in the overcrowded hospitals and who died in the streets, from the lethal cold rather than from their wounds.

Oudinot, all for defending the city well stocked with food and ammunition, raged at his impotence but how could he, tied to his bed, rally men demoralized and exhausted and who else, in the horror and chaos, was ready to do so? Two days after his return the Duc de Bassano made a hasty appearance, apologizing for his failure to come earlier as he sank into a chair beside the Marshal's bed.

"About what I shall tell you you will naturally maintain the greatest secrecy, Oudinot. This morning at dawn the Emperor passed through Vilna on his way to Paris."

The Marshal stared at him, incredulous that the Emperor should have abandoned the army.

"Only Caulaincourt and a small escort accompanied him; no one in the city but I knows he has been here and my time with him was brief as he was in urgent haste to be on his way. He informed me that the sum total of our disaster is told in the 29th Bulletin which has been sent forward to Paris but, though I might guess, not even I had realised its magnitude."

Bassano covered his face with his hands, his grief as much for Napoleon whom he adored as for the fate of the Grande Armée.

"That bulletin was issued on December 2," he moaned, "my God, December 2, the date forever glorious in the annals of the Empire, the day of the Coronation, the day of Austerlitz."

--◦◖▌◗◦--

The stunned silence which followed Bassano's revelation did not last long as Oudinot suddenly exploded in an outburst more violent than Eugénie had ever heard, but she dared not remonstrate with him although fearful lest he work himself into a fever which would further inflame his wound.

"Oudinot, believe that I share your feelings." The Duc de Bassano interrupted the tirade. "The Emperor is not to blame; no one expected so early or so bitter a winter which alone has beaten him. In returning to France he has taken the only course possible because it is imperative to raise new armies to crush the Russians in pursuit. He told me that only from the Tuileries could he impress himself on Europe and it is only in France that you can be of use to him—you, too, must leave Vilna without delay."

Bassano waved aside the Marshal's attempt to speak.

"I am not thinking of your personal safety. Were that alone in question I would urge you to remain but too many commanders have been lost and the Emperor will need those who have survived. My friend, your duty is not to organize resistance in Vilna but to return to France to recover your health in readiness to answer the Emperor's call when it comes in the spring."

Had Oudinot been able to stand on his own two feet he would have resisted Bassano's bidding but, given the choice between two duties, duty to the Emperor was decisive. As soon as Bassano had taken his leave, wishing the Oudinots Godspeed, the Marshal gave orders to prepare for immediate departure.

To Eugénie her husband's decision was a great relief; she was anxious to put as much distance between herself and Vilna as possible but, if they were to go, they dared not linger. She packed in haste, abandoning everything but the essential. The cold was already beginning to bite, the thermometer standing at 28 degrees below zero, cold which penetrated the very marrow of the bones, cold to which hunger was a thousand times preferable.

Two carriages only made up the little party, in the first Eugénie with the Marshal laid on a mattress on the floor while Pils sat on the box with the coachman. The Chevalier de Coucy, the doctor, de Bourcet and Jacqueminot crowded into the second carriage where room had to be found for the Marshal's maître d'hôtel. Twenty cuirassiers escorted the carriages as they left the city, their voluminous white mantles melting into the landscape, but at nightfall Eugénie counted only two men, icicles hanging from their long moustaches on faces burnt black with the cold.

"I am the fittest of the party," Letellier had declared with a glimmer of his old gaiety, although his cadaverous cheeks belied his words. He elected to act as guide, riding beside the carriages, determined, should the Marshal not survive the perils of the journey, to see Eugénie and her uncle safely back to France.

She was thankful that from the floor of the carriage Charles was unable to see the way they travelled, especially when they reached the incline called Ponary. When she and her uncle had descended it only a few months before the trees were still green with barely any signs of autumn. Now the gentle slope was a waste of snow, its whiteness stained only by the blood gushing from the nostrils of men who had frozen to death as they attempted to climb up that wall of ice. As the horses struggled valiantly to mount the obstacle, the carriages passed groups of the living, some bravely carrying their wounded comrades on their backs, determined that, if death met them at the hands of the Cossacks, it would do so with their faces turned towards France.

Eugénie held her breath in agony until they reached the summit of that terrible ascent. Now they were able to go like the wind on the plain covered deep in snow, but they could only trust that they were travelling in the right direction because no road was visible in the blank whiteness. The oppressive silence was only broken when from time to time Eugénie bent to ask if her husband were comfortable or he muttered a few words of concern for her. The sight of Letellier doggedly galloping alongside of them alone gave her some reassurance. On, on, with never a pause until the interminable day wore to nightfall and he shouted that he saw a building in the distance which might offer shelter for the night, but they must hurry.

How Pils and the coachman, exposed on the box to the worst of the weather, found strength to lift the Marshal from the carriage Eugénie could not guess, only be grateful that they did so as she herself stumbled into the building, some kind of barn surrounded by black circles of men huddled over a miserable fire. For them there was no room within the barn, filled to overflowing.

But for Letellier the Marshal and his companions would have been forced back into the carriages, perhaps never to wake from snow-drugged sleep.

"Make way for Marshal Oudinot who is wounded unto death," he cried, but no one moved though once the name of Oudinot would have brought every man to his feet, not now! *Sauve qui peut!* The men were lost to all discipline or human feeling other than self-preservation. Save a Marshal at one's own expense? Not after the plight to which generals and marshals had brought them, never the Emperor, still the god of the old moustaches, unaware that he was speeding on his way to Paris to raise new armies to fight new wars. Yet those who survived this terrible retreat would continue to fight with him again and again until all fighting ceased, to relive in their old age the great battles they had fought under the eagles of their Little Corporal, *Le Tondu*, their affectionate names for their great Emperor.

Inch by inch, drawing on reserves of strength he himself did not know he possessed, Letellier battled his way to the inner part of the barn, the little party crowding behind him as ruthlessly he dragged away the corpses ranged round the fire, left by men too apathetic to shift them. *Sauve qui peut!* or they themselves would die to become stepping-stones for the living to trample on.

Had it lain within Eugénie's power to save what was left of the Grande Armée she would have done so, but not by sacrificing her husband, possessed by a fierce determination to take him home alive, his weak and helpless state arousing a tenderness absent when he was strong and overpowering. Even her longing for a child was thrust into the background; only if Charles lived would that hope revive and how little certainty there was that he could do so!

The boundless confidence she felt in Letellier was justified when they reached a tiny space where Eugénie and the Chevalier were overcome to find General Loison and his staff marching eastwards from Königsberg to reinforce an army which no longer existed. The Marshal managed a wry smile at the General and his little contingent, still well found but able only to guess what lay ahead of them.

General Loison added his efforts to Letellier's to clear some room by the fire for the Marshal's mattress, sleep for all an urgent need not from fatigue alone but to blot out the horrors of the present and those which lay ahead, but there was space neither to sit nor lie, nor did they dare so much as doze lest they fall on the Marshal and do him damage.

With some protection now from the cold their hunger awoke but the provisions they had brought with them were frozen too solid even to hack apart like the dressings which might have given the Marshal some relief. There was no hope of thawing them as the fire had now died down to mere embers but the doctor bravely elbowed his way through the barn to return with a broken gun wheel which reanimated the fire and their frozen blood.

When morning dawned grey and snow-laden the Marshal was moved in haste into the carriage, spared the sight which horrified the rest. Against the dazzling snow the black circles of men were still where night had overtaken them, but now stirred by no movement, stiff as on parade. In that merciless murderous night of cold they had died where they huddled round the fire.

For pity there was no time, they must be gone as fast as their wretched beasts could take them, all their courage needed not to think what their own fate might have been. Iron determination alone kept Letellier in the saddle, some sixth sense guiding him to a village still intact where the travellers fell on a steaming plate of potatoes, their first meal since leaving Vilna, but the Marshal's state was giving rise to great alarm as so inflamed was his thigh that he was uncomfortable whichever way he turned.

At this village they were overtaken by de Lamarre, who had left Vilna shortly after the Oudinots had departed.

--·◄€( )€►·--

"What news?" demanded the Marshal eagerly, but his voice was faint.

"Bad, Monsieur le Maréchal, bad."

The city was in ever greater disorder, the incline called Ponary so encumbered with dead and dying and abandoned equipment as to be impassable; de Lamarre himself had been fortunate in finding by chance a way round it. Oudinot groaned when he learned the loss of the artillery he had rescued at the Beresina but, if he and his party were to be saved, they must be blind and deaf to disaster until from the box Pils shouted that he lost sight of the second carriage, news which aroused all Eugénie's latent fears.

To her distraught mind the blackened stumps of chimneys were lone Cossacks ready to swoop down on the unprotected carriage in which she and the Marshal were cocooned in a winding sheet of grey sky and white snow. Her fear even infected the Marshal who, for the first time in his life was afraid but, if the Cossacks were indeed in pursuit, he was ready somehow to give a good account of himself. Happily there were no Cossacks. Added to her fear was Eugénie's guilt that for her sake alone her uncle had left his home and family; he was the only volunteer moved by love of her while all the rest were where they were by reason of duty. If he were lost how could she ever again face her aunt, if indeed she survived to do so?

"Oh, let us stop and search for my uncle," she cried, but Charles refused; they dared not halt or turn back which Eugénie, distressed as she was, had to admit was right. At least, when by some miracle Letellier recognized the place occupied by the Marshal and his staff at the beginning of the campaign, in another life, another world, there would be some shelter and the hope that the Chevalier's carriage would find them.

In spite of her anxiety about her uncle Eugénie's spirits rose when, on the threshold of the Château d'Antorowna, she saw the mistress of the house lit by flambeaux waving in the wind, but her greeting sent a chill through her icy as the weather.

"How happy I should have been to welcome you," she

cried in a voice cracked with fatigue, "had you not arrived at such a cruel moment. We have typhus in the house, seven people, members of my family and refugees who sought shelter here, have died, but I can at least offer you beds and food."

With no alternative but to accept the proffered shelter the impulse to flee the pestiferous house had to be overcome but, famished as she was, Eugénie could not eat. Might not the food be tainted with the dread disease? Even while she was indulging her distress at her uncle's disappearance his carriage arrived. A slight accident had delayed it, but Jacqueminot had also recognized the way to the Château d'Antorowna and guessed that Letellier would make for it. Glad though the party had been of its shelter, at daybreak they left the château with relief even though it meant plunging again into the white, icy waste.

Freed now of the menace of Cossacks, the little party still had to face their enemies, cold and hunger. Wiser than his young men as to the limits of the human frame, the Marshal decreed that as soon as they reached a place offering any resources they must rest. To the exhausted travellers the sight of Gumbinnen, over the border in Prussia, smoke curling into the air from the chimneys of snug little houses which offered warmth and shelter, was beautiful, nor would they ever forget the taste of the soup, the beefsteak and the potatoes in which they satisfied their hunger, but perhaps, for Eugénie at least, the greatest luxury was soap and water, clean linen and the chance to comb and dress her hair, all missing during the ten days of their ordeal when cleanliness and even propriety had gone by the board.

To her uncle she whispered so that Charles should not hear the gloomy thoughts she had been entertaining, "I do now allow myself to believe that we shall reach France."

"My dear niece, I have never doubted it," was the Chevalier's simple reply nor would he accept Eugénie's praise for his fortitude. "I am a de Coucy," was all he would say.

Rest brought an appreciable improvement in the Marshal's condition but when he learned from some officers who

---◆❚❱◆---

had caught up with him of the evacuation of Vilna, where the wretched wounded had been left to the mercy of the Russians, his anger almost brought about a relapse. In the men's appearance, senior commanders clothed like ragbags, the lucky ones befurred like bears, the others swaddled in a motley collection of bits and pieces, he found nothing at which to smile.

"Deserters!" he spat at them. "And where, gentlemen, do you think you are going, unwounded and in good health? You are leaving the army? Do you for one moment imagine that if I were able to walk I should have turned my back on my less fortunate comrades?"

The men shifted their feet uncomfortably until one bolder than the others spoke.

"Monsieur le Maréchal, you are our direct leader, we must follow you. What is there for us to do now that the Emperor has returned to France and the army no longer exists?"

So enraged was the Marshal by this speech that he struggled to get to his feet but Eugénie, who never left his side, restrained him.

"So, gentlemen! I will tell you this—the army will be reorganized and in the spring it will march again, drums beating, flags flying, to the Vistula. You will await me there but meanwhile you will offer your services to those chiefs of army corps more fortunate than I since they can remain usefully at their posts."

Silently the officers bowed and left the room, but neither they nor Oudinot were aware that all French resistance had ceased with Marshal Ney's heroic rearguard action, fighting his way out of Russia, with a musket firing the last shot of the campaign on the bridge at Kovno, but bringing his few survivors safely into Prussia.

"Men are nothing," said Oudinot gravely. "France is all and France is in danger. Our duty is to preserve her—and the Emperor."

To Eugénie's surprise the Marshal raised no objections when Letellier sought permission to return to France to join the new armies the Emperor was raising. After all, had he

not nobly fulfilled his undertaking to bring Oudinot and
Eugénie out of Russia? She was deeply moved when Letellier
came to take farewell of her.

"Words fail me, dear Captain Letellier, to express all that
is in my heart for what you have done for us, for your devotion to the Marshal and for your unfailing care of me. We
owe our safety to your courage, your determination and your
gaiety. Believe me when I say that, so long as I live, so long
shall I honour the name of Michel Letellier."

Her voice choked by tears, she could only hold out her
hands which Letellier kissed repeatedly, murmuring, "Madame la Maréchale, Madame la Maréchale," when a sound
from the Marshal's bed caused him to drop her hands
abruptly, salute, turn on his heel and go.

"*Eh, bien*, madame," growled Charles, "are you trying to
create as much havoc as the enemy among my staff? Is it not
enough for you that *I* am grateful for your care of me?"

Eugénie recoiled as if from a blow. Was that all Charles
had to say to her? The compassion she felt for his suffering
borne with such patience had been trembling on the verge of
developing at last into something much warmer, more akin
to what a wife should feel for her husband, but it vanished
with his coldness. She had not wanted gratitude, but since
that was all that was offered her she would no longer resist
the feeling which had stirred her heart since the day of her
wedding. From her first sight of him she had been attracted
by Michel Letellier, but she had done her best to overcome
what she had believed to be no more than a passing fancy.
Now, Charles's indifference allowed her to indulge her satisfaction that, filthy and unkempt though she had been during
their nightmare journey from Vilna, she had still aroused the
feelings made apparent by Letellier's farewell.

Jacqueminot now took his colleague's place as guide, for
the hazards of their journey were not yet ended but, although he was competent, he lacked the charm and gaiety
which had done so much to make the intolerable days bear-
able.

Now they were travelling through more civilized country
and, even if the weather was still abominable, at least they

had enough to eat. At Königsberg Eugénie thought sadly of General Loison. Was he still living? No one knew who lived, who had died. Here, however, they had an unwelcome reminder of the disaster which had overtaken the French. When Jacqueminot approached a group of Prussian officers drinking toasts to the débâcle to ask them to moderate their noise because next door a French Marshal was lying gravely wounded, they laughed in his face, redoubling their noise and rejoicing.

"This insolence we must keep from the Marshal," Jacqueminot told Eugénie. "He, always so courteous to his enemies, would be distressed beyond measure to know how low French prestige has sunk in Europe."

Nevertheless the Marshal must have divined the hostility because, although he needed to rest longer, he ordered the horses to be put to on the following day and nobody tried to dissuade him even though Elbing, their next stage, was another pest house. On now through Danzig to Berlin, confident that no further difficulties awaited them, but on the Oder the ice was beginning to thaw. The Marshal, on fire to return to France, insisted on crossing although Eugénie was terrified that the cracking ice would not bear the second carriage but providence was on their side and all together they entered Berlin on New Year's Day, 1813, only to read the fatal 29th Bulletin.

> The cold which began on November 7 suddenly increased and from the fourteenth to the fifteenth and sixteenth the thermometer registered eighteen degrees of frost. . . . Men whom nature had not tried sufficiently to surmount all the hazards of fate and fortune seemed overcome, losing their gaiety and good humour, dreaming only of disaster. . . .

Napoleon had concealed nothing, telling the whole truth, only attributing the disaster not to the enemy but to the weather.

Whatever the harm done by the Malet conspiracy, however disturbing the news from Russia, in France faith in the Emperor's star had not wavered, but when the stark bulletin revealed the defeat of the once invincible Napoleon and his armies, he himself seemed to have reached for that star to bring it down from the sky.

Marshal Oudinot, who had upbraided his men so passionately for daring to speak of disaster, was forced to admit the bitter truth, made more unbearable by learning it in Berlin which twice the French had entered as conquerors and where now the Prussians were blatantly jubilant at the collapse of the Grande Armée.

Leaving Berlin behind, now every mile brought them nearer to friendly faces, to France and home. At Mayence Eugénie was specially touched, since she had liked old Marshal Kellermann, when he paid Oudinot a well-deserved compliment by ordering the password for the day to be "Beresina, Reggio."

Then at last on January 13, 1813, it was Bar-le-Duc, an ecstatic welcome from the family and the indescribable relief at being once again in the comfort and security of home but, now that she took a good look at him, relief from tension sent Eugénie into hysterical laughter at the comical figure cut by the Marshal in a brown fur cloak, an astrakhan bonnet pulled down over his ears, his legs encased in boots of blue and white striped mattress ticking well lined with fur.

"Charles, you look like a nicely tended bear," Eugénie told him.

A year ago, less than a year ago, when they were first married, she would not have dared to speak to him thus, but she had lost a little of her awe of him, although her latent resentment revived when she realised that Charles thought only of a new war. Was there to be no end to days without care or anxiety? Fervently she prayed that there might still be peace even though the Emperor himself had declared that peace could only be won by war.

The impulse which had driven her to Vilna had dissipated. Eugénie was dismayed to find herself drearily apathetic, not realising that she was suffering reaction from all that she had been through. And she could only marvel at Charles's young men who danced and sang and hunted while the Emperor was bent on a chase far more dangerous than those which took place daily at Jeand'heurs.

--◦⊰ ⊱◦--

-⚜{ 6 }⚜-

As Eugénie Oudinot mounted the grand staircase of the Tuileries her nervousness increased with each step she took until she feared that her legs would give way under her, nor did her companion make any effort to restore her confidence. Beside the Duchesse de Bassano, taller by a head, she felt insignificant, wishing that someone less coolly condescending might have been chosen to sponsor her presentation to the Emperor, but the offer of his wife's services made by the Duc de Bassano to show his appreciation of Eugénie's conduct in Vilna was impossible to refuse.

With the careless ease of familiarity the Duchesse de Bassano threaded her way through the crowds gathered in what to Eugénie seemed an endless series of galleries, the Salles des Maréchaux, des Officiers, de la Paix and du Trône, until they reached the Galerie de Diane. Here Madame de Bassano seated herself, motioning to Eugénie to do likewise, thereafter ignoring her protégée to chat animatedly to the men and women who came up to greet her.

Unconscious of the glances in her direction and the whispers that she was the young woman who had accompanied her husband in the retreat from Russia, gradually Eugénie recovered herself sufficiently to notice her surroundings. Once she had believed that nothing could exceed the luxury of Jeand'heurs, but she had not then seen the magnificence of the Tuileries, the superb mahogany furniture richly encrusted with ormolu, the allegorical scenes painted on the lofty ceilings, the tapestried walls and beneath her feet the rich Savonnerie carpet woven in an intricate design of Imperial bees and eagles, but it was less the grandeur that impressed Eugénie than the contrast between the brilliant uniforms of the officers and the torn, discoloured rags of their flight from Russia. Remembering her own unkempt appearance during that journey, she smoothed the white satin of her robe, marvelling at the changes so short a time could bring.

Eugénie had expected to wear her wedding dress for her presentation at Court but she was overruled by Charles.

"No, Eugénie, you cannot wear a dress worn even once and, remember, it is not every day one is presented to the Emperor of the French! You must wear white, not only because you will be making your first appearance at Court since your marriage, but because white is Napoleon's preference for ladies—Josephine rarely wore anything else. You may go to Leroy and spare no expense; the rest you can safely leave to him."

Eugénie was overawed by the prospect of a dress from the great Leroy whose fame had penetrated even to Vitry-le-François. Sometime when Josephine de Beauharnais was one of the slightly shady stars of the Directoire, her path crossed that of Hippolyte Leroy and thenceforward they rose in the world together, she to the shaky position of Empress of the French, he to the solid eminence of dictator of taste and fashion.

Leroy's was the creation of the Empire line, the long graceful skirt, small puffed sleeves, the waist below the armpits and décolletage so low that much of the bosom which should have been concealed escaped voluptuously from the tiny bodice moulded to the body. All over Europe empresses, queens, princesses and accredited beauties eagerly sought Leroy's masterpieces, submitting to his domination as great in his own sphere as the Emperor Napoleon's in his.

The price demanded by Leroy seemed extortionate to Eugénie, who had not yet shaken off the habits of strict economy in which she had been brought up, but all thought of cost vanished in her delight at the dress created for her, more exquisite than any she had ever dreamed of possessing.

To match the colour of her eyes the hem of the white satin under robe was embroidered in a design of forget-me-nots, the same motif repeated on the overdress and train of pale blue velvet.

Framing her head and neck was the tulle *chérusque* stiffened by wires, as obligatory for a Court lady as his epaulettes to an officer. On her head Eugénie wore the diamond tiara which was one of Charles's wedding gifts, while her neck was encircled with a rivière of the same glittering stones. Over one piece of jewellery she hesitated, Charles's name bracelet. Thinking that it went ill with diamonds she discarded it before, shrugging her shoulders, she clasped it round her wrist. After all, it was an easy way of pleasing him.

Charles was delighted with her appearance.

"I knew Leroy would do well with you," he beamed but he only laughed at Eugénie's obvious embarrassment at the amount of her still childish bosom the dress displayed. She managed to fend him off when he stooped to demonstrate his satisfaction by kissing the tender white flesh.

"No, no, Charles, not now—you will disarrange my coiffure and I think I hear the sound of a carriage. The Duchesse de Bassano must have arrived to take me up with her."

Eugénie was more gratified than by her husband's pleasure when, after a quick appraisal, Madame de Bassano unbent a little to compliment her protégée on her gown. Had she expected to find a dowdy little provincial? Eugénie already knew that the Duchesse was one of the most elegant women in a Court renowned for its elegance, but she compared her unfavourably with the Polish ladies of Vilna. Even in the cruel circumstances they had maintained their chic, but their manners had nothing of the freedom and coquetry of the Frenchwomen. Where were those Polish ladies now? Eugénie could only hope that they had been reunited with their husbands and that no dreadful fate had overtaken them now that the Allied armies had streamed across Poland into Prussia but, as a sudden stir in the crowd heralded the Emperor's imminent arrival, this was no time to dwell on those days in Vilna nor the probability of another war.

Quickly the men and women divided themselves into two ranks as the double doors at the end of the Galerie de Diane were thrown open and the Emperor appeared, walking briskly to his own apartments from the chapel where he had been hearing mass. A few minutes later, which to Eugénie seemed interminable, the doors which had closed behind him reopened for a gentleman usher to call:

"Madame la Duchesse de Bassano to present Madame la Maréchale Oudinot, Duchesse de Reggio, to his Imperial and Royal Majesty."

The Duchesse de Bassano rose, followed by Eugénie, sure that the thudding of her heart must be audible, but her sponsor showed no emotion as she led the way to the end of the long gallery, and the presence of the Emperor; never thereafter could Eugénie remember how she succeeded in making the three reverences required by etiquette.

Napoleon bade the two ladies good morning before asking for news of the Marshal, adding, "You're an old married woman, Madame la Duchesse de Reggio."

Eugénie ventured to raise her eyes which had been bent on the ground, to be completely subjugated by the sweetness of the smile no painter ever succeeded in capturing. The prejudices inculcated in her from childhood vanished as she no longer marvelled that men like Charles should be devoted to the Emperor, only that Jacqueminot and Letellier should have raged against his insensate ambition. In that fleeting moment she understood what made soldiers eager to fight, even to die for him like those blackened heaps on the dread incline called Ponary.

--◦◖╫◗◦--

"You are a Champenoise, are you not?"

"My family come from Champagne, sire, but I have always lived in Lorraine."

"Of course."

But Eugénie bit her lip when the Emperor's dark blue eyes ranged over her slender figure as, in answer to a further question, she replied, "Yes, sire, I have been married for fifteen months."

Was it an implied reproach that Eugénie was still childless when the Emperor turned to the Duchesse de Bassano to enquire after her five children but no, still with that ineffable smile, he addressed Eugénie with the same sweetness:

"You took a long journey, Madame la Duchesse de Reggio—and you were very cold."

A further query about Oudinot, a nod and the audience was at an end, but the Emperor had made another conquest.

Short though her audience with Napoleon was, Eugénie walked away from it in a state of enchantment, but not from her reception by the Empress. She had always felt sympathetic to the girl of her own age, married for reasons of state to the man she called the Grampus, enemy of her family and her country, but Marie Louise's hauteur quickly dissipated that sympathy. Between her introduction by the Lady of Honour, the Duchesse de Montebello, and her dismissal two minutes only elapsed, two minutes in which the Empress uttered two or three banal phrases, so cold and distant as if determined to underline the enormous gulf between an Archduchess of Austria, Empress of the French, and the wife of a plebeian Marshal.

To the visits of ceremony Eugénie should have paid on her marriage and was now belatedly obliged to pay there seemed no end. Fortunately the Emperor's three sisters were in Italy, which reduced the number of her obligations, but their formidable mother was in residence at her mansion in the Faubourg St. Germain, the entrenched stronghold of the old nobility, bitterly hostile to her son.

Madame Mère, still beautiful in spite of her age, sat straight in her chair as she extended a kindly welcome to

Eugénie, but she did not hide her disapproval when her questions elicited the fact that the Oudinots had no child nor expected one.

"I have had twelve children," she told Eugénie proudly. "I was married at the age of fourteen and my first child was born nine months later. Four of my children died in infancy but the others were strong and healthy, as they have grown up to be. I hope that you will soon have a family as large or larger than mine. Nothing is so important as bearing children."

Eugénie forced a smile but Madame Mère's words distressed her so much that she repeated them to Charles, who soothed her by saying, "Do not take it to heart, Eugénie, all Corsicans have this obsession. The Emperor is known to consider the greatest women those who have borne the most children."

Eugénie had no desire to earn the Emperor's respect for the size of her family; all she wanted was one child but, even with Charles's almost miraculous restoration to normal health, the longing which had revived remained unsatisfied.

Eugénie encountered no reproaches at Malmaison when she paid her visit to the "old Empress," Josephine, whose charming welcome was far removed from the oppressive formality of the Tuileries.

"You must visit Malmaison often," she told the Oudinots as she led Eugénie and Charles through her picture gallery. "Come when the weather is warmer and I will take you to see my hothouses, my menagerie and above all my roses. Today it is too cold even to venture out-of-doors, although I know, dear Duchesse de Reggio, how inured you are to the cold."

With an apparently spontaneous gesture Josephine handed Eugénie the spray of white camellias she was holding before turning to chat with the Marshal who, as an old friend of the ex-Empress, had accompanied his wife. From time to time Josephine interrupted her conversation with him to ask Eugénie about her reception by Marie Louise with such studied artlessness that Oudinot was obliged to hide a smile.

--◦◆[ ]◆◦--

"You will both dine with me next week?"

The invitation was gratefully accepted, Eugénie voicing her astonishment as they drove away from Malmaison that the Emperor had abandoned so fascinating a woman for one as charmless as Marie Louise. Even though Josephine's appearance owed much to artifice she was still far more attractive than her successor, whose youthful freshness had vanished with the birth of her son, the King of Rome.

"You forget," Charles reminded Eugénie, "that for all Josephine's seductive powers she could not give the Emperor a son. To her marriage she brought only a tarnished reputation and debts, while Marie Louise not only gave Napoleon his heir but as her dowry peace with Austria."

Eugénie conceded that peace was welcome, but she could not like the Empress any better, nor was she sorry, though Charles was furious, when she was not invited to attend Marie Louise's *cercle*.

Only one final visit remained to be paid, to thank the Duchesse de Montebello for arranging her presentation to the Empress. Eugénie was eager to meet the woman she had glimpsed in Marie Louise's carriage when she passed through Vitry on her way to marry Napoleon, but she had been long enough in Paris to hear the generally unfavourable opinion of the Lady of Honour. Imperious with her equals and haughtily proud with her inferiors, no lady of the Court found favour with the Duchesse de Montebello who exercised a ruthless domination over the young Empress.

As Madame de Montebello was another old friend, widow of Marshal Lannes, mortally wounded in 1809 at Essling, Charles again accompanied his wife, to whom the Duchesse paid scant attention, until she suddenly broke off her conversation with the Marshal to address her.

"You are fortunate, Madame la Duchesse de Reggio, in holding no Court appointment. My earnest advice is that, should one be offered you, have the courage to refuse."

Madame de Montebello paid no further attention to Eugénie to burst out to Oudinot, "I could scream at this awful charge the Emperor has imposed on me in the mistaken belief that thereby he was showing his friendship for my husband, but this so-called honour is nothing but slavery, gilded slavery perhaps, but slavery nevertheless. All I want is to return to my own home to bring up my children, made fatherless by the Emperor's passion for war."

This outburst astonished Eugénie and infuriated the Marshal. Had the Duchesse de Montebello seen, as he himself had seen, the tears rolling down the Emperor's cheeks as he held the hand of the dying Lannes, one of his oldest and dearest friends, she might have spoken differently! The Oudinots were both glad to take their leave.

Her duties now at an end, Eugénie was free to enjoy her first visit to Paris. Charles made light of his limp to take her to admire all the buildings with which the Emperor was embellishing his capital in his determination to make Paris the finest city in the world. Disdaining to use the carriage Charles marched Eugénie from the Arc de Triomphe du Carrousel, erected by the Emperor to the army he "had the honour to command," through the arcaded Rue de Rivoli to the still unfinished Arc de Triomphe de l'Etoile, dominating the crest of the prettily wooded Champs Elysées but nothing she saw of the great monuments impressed Eugénie as much as the sight of the little King of Rome in his miniature carriage drawn by two white does.

Eugénie enjoyed her guided tour of Paris far more than the succession of receptions, balls, theatrical performances, hunts, diplomatic audiences, parades of the guard and the Paris garrison. Although attendance at the Tuileries afforded her a glimpse of the Emperor the etiquette was oppressive and even a newcomer to Imperial society was conscious of how superficial was the gaiety enforced by Napoleon, as if gaiety could be imposed by will, but he was intent on demonstrating to the world that, although a campaign had been lost, the war had not, though so many had died, his genius was still alive.

The losses were most apparent at the balls; no mourning might be worn, but none was needed; the faces of many women bore witness to their grief for a husband, a son or a brother lost in the Russian snows. As the Empress sulked, pettishly declaring that she no longer cared to dance, the balls lacked animation; too many danced with empty sleeves, too many wore the marks of frostbite, too many, hobbling on sticks, did not dance at all, and the Faubourg St. Germain jeered at the Emperor's "balls of the wooden legs."

Of all the attempts to revive the previous year's gaiety, none was more disastrous than the Inca quadrille, devised by the ex-Queen of Holland. Few of those who had taken part survived while others were prisoners of war. By tacit consent no further attempts were made for performances of the quadrilles which had once enchanted by their lavishness and ingenuity.

Eugénie was surprised that the Marshal no longer raised any objection to her dancing but she now took little pleasure in it as none of her partners' steps matched her own as well as Letellier's had done. She wondered where he was now; there had been no news of him since he had left the Oudinots in Prussia. No doubt, like the other aides-de-camp, on his return to France he had gone on well-earned leave, Jacqueminot alone remaining in Paris on duty with the Marshal.

Soon all the Marshal's staff would be obliged to resume their duties because, as spring advanced, it was apparent that the uneasy interlude of peace was drawing to a close. The Emperor's determination to avenge the Russian disaster was strengthened by the defection to Russia and Sweden of his former ally, Prussia, as he busied himself with reorganizing his armies, daily reviewing fresh drafts of recruits until, as France braced herself for a new war, the waltz music was drowned by the beat of fife and drum.

Paris was emptying rapidly, the men taking up their stations in the east while the women returned to their country estates or to take the waters at Aix-en-Savoie or Plombières. Charles, pronounced by his doctors fit to take the field, had been given command of the Twelfth Corps and now had little time for outings with Eugénie or showing her off to his friends.

Eugénie was left very much to her own devices with no
intimate friend with whom to eat ices at Tortoni's, stroll
about Frascati or marvel at Leroy's latest creations, so that
when the Duchesse de Castiglione paid her a long-overdue
visit she was delighted, but not for long.

Adèle was so full of herself and her own consequence, so
obviously dazzled by her title, her position at Court and her
husband's fortune that Eugénie was repelled by so parvenu
an attitude in one born a Boulon de Chavanges, but what
disgusted her was Adèle's jeering at her husband's vulgarity.
Eugénie had not forgotten Marshal Augereau's kindliness on
her journey to Vilna.

Coldly Eugénie turned the conversation to their youthful
days at Vitry nor was she sorry when Adèle rushed away;
they would, of course, meet from time to time at the Tuileries, but any wish for a renewal of their former intimacy
had vanished.

Eugénie's next caller was assured of a very different reception. She was flattered that the Maréchale Marmont,
Duchesse de Raguse, had sought her out, particularly as she
was curious to see the woman whose husband the Emperor
had urged to divorce her. Charles had told her that rumours
of a divorce must be untrue; Hortense Marmont was an
heiress and Marmont, who spent money like a drunken
sailor, would not be so foolish as to throw the money bags
out of the window.

"She's a charming woman anyway," he added. "They
should learn to live comfortably together like us, eh,
Eugénie?"

If he had forgotten how coldly he had thanked her for
her care of him on their journey from Vilna, she had not. His
words had been like a blow, an icy draft which had extinguished the nascent warmth of her changing attitude to him.

Eugénie liked Hortense Marmont on sight, she was so
lively and totally lacking in condescension although so much
older. As she threw off her furs Hortense said impetuously,
"I have been so eager to meet you, Madame la Duchesse de
Reggio, but while Marmont was away in Spain I had so

much to do. I want to hear all about your escape from Russia—indeed everyone wants to see the brave young woman who braved such dangers."

Blushing furiously, Eugénie disclaimed any heroism on her part, always embarrassed when praised for devotion to her husband. As briefly as was compatible with politeness, Eugénie related her journey, even to her own ears making its rigours sound colourless but nevertheless Madame Marmont looked at her in admiration.

"And now tell me what you think of Paris and the Court. We who have known the Emperor since he was General Bonaparte no longer feel the same about going to the Tuileries, it is so insufferably dull and etiquette, they say, stiffer even than at Vienna, but Napoleon wanted the most splendid Court in Europe and its most magnificent capital and that he undoubtedly has, but it is all spoilt by Marie Louise—no one likes her."

With this opinion Eugénie expressed her hearty agreement. Her glacial reception by the Empress still rankled.

Hortense Marmont fell into a reminiscent mood.

"You were only a child when Bonaparte became First Consul, Madame la Duchesse de Reggio, so you would not know that at that time there was nothing which might be called society, only a raffish mob of get-rich-quicks, army contractors and women of doubtful reputation—morals were loose as everyone was intent on forgetting as quickly as possible the years of the Terror in an orgy of pleasure and licence. The First Consul quickly put a stop to all that and, of course, Josephine's charm and grace of manner were invaluable in re-creating a stable society. I wish you had known the Tuileries in her day—it's certainly more magnificent now but the magic is lacking. Did you not find her charming when you went to Malmaison?"

"No one could have been kinder—" Eugénie's face lit up—"when Charles and I dined with her; she made me feel so much at home."

"That's because no one else has the same tact as Josephine or a greater gift for making the best of herself." Hortense Marmont chuckled. "At the Coronation she managed to look twenty years less than her age—all skilful make-up but her graceful figure needs no artifice."

Eugénie hung fascinated on her words as Hortense continued talking about the Coronation, of which she had known little since it had caused Madame de Coucy so much distress.

"Nothing will ever be like it again, so gorgeous, so impressive, the Emperor himself almost godlike in his Imperial purple mantle worn over a long white satin tunic so heavily embroidered in gold and doubled in ermine that the weight must have been unbearable. Only some of the older Marshals struck a discordant note. They peacocked in their deep blue tunics and mantles but behind their hands they sniggered at what they regarded as the mumbo-jumbo of the mass. Marmont wouldn't have done so; he comes of a good family and was properly brought up, anyway he wasn't yet made Marshal."

Hortense broke off to say with a laugh, "Do you know what we have in common, Madame la Duchesse de Reggio?" Eugénie looked puzzled, unable to imagine in what way she shared anything with the lively Duchesse de Raguse, who smiled as she saw Eugénie's brow wrinkle.

"Our husbands were raised to the Marshalate on the same day, but, of course, you were not then married."

Softly Eugénie murmured the catch phrase she had already often heard repeated.

"France nominated Macdonald, the army nominated Oudinot and friendship nominated Marmont."

Hortense Marmont's face, a moment before so mischievously gay, now wore a pensive look.

"Yes, friendship nominated Marmont. He is one of the Emperor's oldest friends. He had money and General Bonaparte, who had none, frequently dipped his hands in Marmont's pocket for which he was grateful. That, I think is his fatal weakness, gratitude. He wanted my husband to marry his sister Pauline but Marmont was brave enough to refuse, saying that he would not find with her the domestic felicity of a young man's dream—as if anyone would find domestic happiness with such a flibbertigibbet! Of course she's beautiful—her brother calls her the most beautiful woman of her time—but women have another name for her."

As Hortense Marmont continued talking about her husband Eugénie felt increasingly embarrassed, certain that she herself would never reveal Charles's weaknesses to a stranger. Perhaps he was mistaken when he had told her that, after so many storms in their married life, the Marmonts were again in charity with each other.

"Marmont was bitterly resentful that he did not figure in the first creation of Marshals in 1804 and his resentment grew until he became jealous of everybody else and obsessively ambitious."

"But Marshal Marmont did get his baton at Wagram," Eugénie put in with some hesitation.

"But only after the Emperor upbraided him for manoeuvring like an oyster, though how an oyster manoeuvres he did not explain."

With a quick change of mood Hortense laughed, to Eugénie's relief.

"The Emperor told Charles, my husband, that he deserved to be shot."

"We all know that was because, by disobeying orders, the Duc de Reggio helped to win the battle."

The Duchesse de Raguse rose to take her leave, once again vivacious as she impulsively kissed Eugénie.

"You must forgive me for running on so—I get carried away when I find a sympathetic listener and you are a very good one. You must come to see me soon, Madame la Duchesse, or may I not call you Eugénie?"

As Hortense Marmont bustled away Eugénie felt that she had found a friend in her, promising to return her visit as soon as possible but she was not deceived by her liveliness. With unusual perceptiveness in one so young Eugénie felt that the underlying cause of Hortense's revelations of her husband's weaknesses was that, after a marriage of nearly twenty years, small hope of bearing a child remained to her

—◦◦⊱❦⊰◦◦—

128

and that perhaps the Emperor's advice to Marmont had reached her.

When Charles returned home that evening Eugénie told him of the Duchesse de Raguse's visit but not what she had said, only asking a little mischievously whether the army were not as much involved in gossip as in war, a sally which made the Marshal laugh.

"You may be right but it is essential that the Emperor be informed of everything—nothing is too trivial for him to know. That marvellous brain seizes on what is important and discards what is not."

Eugénie's hope of pursuing her acquaintance with Hortense Marmont was dashed when, to her dismay, she heard the Marshal humming the fateful air, *"Malbrouck s'en-va-t'en guerre,"* although about the outcome of this new campaign he showed less than his usual confidence. Despite the horrific losses sustained in Russia, the Emperor was preparing to put 300,000 men into the field but, as Oudinot patiently explained to Eugénie, not only soldiers were needed in war.

"Horses are less easily replaceable than men and in Russia we lost not less than sixty thousand horses. I wish to God I had been mistaken about Frederick William's hostility to France, but I was not. Prussia is already supporting the Russian advance towards the Oder while withdrawals of troops from Spain leave the remainder of our army in the Peninsula dangerously exposed, although the Emperor is convinced that the British will not go over to the offensive."

Oudinot's lips were set in a hard line as he threw back his shoulders to continue, "With us we have Westphalia, Bavaria and Saxony, Allies who will enable us to teach the King of Prussia that France can still muster an army capable of defeating him, as she has so often defeated him before."

But to Eugénie his words lacked conviction.

Soon it was time for the Oudinots to leave Paris, where few people now remained with the exception of the Empress, appointed Regent and the household.

Eugénie was surprised to see only one carriage, the Oudinots' own, drawn up outside the house in the Rue de

Bourgogne and to find that Jacqueminot alone appeared to be accompanying them but she supposed that, as the street was so narrow, the other carriages awaited them in the open space behind the Corps Législatif. When she questioned the Marshal he merely growled, not being in the best of tempers. Jacqueminot answered for him.

"My colleagues are coming from many parts of France so it has been arranged that they will meet the Marshal on his way to Mayence. So far as I am aware the only change in the staff is General Lejeune for General de Lorencez who now has an independent command."

This was not the answer for which Eugénie had hoped but with it she had to be content, promising herself that, when Charles recovered his good temper, she would try to find out where and when Letellier would join him, resolutely refusing to acknowledge why it was important for her to know.

As the Marshal's route eastwards always took him through Bar-le-Duc he would deposit Eugénie at the Hôtel Oudinot before proceeding on his way, but on their arrival at Bar they were horrified to find that the mansion had been virtually destroyed by fire and little more of it remained than ruins. For Oudinot this disaster was far more than the destruction of a home; it had been the visible sign of the success he had won so hardly, built not with bricks and stone but with his blood and wounds. As he stared at the shell of what had been so splendid a house, his silence was more eloquent than words until finally he said in a flat voice without a trace of emotion, "We will drive on to Jeand'heurs where you may stay until my return. Meanwhile you will superintend the rebuilding of the house which I will have put in hand forthwith."

He took his seat in the carriage beside Eugénie with no further word until they reached Jeand'heurs, where he did not linger with his farewell, for once anxious not to go to war but to have done with this campaign.

After her exhausting stay in Paris Eugénie would have been content to exchange Bar for the peace of Jeand'heurs had it not been for the shock of the catastrophe, but she had scarcely begun to unpack her trunks before her maître d'hôtel asked if she would receive Colonel Letellier. Although surprised by this unexpected visit she said, "Certainly. Please tell Colonel Letellier that I shall be with him immediately."

Pausing only to see that she looked reasonably neat, she ran downstairs, greeting Letellier with the words, "What good wind blows you here, Colonel Letellier? Did I not understand that you would be meeting the Marshal on the way to Mayence?"

"I must beg your pardon, Madame la Maréchale, for intruding on you so unceremoniously—" holding Eugénie's hand a little longer than courtesy demanded. "That was my intention until I found that I could as easily meet the Marshal at Bar and travel with him."

No doubt Eugénie did not know, nor did he feel the need to tell her, that Bar-le-Duc was by no means on his direct route from the Vendée to Mayence, but the chance of seeing her was one he could not forego.

"I was shocked by the disaster to the Hôtel Oudinot and guessed that you were probably here at Jeand'heurs. I could not go on my way without tendering my condolences for the dreadful loss you and the Marshal have sustained."

"Thank you for your kind thought. Naturally the Marshal and I are deeply distressed, he even more than I since the house was so much longer his home, but you know his wonderful powers of recovery. I am hopeful that, by the time he returns, the house will be in a fair way to being habitable again, but I am sorry for your disappointment in missing the Marshal, who left only a short while ago. He, at least, has Jacqueminot with him but you will be obliged to travel alone."

No sign of disappointment was visible on Letellier's face, only a dancing light in his eyes as he accepted Eugénie's invitation to sit down and take some refreshment.

"Do you know, Madame la Maréchale, that we have not met since we parted company in Russia? I am delighted to see that you have recovered from that terrible experience."

He thought that she showed no signs of that ordeal but there was a subtle change in her, not only her greater elegance but more poise and a quiet self-confidence.

"Of course I have recovered." Eugénie laughed. "As you well know, I was the one who suffered least."

This he would not have, protesting that her sufferings had been as great, if not greater, than anyone else's since she was not inured to the hardships which were a soldier's lot. For a little while they argued gaily, increasingly conscious of the idleness of their talk until silence fell between them as each covertly took stock of the other.

Eugénie was distressed to see Letellier's gaiety fall away to give place to the melancholy always so close to the surface while he, who had thought it would be enough to sit near her, to look at her sweet face and steadfast eyes, discovered that he wanted far more, but dared he risk a rebuff by avowing his feelings or should he be content with a brief hour of conversation?

From their very first meeting he had been drawn to Eugénie; it was the knowledge that his feelings were developing into something infinitely warmer which had impelled him to leave her and the Marshal in Russia at the first opportunity. He had long suspected that, although she had cared devotedly for Oudinot in Vilna and on their homeward journey, she acted from a sense of duty not love. Why he should know this he failed to understand except that he was sensitive to everything concerning her. He longed to know if she regarded him in a different light from the other aides-de-camp but he realised that it would be grossly improper to take advantage of a woman alone, one moreover the wife of his superior officer.

Letellier rose, conscious of the temptation of staying longer.

"If I am to overtake the Marshal—no great problem since he is little more than a day's march ahead—regretfully I must take my leave."

At least he would be able to meet the Marshal without the burden of guilt!

"God willing, we will meet again, Colonel Letellier," Eugénie said gently as she proffered him her hand. "I rely on you, on you all, the Marshal's aides-de-camp," she corrected herself hastily, "to take good care of yourselves. You are in some sort my family as you are his, perhaps the only family he will ever have."

The words were spoken so low that Letellier scarcely caught them, but they comforted him; at least he need have no cause to be jealous that she was carrying the Marshal's child.

Eugénie accompanied him to the door, remaining to watch him until he reached the end of the drive where his carriage was waiting. He waved his hand, she waved hers in reply, then he was gone.

She went back into the house, feeling more forlorn than when she had parted from her husband. Was it wrong to care whether or not she would see Michel Letellier again? She was not as unaware as he had imagined of what had been unsaid, even perhaps undone. Would her resolution have wavered? There was no need to answer her own question. It was too late.

Charlotte, Gräfin von Kielmansegge, lost count of time as she awaited her guests in the colonnaded porch of her Schloss Lübbenau, shading her eyes from the glare of the sunset gilding the ornamental water lying in front of her, but twilight had already fallen before the distant sound of horses' hooves signalled the arrival of Marshal Oudinot and his staff, assigned to the Schloss as their quarters for the duration of the armistice recently signed at Pleswitz. Minutes later the plumed troop trotted into view to draw rein at the portico, Oudinot the first to dismount to kiss the hand the Gräfin held out to him, saying with his easy courtesy, "It gives me great pleasure, Frau Gräfin, to renew our all too slight acquaintance and to beg you to accept my grateful thanks for your hospitality to me and to my staff. Please rest assured that, so long as we occupy your home, we shall make every effort not to disrupt your life more than is absolutely necessary."

Charlotte von Kielmansegge graciously inclined her head.

"In welcoming you to Lübbenau, I trust you will regard as your own the house I now invite you to enter."

Before he accepted her invitation the Marshal asked permission to present his chief of staff and his aides-de-camp. As he named General Lejeune, Lachaise, de Lamarre, de Bourcet, Jacqueminot and Letellier, they were hard put to it to conceal their surprise that, instead of the stiff elderly German dowager they expected to see, a beautiful young woman, whom they judged to be in her early thirties, smiled as they saluted her. Charlotte von Kielmansegge herself was delighted by the group of handsome young men whose presence would undoubtedly enliven the old Schloss, too vast for a woman alone and lonely, but it was on Michel Letellier that her gaze rested longest. His exceptional good looks and splendid physique, enhanced by his light blue hussar's uniform, the befrogged dolman thrown negligently over one shoulder, the shako with its tall black plume adding to his commanding height, impressed her as no man had ever impressed her before. The heart, which for too long had beaten in a vacuum, pounded in Charlotte's bosom as she fell madly in love at first sight.

As the little party trooped into the house, although Charlotte was filled with excitement, she could not avoid the thought that, in assigning her home as his quarters to the Marshal, the Emperor had some mischievous intention since he had once suggested Oudinot as a suitable husband for her, careless of the fact that her husband was still living. She did not want Oudinot but she was piqued that to the full bloom of her beauty, her grace and her superior intelligence he had preferred an immature young girl. Her surmise was, however, mistaken. Napoleon was not responsible for the arrangements made when his army was dismissed to quarters and he had other matters far more important on his mind.

By the superhuman effort of which he alone was capable, the Emperor had put a large army into the field, beating the Russians and the Prussians in a hard-fought campaign first at Lützen and more decisively at Bautzen. To the battle-weary troops on both sides the armistice offered a welcome respite even, it was whispered, to the Emperor himself. Nevertheless he regretted the lost opportunity of following up his victories with a final blow, his consent to an armistice motivated by his shortage of cavalry and the ambivalent attitude of Austria.

Once again Napoleon took up his residence at Dresden, not at the royal palace but at the Marcolini palace where he maintained his usual state, though shorn now of the parterre of sovereigns to whom a mere year ago he had acted as arrogant host. Only the King of Saxony, whose capital he now occupied, remained as his staunchest ally.

Before he left Paris the Emperor had declared to the Corps Législatif:

"I wish for peace but the peace I shall make will be an honourable one."

That honourable peace could be achieved only if Austria consented to terms acceptable to Napoleon but the conference deliberating at Prague was dominated by the Austrian Chancellor, Metternich, who held the Emperor of Austria in the hollow of his hand. Already it was clear that the demands made on France would be severe.

"How much is England paying you to oppose me?" The Emperor harangued Metternich to whom he had granted an audience. "Never shall I agree to cede an inch of territory! Your sovereigns, who were born to thrones, can be beaten twenty times and still return to their capitals. I cannot do that. I am a self-made soldier!"

Watched with cold irony by Metternich the Emperor furiously threw his hat across the room which the Chancellor made no move to pick up, obliging Napoleon to retrieve it himself.

"Tell me, Metternich," he continued, "was I not a fool to marry an Austrian princess?"

"Since you seek my opinion, sire, I must say that the great conqueror, Napoleon, was mistaken," was the urbane reply.

"And the Emperor Francis would chase his daughter from the throne of France?"

"Sire, the Emperor of Austria thinks only of the good of his empire and will not be guided by personal considerations, not even his daughter's fate. He will not hesitate to sacrifice his family for the good of his empire."

In a muffled voice Napoleon muttered, "What you say does not surprise me, only shows me how great was my error."

All he had crudely wanted was a womb more fertile than Josephine's but he had been flattered to ally himself with the "daughter of the Caesars" who brought peace as her dowry. He was fond of Marie Louise and grateful that she had borne him a son but, although he would not confess it even to himself, a young wife who had inherited her father's exaggerated sexuality was a burden to a man of middle age.

With a sudden change of mood Napoleon screamed at Metternich, "I know how to die—if you want war you shall have it. Very well, we shall meet at Vienna."

The Emperor indicated that the audience was at an end but, as he escorted the Chancellor to the door, he put his hand on Metternich's shoulder, murmuring persuasively, "Surely you will not start the war again?"

Metternich had the final word.

"You are lost, sire. I had a presentiment before I came here. Now I am certain of it."

As the door closed behind him Metternich smiled thinly; it was all up with Bonaparte.

Small wonder that the Emperor's most intimate associates were conscious of a change in him. He was often distrait, alternating between gaiety and gloom, so depressed by the loss in battle of two of his oldest and dearest friends that he seemed to be losing confidence in the star which had guided an insignificant lieutenant of artillery to the mastery of Europe. To add to the problems bedevilling him was the loss in battle of many generals and the absence from the campaign of a number of Marshals which increased Oudinot's importance.

Rarely in the course of their campaigns had the Marshal and his staff found quarters as pleasant as Schloss Lübbenau, which offered every kind of sport for their entertainment during these idle days, but the greatest attraction was the Gräfin herself. Bewitched by her charm and the message of her lustrous black eyes, the aides-de-camp fluttered round her with the exception of Jacqueminot who, arrogantly conscious of his own claims to preference, disdained to enter the lists for Charlotte von Kielmansegge's favours. Any one of the others was hers for the asking but, as de Bourcet observed ruefully to Letellier, "It's you alone she wants."

As a fighting man whose tomorrow was always a question mark Michel Letellier had learned to live for the day. In the countries occupied by the French the temptations they met were frequently too great to be resisted and why should they resist when women made themselves so easy, ready to buy favours for husbands and brothers with the only coin they possessed? From Letellier Charlotte sought one favour alone, himself, a desire she betrayed by the special radiance surrounding a woman passionately in love, by her brighter eyes, more translucent skin and whole body nervously alive.

Michel, whose heart was armoured by another love, was ready enough for a pleasant interlude with a beautiful and desirable woman but fond though he grew of her, his heart was not involved so that, as time passed, he was frequently irritated by her increasing demands on him. Whenever he was on duty at the Schloss she contrived that he spend the larger part of his time in the privacy of her own apartments, stifling his protests with wild kisses until, in spite of himself, he responded to her ardour.

At other times, exhausted by her passion, he would disentangle himself from her arms to beg, "May we not sit quietly for a while? I have been out riding with the Marshal and am exhausted."

Contrite, Charlotte would sit beside him on a sofa, smoothing his hair, caressing his shoulders as she murmured, "My Saint Michel, my angel, my archangel!" until she could restrain herself no longer and Michel's fatigue and reluctance were overcome.

Charlotte von Kielmansegge was wise enough not to ne-

138

glect her principal guest, making it her practice to take a daily stroll with the Marshal in her magnificent park where the trees were in their early summer green. With Oudinot she talked freely about the Emperor for whom she cherished a devotion compounded of respect, awe, admiration and a love in its purest sense far removed from her sensual passion for Letellier. Particularly during her promenades with the Marshal Charlotte questioned him eagerly for news of the progress of the peace conference to meet the same reply.

"All I know is that the original six weeks of armistice have been prolonged until August, but I have been warned that celebrations of the Emperor's birthday, which should take place on August 15, have been put forward in case hostilities are resumed."

In reply to a further question he shook his head.

"At Prague they are still talking but what, if anything, has been decided I am ignorant. No doubt in a day or two the Emperor will send for me and I shall have some definite news for you."

"Do you think," Charlotte asked wistfully, "that the Emperor will send for me?"

"*Meine liebe Frau Gräfin*," Oudinot laughed, "the Emperor is so incalculable that we never know what he will do from one day to the next, but why do we talk about him when I had so much rather talk about ourselves?"—words which sounded a warning bell in Charlotte von Kielmansegge's ears.

Early in his married life Charles Oudinot had assured his wife that she need not fear he would imitate the conduct of his fellow Marshals in Spain, that she would always find him a faithful husband. If he now remembered this declaration, he had forgotten that he had also told her that a woman was necessary to him, forgotten, too, Eugénie awaiting his return at Jeand'heurs and painstakingly carrying out his instructions about the rebuilding of the house at Bar. All that the Marshal remembered and thought of was his desire for the Gräfin walking beside him.

Charlotte von Kielmansegge was perfectly conscious of

her effect on men. Although she would indignantly have disclaimed coquetry on her part in fact she found it impossible not to encourage any man with whom she came in contact to fall a little in love with her. For once her obsession with both Letellier and Napoleon had blinded her to Oudinot's mounting admiration. Now, suddenly aware of it, she would gladly have staved off the declaration it was obvious he was about to make.

"You must have observed, my dear Comtesse, the great admiration I have for you though admiration is too pale a word to express my feelings," he began in a voice charged with emotion. "Dare I look from you for some sign that you share those feelings? My own are ardent and long to be fulfilled."

Aware of the extreme delicacy of the moment but even more of the embarrassment that this unwelcome declaration might cause in the future, Charlotte von Kielmansegge gently withdrew her hand from the Marshal's grasp.

"Believe me, my dear Marshal," she said softly, "that I am deeply touched by this avowal of your affectionate regard. Never could I have dreamt that, in the midst of a terrible war, I should meet with such warmth of feeling. So long as I live I shall be a friend to you and to all your happy family of young men, but to my sorrow I can promise nothing more."

Oudinot was obliged to accept the Gräfin's rejection of his advances with as good a grace as he could muster and for a time they strolled on in silence, but he was shrewd enough to realise that a woman of Charlotte's ardent temperament would not lack a lover. The Marshal was conscious of a spurt of jealousy as he asked himself who of his entourage was more fortunate than he?

Determined to find out, Oudinot increased his evening visits to the Gräfin's salon where, the war temporarily forgotten, the aides-de-camp laughed and joked while as usual de Bourcet sat at the piano, showing a preference for playing sad love songs with a quizzical look at Letellier. When he softly sang the words of Queen Hortense's air, *"Partant pour la Syrie,"* his gaze rested so compellingly on Letellier as he repeated the refrain that the brave Dunois should love the most beautiful woman that the Marshal's suspicions were aroused. Glancing in the Gräfin's direction Oudinot observed that her eyes strayed so constantly to the hussar that he drew his own conclusions. Perversely the resentment he felt was with his aide-de-camp, not the Gräfin herself who, sensitive to everything concerning Michel, was uncomfortably conscious of being the cause of the Marshal's increasing coldness to him.

The strained atmosphere was relieved by the Emperor's command to Oudinot to attend him at Dresden, the same courier bringing a letter to the Gräfin inviting her presence at the Marcolini palace.

"See, Monsieur le Maréchal." With a radiant smile Charlotte held out the Emperor's letter. "His Majesty has invited me to Dresden."

"Then, Madame la Comtesse, as the Emperor has summoned me also I shall be most happy to escort you if you will do me the honour of accompanying me."

The journey from Lübbenau was made in great state, the Marshal in one carriage with Lachaise and Jacqueminot, Charlotte and her small daughter in another, the cortège escorted by a piquet of cavalry and from one stage to the next by officers of the Marshal's Corps. Charlotte's initial reaction to the omission of Letellier from Oudinot's suite was one of disappointment but on second thoughts she conceded that it were better so; her whole heart and mind could now be concentrated on the Emperor.

In general Napoleon had only one use for women, convinced that when they meddled in serious matters they always intrigued but for Charlotte von Kielmansegge he made an exception. During a long stay in Paris she had earned his esteem by the discretion with which she had acted as his eyes and ears but, while no means insensible to her charm and beauty, he valued her services too highly to make her his mistress.

"It gives me great pleasure to see you again, Madame la

Comtesse," the Emperor greeted her when she was ushered into his presence, bending with awkward gallantry to kiss her hand before demanding peremptorily, "What's this I hear? Your property at Schmochtitz was plundered by an Italian regiment under the command of Marshal Marmont?"

"Yes, sire, that unfortunately is so."

"Marmont shall compensate you for this want of discipline. I myself will see to it." He smiled the smile that Eugénie Oudinot was not alone in finding irresistible. "In exchange you shall have a house in Paris, then you will always be near me."

Charlotte's adoring eyes never left Napoleon's face as for a while they talked about the present situation until he was obliged to take leave of her, but saying, "You will come to lunch with me tomorrow."

She did not expect the honour of a tête-à-tête luncheon with the Emperor but next day she found only a few other guests, the Duc de Bassano, Marshal Oudinot and Marshal Berthier, the indispensable chief of staff. Standing a little apart, the men discussed the war in general and the advantages and disadvantages of the prolongation of the armistice. Charlotte listened attentively, taking no part in the conversation, but she was struck by Berthier's gloom, who was depressed by the news he had just received from Spain of an English victory at Vittoria with heavy losses in men and equipment by the French.

The Emperor, already infuriated by the ineptitude of his brother Joseph, King of Spain, had also listened in silence but with increasing irritation until the two Marshals and the Duc de Bassano gave their decided opinion in favour of peace, even though it might involve surrender of the Rhine frontier.

"No!" shouted Napoleon, thumping the table so vigorously that the plates and cutlery rattled. "I am ready for any sacrifice but make peace under such conditions I will not."

Angrily the Emperor turned his back on his Marshals and Foreign Minister to address himself to Charlotte von

Kielmansegge, his wrath dying as he reminded her of his promise to look after her affairs. Oudinot, anxious to restore harmony, intervened to praise her kindness and the warmth of her hospitality.

"I assure you, sire," he said earnestly, "that next to my own Jeand'heurs there is nowhere I would rather be than at Schloss Lübbenau."

This tribute to the woman whom he held in such affectionate regard so mollified the Emperor that he suggested that Oudinot recount some of his exploits which the Marshal was pleased to do. Turning to the Gräfin, he began to tell her about his narrow escape from the Cossacks after crossing the Beresina but the Emperor, who had ceased to listen, interrupted the recital to bark, "Then we make war?"

"Yes, sire," was Oudinot's quiet reply, "a bad thing."

In horrified silence Charlotte watched Napoleon spring to his feet, stride to the door which he opened and gestured to the Marshal to get out, but Oudinot merely bowed, smiled and left the room in the most natural way possible. Was it her fancy or did she really hear the Emperor mutter, "I have no illusions about the Marshals; they do not love me but they fear me. If I should meet with a great misfortune they would be the first to abandon me."

It must have been fancy Charlotte decided because, with the mercurial change of mood characteristic of him, the Emperor, apparently oblivious of any contretemps, immediately began to talk to her about the theatrical performances he had ordered to take place nightly at the Marcolini palace.

"You must come tomorrow evening—they will be giving a comedy of Marivaux, though as you know my preference is for tragedy. It is my firm belief that drama lifts up the heart and inspires heroic deeds. Were Corneille alive today I would make him a prince but, since that gratification is denied me, will *you* not give me the pleasure of lunching with me tomorrow? Now, my dear Comtesse, if you will forgive me I have work to do."

Overwhelmed by this evidence of Napoleon's regard for her Charlotte eagerly accepted both invitations, troubled nevertheless that Oudinot might suffer some punishment, even degradation, for his temerity in offering advice so patently unwelcome but her fears proved groundless. When she returned to the inn where she was lodging she found the Marshal placidly playing with her small daughter without the slightest sign of anger or fear at the Emperor's wrath.

"Do not distress yourself, dear friend—" he laughed at her anxious face—"about the scene you witnessed; such rages are of frequent occurrence. The Emperor needs me. I wager that he will send for me tomorrow and behave as if nothing had happened. If he fails to do so I'll come to drink my coffee with you, but don't count on it!"

Oudinot was right. Next day he was again Charlotte's fellow guest at Napoleon's table. As they took their seats the Marshal whispered in her ear, "You see, the Emperor needs me."

The subject of peace or war was carefully avoided and the Emperor appeared to have recovered his good humour which so relieved Charlotte that she showed more warmth than she intended to the Marshal, who escorted her to the theatre, which encouraged him to exert all his charm, with the intention of making her regret her rejection of his advances. To emphasize that he bore her no ill-will, he showed her a miniature of Eugénie on which the Gräfin complimented him.

"You are fortunate in possessing so young and charming a wife," she said as she handed the miniature back, managing to imply at the same time that he had no need to look elsewhere.

Oudinot was on the point of following up what he assumed to be some slight encouragement when he had to make way for the Emperor, who took the Gräfin's hand to lead her up to the King of Saxony, saying, "May I recommend this dear lady to Your Majesty? She has been of inestimable value to me in looking after one of my Marshals so well that I am doubtful of being able to prize him away from Schloss Lübbenau."

The King of Saxony smiled wryly; he knew that this subject of his own was valuable to Napoleon, not merely in the hospitality she showed to Marshal Oudinot but as one of his agents and no doubt as his mistress also.

The Emperor's graciousness made the evening one of unalloyed happiness for the Gräfin but, when next day he sent for her, she found him alone and sombre, in great contrast to his geniality at the theatre.

"I have sent for you, Madame la Comtesse, because I wish to repeat to you in person what I bade Oudinot tell you—that you are one of the rare women I have loved with my whole heart. Perhaps it is because of the high opinion I hold of you that I have never attempted to alter our relationship, a compliment I have paid to no other woman. Because of my regard for your intelligence and devotion to me I wish to entrust you with a mission of the greatest importance."

Tears started to Charlotte's eyes at this praise from a man whom she held above all others. Words were beyond her, but they were not needed as Napoleon continued, "Whatever results from the Prague conference I can see only difficulties ahead. All now depends on Austria although I cannot believe that Papa François will join the Allies to fight against me but Metternich is the man with whom I must reckon, not my father-in-law."

An angry look passed over the Emperor's face as he recalled Metternich's biting words, but his tone was still equable.

"What the future holds none of us can foresee," he said with a point of sadness, "but of one thing I am certain, that your devotion to me will never waver. That is why I asked you to come here today."

Followed by the Gräfin's eyes, Napoleon walked over to a desk to take out a small packet which he handed to her, saying with great solemnity, "I am entrusting this packet to your safe keeping until I send for it; it contains a letter for the Czar whose evasions and perversions of the truth are responsible for much that has happened to me of late. I have told him of my regret that we have ceased to understand each other and my hope of mutual forgiveness. Finally, as Alexander considers himself the greater sufferer I exhort him to fulfil a ruler's primary duty, to propagate religion which has an influence far greater than philosophers realise."

Charlotte's tears were now flowing freely as she sensed despondency in the Emperor's words so that only with difficulty did she find enough voice to ask, "What should I do if my house is searched?"

"You must act as you think fit in the circumstance, only be cautious. If the Russians search your house you may deliver the packet to their senior officer, but be sure to obtain a receipt."

That Napoleon could give such businesslike advice in a moment so charged with emotion brought a tremulous smile to Charlotte's lips but her tears returned when the Emperor took her hand, pressing it slightly as with deep seriousness he urged her to consider abjuring the Protestant faith to join the true church.

"Become a Catholic and we shall then be certain of meeting in the next world."

Napoleon turned aside to blow his nose, a homely gesture which touched Charlotte more than anything he had said. Then, with his most attractive smile and his arm about her shoulders, he led her to the door, his voice very tender as he uttered his parting words, "I have not forgotten about the house for you in Paris—there we shall most surely meet again. *Lebwohl!*"

All that the Emperor had said during this interview but most of all his solemn injunction to change her faith filled Charlotte von Kielmansegge with foreboding that she had seen him for the last time, a conviction strengthened by sensing that, despite his promise that they would meet again in Paris, this was also his belief.

With so much on her mind Charlotte was not sorry that her return journey to Lübbenau was made alone as the Marshal had gone to review his troops. Somewhat shamefacedly she confessed to herself that, during their stay at Dresden, her admiration of Oudinot's character and conduct had grown to such proportions that, had they remained only a few days longer, she might have been in danger of yielding to him. Surely it was possible to love two men at the same time? Did she not love the Emperor? In all honesty Charlotte recognized the great gulf which lay between her attachment to Napoleon and what she felt for the Marshal and still more for Michel. It was on him alone that her mind was fixed the nearer she approached the Schloss, but his welcome disappointed her.

"Of course I am happy that you have returned," Letellier protested as soon as he and Charlotte were alone, "but while you were away I received news of my father's grave illness. I long to go to him but, even if the Marshal were indulgent enough to grant me leave of absence, I could not go. My home is in the Vendée in the extreme west of France—impossible to make the return journey in time to resume my duties should war break out again."

Charlotte was all sympathy but Letellier was only partially truthful in ascribing his coolness to his anxiety about his father. Her absence had released him to enjoy the happy companionship of his friends, to share in their sport and their amusements. He was angry with himself that he had allowed Charlotte to take such total possession of him, sated with her embraces, with her peremptory demands on his time, her abject apologies when she feared she had offended him, above all her failure to recognize the impermanence of their liaison. Although Letellier had taken no vow of chastity he now regretted that he had not been as chivalrously faithful to his true love as Raoul de Coucy, whose story Eugénie had told him during the interminable days of their flight from Russia.

The obligation to attend the Marshal when he reviewed his whole Corps was a welcome break for Letellier but Charlotte was desolate at even a short absence so soon after her return home.

"Let Jacqueminot or Lachaise or any one of the others go in your stead," she urged. "Stay with me!"

Letellier only laughed as he unclasped her arms from his neck.

—◦◦❦ ❧❀◦◦—

"You do not understand! When the Marshal reviews his Corps he is attended by *all* his aides-de-camp. Am I to tell him that I failed in my duty because you wish to keep me beside you?"

He flung out of the room but Charlotte's entreaties had so delayed him that his colleagues had already gone, leaving him only two wretched nags in the stables. He jumped into his carriage, hoping that by ample use of the whip he could summon some speed from the miserable beasts but, to avoid a child straying across his path, Michel was obliged to swerve with disastrous results. His carriage overturned, hooking on to a tree, while he himself was sent headlong into a canal running alongside the road.

Only with difficulty did he succeed in climbing out of the water because he had injured his leg which he realised would make it impossible for him to ride beside the Marshal. Dripping wet and shaken by the accident, he abandoned all hope of reaching the review but his absence must be explained.

Fortunately the mishap had occurred near a posting house to which Letellier limped, calling urgently for the postmaster.

"Send a man at once to Marshal Oudinot," he ordered, "to inform him that Colonel Letellier has met with an accident which regrettably prevents his attendance at the review."

The postmaster promised to send the message, and found a conveyance for Letellier who had no alternative but to return to Lübbenau.

"What has happened, dearest Michel?" Charlotte wailed when she saw her lover descend painfully from a peasant's cart, but her alarm paled beside the Marshal's fury when he returned to the Schloss. He sent for Letellier to storm, "How is this, sir? You fail to attend me at the review without sending me an explanation of this dereliction of duty? Is this insouciant neglect the way in which you regard your obligations as my aide-de-camp?"

"But, Monsieur le Maréchal," replied Letellier in some consternation, "I did send a message by the nearest postmaster to tell you that I had an unfortunate accident to myself and my carriage and was in no state to proceed."

The Marshal refused to pay any heed to this attempt at explanation and Letellier realised with dismay that the postmaster had failed to send the message.

"Broke his shin, did he?" The Marshal glared at the other aides-de-camp standing silent and uncomfortable when Letellier had been ordered from the room. "Well, I'll break him and his career in the army."

What was irretrievably broken was the peace of Lübbenau but, had it not been for an error of judgment on the part of de Bourcet, who believed he was acting in Letellier's best interest, the Marshal's anger might have cooled and the storm blown over. Unwitting that he was precipitating a crisis, de Bourcet indignantly repeated the Marshal's words to his friend.

"He said, Michel, that he would break you, but he cannot intend to disgrace you. It would be too cruel and unjust."

Impetuously Letellier rushed to seek out the Marshal, whom he found lunching in oppressive silence with his other aides-de-camp.

"Monsieur le Maréchal," Letellier demanded, controlling his voice with difficulty, "may I ask you to repeat the words spoken to my colleagues?"

For a moment Oudinot hesitated but jealousy of his aide's good fortune with the Gräfin and his latent jealousy of Eugénie's kindness for Letellier erupted into a fierce attack.

"You dare insult your superior officer, Colonel Letellier?"

"Sir, I have the right to justify my conduct."

The icy rebuke served only to infuriate the Marshal further. Losing all control of himself, he seized a silver dish from the table to throw it at Letellier, who stood his ground as he said in an even voice, "You will not do this, Monsieur le Maréchal, as you are dealing with a man of honour."

The Marshal was beyond listening. As he lunged at his aide-de-camp the dish fell from his hands but General Lejeune and Jacqueminot thwarted his attempt at attacking Letellier, who stood firm although, as a precautionary measure, Lachaise and de Bourcet seized hold of his arms.

Shaking off the restraint of the General and Jacqueminot, the Marshal, panting with rage, hurled at Letellier, "Consider yourself under arrest!" before flinging himself out of the room, leaving his staff to gaze at one another in consternation as in his turn Letellier left.

"This deplorable quarrel is my fault," de Bourcet burst out. "I should never have repeated what the Marshal said, but I thought I was acting for the best. What are we to do now? We cannot let the Marshal carry out his threat to break Michel."

After a brief discussion they reached the conclusion that only the Gräfin could help them, certain that she would appeal to the Marshal to pardon Letellier.

Charlotte, who knew nothing of the quarrel, was surprised when the aides-de-camp trooped into her salon, standing a little awkwardly while Jacqueminot acted as their spokesman. When he told her how the quarrel had arisen, he continued sadly, "In all the years we have spent in the Marshal's service we have never seen him lose control of himself like this. Unless he can be reconciled with Colonel Letellier our happy family will be broken up but, far worse, his career will be ruined."

The Gräfin was horrified by this recital. At all costs Letellier must be saved from disgrace! She assured the aides that she would do everything in her power to persuade the Marshal to change his mind. Scarcely had they left her with grateful thanks than Oudinot himself entered, sinking heavily on a sofa and burying his head in his hands to hide the tears of anger and grief which he could not contain.

"Never in my life have I been so angry," he groaned, "but no one honestly believes that I really intended to attack a man who has served me so brilliantly for seven years and on whom I have conferred every honour at my command. Why, oh, why, did not Letellier address me in your presence, madame? I should have accepted his apology but the fool upbraided me in front of my whole staff. When I said I would break him I was making a play on words, ill-judged as I now see."

While the Marshal brooded silently the Gräfin held her breath, desperately hoping that he would calm himself but when he spoke again it was with rising passion.

"I'll send Letellier to prison! De Bourcet I shall simply dismiss from my service, but Letellier comes under army orders."

Charlotte von Kielmansegge was aware that she must use the utmost tact if her appeal for clemency were not to inflame Oudinot further, especially as her liaison with his aide-de-camp made her position one of great delicacy, but what did it matter compared with saving Letellier's career in the army in which he took such pride?

"My dear Marshal, my dear, dear Marshal, will you not reflect before taking so drastic a step?" Charlotte began softly. "I cannot but believe that second thoughts will prevail and your natural kindness and affection for your young men will gain the victory over your anger."

The Marshal made no answer, only muttered, "Eugénie will be greatly distressed to learn that Letellier has been imprisoned; she feels so much gratitude to him for having brought us safely out of Russia."

Finally it was not the Gräfin's appeal but the recollection of Letellier's heroism which decided Oudinot to mitigate the severity of his sentence. Raising his head, he looked straight at Charlotte.

"So be it! Because you and Lejeune have pleaded so eloquently for Letellier I will release him but I shall not see him again nor I am sure will he wish to see me. I'll write to Berthier, asking him to discharge Letellier from my service but, until he leaves the Schloss, he must continue under surveillance with a sentry outside his door."

This decision gave Charlotte a little hope that Letellier's career might be saved from utter ruin but, if he was to continue under surveillance, it would be impossible for them to meet and, so long as the armistice lasted and the Marshal remained at Lübbenau, that was a prospect she could not contemplate. All too soon they would go but there was always the hope that Letellier would return. Desperately Charlotte cast about for some solution to this problem until by a fortunate chance she recalled a few words she had heard at Dresden.

"Will you permit me, Monsieur le Maréchal, to suggest a course less harsh? Do you not recollect your asking the Emperor to nominate Colonel Letellier general of brigade? If you repeat your request it will certainly be granted. You would then be relieved of the Colonel's presence while at the same time performing a noble action and one more worthy of you."

Hope died as Oudinot shook his head.

*"Meine liebe Frau Gräfin,* you should by now know me well enough to know that I do not bear malice but the situation is not as simple as you think. I have suffered a severe shock. I have always treated my staff as if they were members of my own family but in future they will be to me merely officers in my service. My relations with them will be on an official basis only; their orders they will now receive from my chief of staff."

Emotionally exhausted by this trying interview, Charlotte decided not to attempt further persuasion at the moment, trusting that the Marshal would change his mind but, as he rose to leave, Oudinot said only, "I shall at once send a courier to the Emperor but, until I receive word from him Letellier must leave the Schloss."

As the Marshal did not say what message he was sending to the Emperor Charlotte remained in a state of anxiety but, at least, with de Bourcet's connivance, she was able to hide Letellier away in a part of the Schloss where his presence would not be discovered.

Schloss Lübbenau now housed two wretchedly miserable men. Alone in his attic Letellier fell into worse despair even than during the Russian retreat, tormented about his future, anxious about his father, from whom no news had come, anguished by the certainty that, whatever fate the Marshal had in store for him, he would inevitably leave his service, never perhaps to see Eugénie again. Would she be concerned about him? He might never know. All he could hope for was an early resumption of the war so that he could seek oblivion and death in battle.

Shut up in his own quarters, the Marshal was now bitterly ashamed of his loss of control, but at the same time resentful that his staff failed to remember that, however violent his rages, they never lasted long. The chief cause of his regret was that he had allowed his desire for a woman to come between him and the officer he loved as he had loved no other man—and always there was the nagging thought of Eugénie's silent reproach. She would never question any decision of his, but he knew that she would blame him in her heart.

The term set for the armistice was approaching rapidly and whether or no the Emperor accepted the peace offered him, the Marshal would leave Schloss Lübbenau as, in the course of war, he had left so many places but none with such · mixed feelings; its châtelaine would be only a memory but Oudinot, who had suffered and recovered from so many painful wounds, was certain that the wound of his quarrel inflicted at Lübbenau would never heal.

The Schloss, lately so gay, was now a place of gloom. Cut off from one another, the Marshal and the aides-de-camp made the Gräfin their confidante. First it was Oudinot who visited her to repeat his complaint.

"Had I fought Letellier in your salon we should afterwards have been reconciled and I should not now be bereft of a family as my staff no longer means anything to me. I know they are justified in criticizing my handling of this deplorable business because, better than anyone else, they have seen Letellier's bravery in action and are sensible of the extent to which he enjoyed my confidence."

Then it was the turn of the aides-de-camp who bemoaned their banishment from the Marshal's society. Hopeful that, if Oudinot relented towards them, he might also relent towards Letellier, Charlotte suggested, "I have done everything possible to make the Marshal change his mind.

Why do you not approach him yourselves? You can put your case with far greater eloquence than I can."

The young men brightened immediately, sending Pils to request the Marshal to receive them. Although longing to be reconciled with them, he was too proud to make the first move and secretly was delighted to consent to seeing them.

"Monsieur le Maréchal—" again it was Jacqueminot who spoke for them all—"we are deeply distressed to have fallen under your displeasure. Will you not again admit us to your intimacy and let everything be as it was before?"

Although he missed their laughter and good spirits, Oudinot determined not to show himself weak by yielding to their pleading.

"Gentlemen," he told the aides, "I am too upset to resume our old association; I need to be alone for a few days."

Discouraged by the Marshal's obstinacy, the aides withdrew, at their wits' end to find a means of making him alter his decision, when the return of the courier sent to Dresden brought a ray of hope which miraculously turned into a burst of sunshine. In his pouch the courier brought Michel Letellier's nomination as general of brigade. After all, Oudinot's second thoughts had proved best.

Quickly the news spread through the Schloss to the general relief but the aides were unanimous in agreeing that Letellier's reconciliation with the Marshal should take precedence over their own. Obviously de Bourcet must inform his particular friend who as yet was ignorant of the joy in store for him.

"Michel," de Bourcet cried as he burst into Letellier's hideout, "you have been nominated general of brigade!"

Letellier turned pale at the news of his promotion. Incredulous, he asked de Bourcet whether he was joking and it took some time before he was convinced that his friend was serious. His reaction then was, "I must at once seek out the Marshal to beg his forgiveness."

This proved to be less simple than Letellier had imagined. The Marshal persisted in his refusal to see his aide-de-camp, although he made no comment on the deception practised on him when it was revealed that contrary to his orders, Letellier was still at Lübbenau, but Charlotte von Kielmansegge was determined to bring the two men together before her lover left the Schloss. This was the last kindness she could do for him and, although broken-hearted by the knowledge that he would leave the Schloss immediately, her love was real and unselfish enough to rejoice in his promotion.

Since speed was essential the Gräfin sent an urgent message to Oudinot, asking him to come to her salon but, when he arrived, under the stress of her feelings she forgot the speech she had prepared, to plead, "I entreat you, Monsieur le Maréchal, to show Colonel Letellier the grace of heaven by forgiving him for what was, after all, a misunderstanding on both sides. If you will not do this for him will you not do it for my sake?"

The Gräfin looked so lovely as she made her appeal that only a man less susceptible to her charm than Oudinot could have refused her. He fidgeted uncomfortably in his chair, seeking a way of saving his face although he was now anxious for a reconciliation. Charlotte waited in suspense until the Marshal at last blurted out, "Very well, Frau Gräfin, it shall be as you wish. I will see Colonel Letellier—General Letellier—but only if a meeting is contrived as if by chance."

Before the Marshal could change his mind Charlotte sent a servant to bring Letellier down to her salon. When he appeared, accompanied by General Lejeune who had been hovering outside the room, anxiously waiting the result of the Gräfin's démarche, Letellier went straight to Oudinot, put his arm about his shoulders and grasped him warmly by the hand. Deeply embarrassed, the Marshal tried to disengage himself and for a moment everything hung in the balance until Charlotte cried imperatively, "Monsieur le Maréchal, stay—I beg of you."

Seizing General Lejeune's arm she and he withdrew to the adjoining room to watch the two men through the half-open door. To their great relief they saw the tension gradually relax and from a word or two they caught here and there they heard the Marshal and his former aide-de-camp talking about the many battles in which they had fought together, recalling especially the nightmare experience of the Russian campaign until the poignancy of their separation became intolerable. With a final embrace Letellier turned on his heel, leaving the Marshal so dejected that Charlotte rushed back into the salon to comfort him.

"My dear friend," he murmured in a voice broken by emotion, "I can find no words to thank you for what you have done to lighten my heart. Sooner or later Letellier must have left me because he has nobly earned the promotion he now has, but how different then would have been our parting! It is too late to wish that our separation had taken place in happier circumstances but at least, thanks to you, we have parted as friends."

Not for the Marshal only was the parting from Letellier painful, although Oudinot would suffer for a long time pangs of self-reproach for the outburst which had such unhappy consequences. His comrades would sorely miss the gayest and best loved of them while Charlotte von Kielmansegge saw all her happiness go with the man she loved so passionately, but the worst sufferer was Michel Letellier himself.

After the emotional farewell as, with a final wave of his hand, Michel Letellier rode away from Schloss Lübbenau, he asked himself whether Charlotte's passion was compensation for the rift with the Marshal and knew that it was not. He had once heard a Prussian officer contemptuously dismiss woman as the reward of the warrior—he even remembered his name, von Clausewitz. If he was right then he, Letellier, had had his reward and must now seek worthier rewards in battle. He would remember Charlotte's beauty and above all what she had done to bring about a reconciliation with the Marshal but never so often as his close and affectionate companionship with Oudinot and all his friends.

What had he gained from his stay at Schloss Lübbenau? Some physical satisfaction from Charlotte von Kielmansegge but, weighed in the balance of what he had lost, only misery. Misery? General of Brigade Letellier pulled himself erect in the saddle. How ungrateful to call himself miserable when all that mattered was the army which he would now serve in a higher rank. As he rode on towards Dresden with a lighter heart a fortunate chance brought him to the summit of every French soldier's ambition, an encounter with the Emperor.

"Who is this adjutant?" Napoleon demanded of his own suite as Letellier drew rein and saluted.

"Sire," he himself answered, "Your Majesty has just been indulgent enough to promote me general."

"Of division?"

"No, sire, of brigade. I was aide-de-camp to Marshal Oudinot and am now on my way from his quarters at Schloss Lübbenau to assume my new command with the Fourteenth Corps."

"Ah, you come from Lübbenau, eh?" The Emperor's interest was aroused. "Fortunate young man to be the guest of the Gräfin von Kielmansegge! Letellier, is it not? I remember now. Do you know how to command infantry?"

"I have served in all arms, sire."

"Good. How long did you serve with Marshal Oudinot?"

"Seven years, sire."

"So much the better—you will have learnt your job well. On your way now, General Letellier, and be a credit to your new command."

Letellier was overwhelmed by the Emperor's interest as once again he saluted and rode off. Did he remember that he had once railed against Napoleon, that he had blamed him for the Russian adventure? That was now to be forgotten, only a determination remaining to be an even better soldier of the Emperor's army.

Shortly after Letellier's departure from Schloss Lübbenau the Marshal and his staff were obliged to leave when the armistice was broken. Napoleon's acceptance of the peace terms offered him had arrived a day too late and Papa François, led by the nose by his Chancellor Metternich, allied his country with France's enemies to declare war on his daughter's husband, the war Oudinot had called a bad thing.

Schloss Lübbenau was deserted, the rooms so recently

filled with music and laughter intolerably silent until, as the Allied armies advanced into Saxony, the Gräfin von Kielmansegge herself was forced to go. Napoleon won a victory at Dresden but he took philosophically less good news from elsewhere, remarking to Berthier, "That's war for you! Up in the morning, down in the evening."

A refugee now, Charlotte, mourning her lost lover, on her way to Leipzig met young Lachaise, left behind because of illness and now rejoining the Marshal's Corps in the neighbourhood of Berlin.

"Will you not permit me to escort you, Madame la Comtesse?" he begged. "It is not fitting for you to travel alone."

Charlotte smiled sweetly as she refused his offer.

"Much as I should like your escort, dear Captain Lachaise, for you it is too dangerous—the roads are blocked by Austrian troops. Me they will not harm, but you would not be safe."

Reluctantly Lachaise was forced to agree but, as he bade Charlotte farewell, he gazed at her for a long time as if to fix her features on his mind before he said with sad prescience, "Perhaps, Madame la Comtesse, you will be my last kind memory."

It was some time after Lachaise left her before the Gräfin gave her coachman the order to proceed, wishing that she might have the aide-de-camp with her. He was a charming boy but, more than that, he was her last tenuous link with Michel. Now even that link was broken. Would she ever see Letellier again? She could only trust in God's mercy. Was Napoleon right in urging her to change her faith? Unhappy and bewildered, Charlotte von Kielmansegge drove on towards Leipzig, which all too soon would be a sinister name to her and so many others.

---

—◦◦❦{ }❦◦◦—

Bad news, the Chevalier de Coucy had once reminded his niece, always travels fast, but Eugénie had received little news of the Marshal, either good or bad, since the rupture of the armistice and the resumption of the war; even from Lübbenau his letters had been brief. Her anxiety was somewhat assuaged by the Emperor's great victory at Dresden so that for once she was happy enough to enter Marie Louise's orbit to attend the "Te Deum" sung in the chapel of St. Cloud and the grand reception and court which followed.

The optimism was of short duration; where Napoleon himself was in command he was successful but, fighting on a front four hundred miles long, much was left to his subordinates who failed miserably. From the *Moniteur* Eugénie learned of the successive defeats of the Marshals, Ney at Dennewitz, Macdonald at the Katzbach and, almost inconceivable to her, Oudinot at Gross Beeren. Thereafter all was silence.

Eugénie's alarm grew when nothing whatsoever was heard of Charles. Was he again desperately wounded, in enemy hands or dead? Bad news was not long in forthcoming. After a battle lasting three days at Leipzig resulting in a decisive Allied victory the Emperor was forced to admit that "the French army had lost its victorious ascendancy," nor was that all. As the beaten French troops scrambled homewards across the Rhine their enemies moved in for the kill while in Spain Wellington was pressing towards the French frontier and in Naples the Queen, Caroline Murat, the Emperor's sister, opened her ports to British ships.

Once again the silent rooms of the rebuilt Hôtel Oudinot were unbearably lonely but Eugénie shrank from inviting Madame de Coucy to keep her company, preferring solitude to witnessing her mother's jubilation at the Emperor's collapse, yet still marvelling at her own change of heart. Was it merely because Napoleon had smiled sweetly at her that she felt estranged from her mother's blind devotion to the Bourbons?

The onset of winter made the days even more melancholy and still there was no word of Charles. Eugénie had almost given up hope of knowing his fate when a thunderous knocking on the door penetrated to her boudoir. It must, it could only be Charles! But the man who stood on the threshold, travel-stained and so weary that he was obliged to lean against the lintel for support, was Colonel Jacqueminot.

"I come in haste, Madame la Maréchale," he gasped, "to tell you that the Marshal is hard on my heels. He will be here directly but he is exhausted, greatly changed and in need of all your care. Courage!"

Jacqueminot would not stay to answer Eugénie's agonized questions only, as he leapt into his waiting carriage bound for Paris, repeating the one word, "Courage!"

The day dragged on but still Charles did not come. In an effort to keep calm Eugénie set out the chessboard and men but it was impossible to concentrate on the game she was playing by herself, her whole attention strained for the sound of carriage wheels. Only after an eternity did she at last hear them. Jumping to her feet, in her haste the table overturned and the chessmen scattered far and wide as she rushed downstairs.

--◦◦◄‖►◦◦--

Heedless of the icy drizzle she flew outside to see Pils and another soldier lifting Charles in their arms, a sickening repetition of Vilna! As he was carried tenderly into the house and to his own room he briefly opened his eyes, seeming to recognize Eugénie before again relapsing into a coma.

"Typhus!" announced the doctor briefly, the same doctor who had tended Eugénie's eye after her accident. "The whole army is infected with it."

Typhus! Had Charles escaped the horrors of the Beresina, the desperate flight from Vilna and the Château d'Antorowna's typhus-stricken dead only to fall victim to the same dread disease?

For five days Eugénie, careless of infection, stayed by her husband's side, compassion her dominant emotion as she held his hand, now icy, now burning hot. In his delirium disjointed words came from his cracked throat, "column," "attack in column," "the Saxons" and again and again "the traitor Bernadotte." When the fever was at its height he shouted, urging his men on to fight or muttering in despair that the Emperor refused to see reason. Once he cried "Letellier—I'll break him," followed by a sob, "I loved him like a son" and "Charlotte" many times repeated.

What did Charles mean by saying he would break Letellier? Only if he recovered could Eugénie learn the truth.

His indomitable will and strong constitution triumphed. As soon as he was able to speak coherently, the Marshal bombarded Eugénie with anxious questions but carefully she answered only those which might not so alarm him as to cause a relapse. He nodded approval when told that, after a victorious engagement at Hanau, the Emperor had returned to St. Cloud to make a fighting speech to the Senate.

"A year ago all Europe marched with us; today all Europe is marching against us. Posterity will say that, however grave and critical the circumstances, they were not above France and myself."

With studied cheerfulness Eugénie reported that court ceremonial continued normally with balls and command performances while Napoleon had resumed his habit of visiting the various works he had initiated in Paris, but she refrained from repeating the Emperor's sad verdict when he inspected the unfinished Temple of Glory:

"Our grandiose ideas about it all have changed considerably; we must hand over our shrines to the care of the clergy. Let the Temple of Glory be henceforward a church, the church of the Madeleine."

Yet, even the news that the Allies had crossed the Rhine and in the south the British were steadily advancing into French territory was not allowed to interfere with the customary celebration of the New Year at the Tuileries, but, in contrast to the enthusiastic welcome of the populace when he rode among them, the Emperor's reception by his Court was cool. It was plain that the demand was for peace, peace at any price.

The truth could no longer be concealed from the Marshal, who raised himself up in bed with a cry as unearthly as the wailing of a banshee.

"Let me up! Let me up! I must go to him! Why, oh, why would he not listen when at Dresden we begged him to make peace, when I told him that making war was a bad thing!"

This was scarcely the moment to question Charles but, although Eugénie constantly chided herself for thinking too much about Letellier, she could no longer bear the suspense of not knowing his fate. Charles's mention of Dresden gave her an opening.

"In your delirium you said, Charles, that you would break Letellier. What did you mean?"

The Marshal hesitated before murmuring that it was a joke, not a very good one.

"He was due for promotion and I had him made general of brigade," he added hurriedly. "He went to Victor's Fourteenth Corps, but what became of him I do not know. I do not know what happened to so many. Lachaise is dead—he lost a leg at Leipzig and did not recover."

"Poor Lachaise! He loved dancing so much; had he lived he would never have danced again. I will have a mass said to his intention—he saved your life when you were wounded in Russia."

For Lachaise it was permitted to shed a tear, but

Eugénie's tears were as much for Letellier, who seemed to have disappeared who knew where or how?

To rouse Charles from his gloom Eugénie ventured to question him further.

"And who is Charlotte? You spoke often of her."

"Charlotte, oh, yes, Charlotte, sweet little thing, I used to play with her often. She is the daughter of the Gräfin von Kielmansegge. You know that during the armistice we were quartered at her Schloss Lübbenau."

Charles's hesitation puzzled Eugénie. If Charlotte were indeed a little girl why did he sound so embarrassed. Her identity was unimportant, mattering less to Eugénie than his far too casual explanation of Letellier's transfer, but every consideration went by the board when the Allies' advance into Lorraine made it imperative for the Oudinots to leave Bar if they were not to be trapped in a battlefield.

Though weak, the Marshal's health had improved sufficiently for him to travel but progress to Paris was wearisome along roads choked with troops, mainly the new recruits, the "Marie Louises" called out ahead of their class by the Empress-Regent. They were pitifully young but there was no need to seek the veterans. Eugénie had seen them in Russia, dead as the burnt-out embers of their bivouac fires.

In the bitter weather, sinister reminder of the Russian winter Eugénie shivered, less with cold than with a presentiment of disaster, her fears realised on their arrival in Paris when the Marshal told her that he had accepted the new command offered him by the Emperor.

"But you are far from strong enough, Charles," she protested.

"I alone am the judge of my actions," was his acid reply. "I know how many commanders of the highest rank the army has lost. Even though I am convinced that the Emperor was gravely mistaken in making war, nothing now matters but *la patrie en danger*. At whatever personal cost France must be saved."

While Charles proceeded to join his new unit at Provins, Eugénie remained in Paris until, during a lull in the fighting, he sent for her, the bearer of his message young de Thermes whom she had last seen on her way to Vilna.

"The Marshal begs, Madame la Maréchale, that you will take him some food."

"Food, did you say food? I will take him whatever he wants, but why food?"

"Because, madame, the country has been fought over so often that even for the Marshal supplies are lacking."

As Eugénie packed every available space in her carriage with provisions, irresistibly she was reminded of her journey to Vilna; she seemed always to be hearing music for which the composer's inspiration had failed him, able only to repeat endlessly the same monotonous refrain.

As every man counted, de Thermes was obliged to leave Eugénie to travel alone along snow-bound roads to Nangis, even nearer Paris, where Oudinot now commanded the Seventh Corps. She still found it impossible to grasp that the Emperor was fighting on the soil of France but the scant news gleaned at the posting houses was sufficiently encouraging: Napoleon had won several victories and the Allies had been thrown back. A little reassured as to the outcome of the campaign, she wearily closed her eyes, only to open them with a start when her carriage suddenly halted and a head was thrust through the window.

"You must remain where you are, Madame la Maréchale, and not proceed farther. The route everywhere is infested with Cossacks."

Cossacks! In France? Had she slept only to wake to the nightmare of that fearful incline called Ponary? Surely Ponary was fifteen hundred miles away and Paris only thirty! Despite her resolve to be courageous, the trials of the last weeks caused Eugénie to burst into tears.

The opening of the carriage door and the tentative hand laid sympathetically on her shoulder led her for one wild moment to believe that it was Letellier's, only to remember that he was no longer on the Marshal's staff and where he was no one knew, but the hand belonged to de Bourcet, sent to halt her on her way. She was pleased to see him not only for himself but, as Letellier's great friend, he would surely know whether he were alive or dead.

"Please, please, Madame la Maréchale, do not cry. The Marshal would be greatly distressed if he knew."

Poor de Bourcet! His embarrassment helped Eugénie to wink away her tears and smile tremulously at him.

"It was a momentary weakness, dear Monsieur de Bourcet. See, I am myself again, but tell me how you are—I have had no news of any of you for so long. I know only that little Lachaise is dead."

"Most of us were luckier, except Michel—Letellier— taken prisoner by the Austrians at Leipzig. I have no idea where he may now be."

A prisoner of war! Why had she not realised that this was the reason for Charles's ignorance of what had happened to him? Eugénie could only be thankful that, whatever hardships he might be suffering, Michel was safe from further fighting.

"You must miss him very much."

"We do indeed, I particularly but, you know, Madame la Maréchale, he left us to join Victor's Corps."

"So the Marshal told me—he had certainly earned his step up in rank."

Afraid of showing too much interest in Letellier, Eugénie asked when de Bourcet thought she might be able to proceed on her way.

"It would be advisable, Madame la Maréchale, if first I reconnoitred the road—the situation changes hourly."

When de Bourcet had ridden away Eugénie soon tired of looking at the dreary plain to huddle in a corner of her carriage and give herself over to thought. How long it was since she had ceased to think about Eugène de Villers and what she realised was her girlish infatuation! Sternly she banished Michel Letellier from her mind but Charles was not so easily disposed of.

What had he told Monsieur de la Guérivière? That he wanted a wife young enough to adapt herself to his wishes? On that score she had nothing with which to reproach herself; her compliance he had always had. But disillusion with her marriage had not entirely dispelled Eugénie's romantic dreams; if only Charles had offered her his heart would he not have had hers? Her understanding of men and her husband in particular was still so slight that she could not grasp their inability to express their deepest feelings. Had anyone enlightened her, she would have retorted with unusual cynicism, that she doubted if Charles had feelings for anyone other than himself and the army, except those he demonstrated in the way she found repellent.

Conscious of the dangerous ground to which she was heading, the sight of de Bourcet with a small escort was welcome; Eugénie might, he told her, proceed with caution to the camp where, on arrival, the Marshal had time only for a hasty embrace before striding away to a conference with his generals which lasted far into the night. When he finally returned, late and exhausted, to her relief he fell immediately into heavy sleep.

Although next morning he seemed preoccupied he assured Eugénie with a show of confidence that the party was not yet lost.

"The Emperor has recovered himself. He shows the same genius as in the past; it may be said that this campaign is the most brilliant of his career. The Allies will yet learn to their cost that the lion is neither dead nor dying."

"But what if things should go against us?"

"That is unthinkable." Charles paused for a moment before saying decisively, "Should the worst happen you will be guided by the Empress; if she leaves Paris you must leave also. Now, since we shall shortly be on the march again, you must return to the Rue de Bourgogne where I am firmly convinced you will remain. I shall do my best to keep you informed of our progress. Above all, keep a stout heart, little Eugénie, the battle for France continues."

Charles would admit no possibility of being mistaken but had he not said it was unthinkable that they should leave Vilna, yet they had been obliged to go. Even in the brief time she had spent in the camp she had learned that his fellow

Marshals did not share his optimism, that their lacklustre performance in the field had aroused the Emperor's anger.

The battle, as Charles had said with such confidence, was continuing, but in Paris she learnt to her dismay that it was a losing battle. Nearly all her acquaintances had already left the capital. Those still remaining were feverishly packing up their valuables, poised for flight, for the imperious necessity of escaping the Cossacks and Prussians ready to swoop on Paris to despoil, to pillage and to rape. On the outskirts Marshals Marmont and Mortier were heroically defending the city while waiting for the Emperor to appear but, once again, the agonized question was, where was Napoleon? Rumour murmured that he had gone to the eastern fortresses to rally the troops in garrison, but nothing was certain except confusion and fear.

The eyes of the Court were fixed on the Tuileries. If the Empress stayed, they stayed; if the Empress left, they left. Throughout the night of March 28 Eugénie was kept awake by the incessant sound of men, horses and carriages making for the west. At daybreak all Paris hung out of its windows to see the Empire pass with its pomp and splendour, the ministers, the archives, the diamonds of the Crown, finally the Empress and the little King of Rome. Mingling with the great ones of the earth trudged the poor, their carts heaped pell-mell with their meagre treasures. Everyone who could was leaving the city; into Paris came only the sound of guns.

Charles's orders had been formal; if the Empress left Paris Eugénie must leave but, with her faith undiminished that the Emperor would save his capital, only reluctantly did she decide to follow the crowd on the one route now safe from the advancing enemy, the road from Paris to Versailles.

So great was the press of carriages queueing at the posting house in the Avenue de la Reine that a long delay was inevitable, if indeed a change of horses was obtainable. To glean any news she could Eugénie left her carriage, nodding here and there to a familiar face, hearing, as she threaded her way through the mass of people, a mocking voice exclaim,

—◦◦⋖⫯⫯⋗◦◦—

"Oh, if Marshal Marmont told his wife to remain in Paris you may be sure she would do the opposite."

Did this chance remark mean that Eugénie might find Hortense Marmont somewhere here? She would have been happy to meet a friend but, among so great a crowd, it was impossible to find either the woman who had spoken or the Duchesse de Raguse. Forcing her way back to her own carriage, Eugénie gave orders to proceed slowly until they reached another posting house, meandering for several days, taking what accommodation she could for the night, uncertain of her final destination until she succeeded in halting a horseman galloping by.

"What news?" she called anxiously.

"Bad news," he shouted, his words almost lost in the slipstream of air he created. "The King of Prussia and the Czar have entered Paris with their troops—the Emperor has abdicated."

Eugénie refused to believe what she heard. Never would Napoleon have allowed the enemy to enter his beloved city while as for abdication the idea was ridiculous. However angry Charles might be, she would return forthwith to Paris—as if her presence there could alter the situation!

Her horses could manage only a walking pace so the journey was agonizingly slow but at last she arrived at the Rue de Bourgogne to find to her astonishment that Charles was in the house, sitting slumped in a chair, his whole aspect so dejected that Eugénie was afraid to rouse him, but her need to learn the truth overrode her fear.

"Yes, it is true," the Marshal muttered. "The Emperor has abdicated and is exiled to the island of Elba."

Exile, in Elba, a petty little island for the man who had been master of half the world! Before Eugénie had time to digest the full horror of his fall Charles continued dully, "Half a dozen of us were gathered at Fontainebleau while at Essonnes Marmont's Corps was still intact. The Emperor was all for continuing the fight because with those troops he might have beaten the enemy but we, the Marshals, could fight no more. Twenty-five years of unremitting war had left us played out, exhausted, all fight gone out of us."

"But was not the Emperor also exhausted?"

Charles, conscious of the edge in Eugénie's voice, avoided her eyes.

"For him it is different—with so much more to lose than we he was bent at all costs on preserving what he had."

Slowly now Charles related the fatal interview.

" 'We will crush the Allies in Paris itself—we must march on the capital without delay,' Napoleon shouted, but we were horrified that he was ready to make Paris a battlefield. We dared to oppose his plan, Macdonald going so far as to tell him that our minds were made up—we could not expose Paris to the fate of Moscow—we were determined to end it.

" 'I will call on the army,' the Emperor shouted.

" 'The army will not march,' was Ney's dour rejoinder.

" 'The army will obey me!' Napoleon retorted.

" 'Sire,' the formal address was almost a sneer, 'the army will obey its leaders.'

"There was a sudden hush," Charles continued, "as we trembled to think what the Emperor would say or try to do next. After all, he *was* the Emperor and, with the vital asset of Marmont's Corps, intact at Essonnes, Napoleon was still capable of resistance, from beyond the Loire if necessary, but then we heard the shattering news that Marmont had signed the capitulation of Paris and ordered his men to lay down their arms. Never before had I, had any of us, felt such anxiety until, to our great surprise, the Emperor demanded quite calmly, 'Then, gentlemen, what is it you want?'

"I think Ney and I answered simultaneously, 'Your abdication, sire.' "

The Marshal stirred uncomfortably in his chair, his tone almost pleading as if he must justify his actions to Eugénie.

"Do not believe that our advice to the Emperor—and it was advice, not an ultimatum—was given lightly. Had it still been possible to defend Paris would we willingly have forsaken him to hand the city over to an enemy against whom we had made war for so long and so successfully? Only too

well do we know the fate of conquered cities! No one
doubted that in defending Paris from the heights of Montmartre Marmont and Mortier had fought like heroes, but they
had neither men nor ammunition to continue fighting. There
was only one possible solution."

Eugénie stared at her husband, incredulous that Marshal Oudinot, the Bayard of the army, could have uttered
the fatal word, "abdication," had abandoned the Emperor,
a weakness of which she had believed him incapable. She
was thankful that she had not been in Paris to see the consequences of his "advice," the triumphant entry of the
Allied sovereigns into the capital.

Behind a troop of red-coated Cossacks, riding fifteen
abreast, the vanguard of an endless cavalcade of Russian,
Austrian and Prussian lancers, cuirassiers and hussars, Czar
Alexander rode on a grey charger, surrounded by a jingling
group of green-jacketed aides-de-camp. He had looked calm,
even a little sad, thinking perhaps of the promises exchanged
at Tilsit with Napoleon, that each would visit the other's capital. Alexander had intended to be the first to fulfil that promise but Napoleon had forestalled him by entering Moscow,
not as friend but as conqueror. Now at last Alexander came
to Napoleon's capital as victor and in neither case was the
other present to welcome his guest.

Eugénie felt she could have borne the sight of the Czar of
Russia, but not Frederick William of Prussia, trotting meekly
beside the Czar, once again his ally. At least, she thought
scornfully, the Emperor of Austria was absent from the procession which wound its way along the boulevards to the
Champs Elysées, bands playing and colours flying, watched
by a silent and stunned crowd. Prudently Francis, unwilling
to humiliate his daughter by triumphing over her husband,
had remained at some distance from Paris, no doubt engaged
in his favourite occupation of making toffee!

Eugénie's bitter thoughts were broken into by Charles
who curtly informed her that he had rallied to the Bourbons
and been sworn in as a member of the provisional government, as if already Napoleon belonged to the past. Charles's

--·◄€[ ]€►·--

assessment of the military situation she was obliged to accept, but she was stunned and ashamed, even more than by his "advice" to the Emperor as by his precipitancy in allying himself with his enemies.

Abruptly Eugénie left the room. Charles's actions did not accord with her own concept of honour. She conceded that peace was welcome since it meant an end of the terrible carnage, to scenes like those she had witnessed in Russia, but did peace really demand the fall of the Empire? Eugénie knew that she should have rejoiced at the return of the Bourbons, but she could not imagine France without Napoleon; she had never known a Bourbon reign but had grown up in Imperial France ruled by an Emperor who had smiled at her. Yet she was aware of the irony that she, Eugénie de Coucy, of an irreproachably royalist family, regretted Napoleon while Charles Oudinot, the brewer's son who owed his marshalate, his dukedom, his honours and his fortune to the Emperor should have shown such alacrity in rallying to the Bourbons.

Eugénie had not long to wait for practical demonstration of the change in régime when the Comte d'Artois, brother and heir of Louis XVIII, made his entry into Paris. Still supple and elegant in spite of his fifty-seven years, Artois rode into the city on a white charger to end an exile which had lasted for twenty-five years. Cantering beside him in the uniforms worn in so many of the Emperor's battles were four of Napoleon's renegade Marshals: Ney, Marmont, Moncey—and Oudinot. For them all, even for her husband, Eugénie felt the utmost contempt but her heart ached for the humiliation of the Imperial Guard escorting the Prince.

The Marshals were there by their own cynical choice but the guard, grieving for their adored Emperor to whom at Fontainebleau they had recently bidden a poignant farewell, had no alternative but to obey orders. Never had Eugénie seen such rage as on the weather-beaten and battle-scarred faces of these veterans whose fury was expressed in the menacing clash of their weapons as they presented arms.

---◦◦∢[ ]∢◦◦---

Like all France Eugénie needed time to adjust herself to
the changes wrought by the Restoration, to reconcile herself
to the emergence of new faces and the disappearance of the
old. Worst of all she had to learn to live in a city polluted by
the presence of the occupying troops, especially the arrogant
Prussians whose behaviour at Königsberg she had not
forgotten. The savagery of the Cossacks had been expected,
nor could Eugénie repress a shudder when she passed one in
the street. Even their leader, the Hetman Platov, was reported to be so uncivilised as to go to bed booted and
spurred.

Until the King took up his residence in the Tuileries, his
return to France from his English exile delayed by an un-
heroic attack of gout, social life was in suspense, the gap
filled by gossip, the favourite whisper the conduct of the
Marshals, who were believed to have been moved not by war
weariness but the influence of their wives in forcing the Emperor's abdication. Although all the Marshals who were
present at Fontainebleau were hated by the devoted adherents of the Emperor, none was more so than Marmont.

An impulse of sympathy for his wife sent Eugénie to call
on Madame Marmont, heedless of Charles's probable disapproval of her visit, but a hostile reception made her regret
her visit when Hortense demanded scathingly. "Have you
come as a friend or to triumph over me because of my husband's betrayal of the Emperor?"

"How could you think that was my motive?" Eugénie
herself was indignant. "I came because you are the only person I know who will give me an honest answer to a problem
which torments me."

"Forgive me! I should have known *you* came as a friend,
a sincere friend, but so many have not!"

Encouraged by Hortense's softened attitude, Eugénie
hesitated a little then rushed into what she wanted to ask.

"You have heard what people are saying, that their
wives were responsible for urging the Marshals to have done
with the Emperor. Please do not take it amiss if I ask you if

you influenced Marshal Marmont. I know that if I had attempted to influence my husband he would have laughed at me for a silly goose."

"I influence Marmont?" Hortense threw back her head and laughed but her laugh was bitter. "Never! You are too young, *ma chère*, to know the unhappy story of our married life. I had what I now know was the misfortune to fall in love with Captain Marmont as he then was the very first time I saw him. Although my father opposed my marriage in the end/he let me have my own way and often and often I have wished he had not done so."

Eugénie saw a slow tear roll down Hortense's cheek but she quickly regained her composure.

"Vanity is Marmont's undoing and his vanity ruined my happiness. No one knows the true story of what is called Marmont's betrayal of the Emperor. When he returned home after the capitulation, unrecognizable with a week's growth of beard, blackened by gunpowder, his greatcoat in tatters, he expected reproaches for delivering Paris to the enemy. His vanity led him to fall into the trap laid for him by Talleyrand, who hailed him as the saviour of his country, and avid always for praise, Marmont believed him."

All Hortense Marmont's pent-up resentment against her husband tumbled out to Eugénie's acute embarrassment.

"Do you know, my dear Duchesse, what he said? How impudent for a Marmont, preening himself like the peacock he is, to speak thus of a Napoleon Bonaparte, who called him his son, the man of whom he made everything. Marmont was always able to use his undoubted talents as a speaker to his own advantage. Listen to what he said: 'When Napoleon said, "Everything for France," I served with enthusiasm. When he said "France and I," I served with zeal. When he said "I and France," I served obediently but, when he said, "I without France," I felt I must dissociate myself from him.' Phrases, phrases from a pigmy about a giant."

For a moment there was silence but once the floodgates had opened Hortense could not close them.

"It was vanity which lost Marmont the battle of Les Ara-

--◦◦⟨ ⟩◦◦--

piles—which the English call Salamanca. He was so determined to have the sole glory of beating Wellington that he
refused to wait for reinforcements and attacked too soon. I
admit it was not his fault that he had been on the field for a
bare half-hour before his arm was shattered by a shell and he
was carried off. I cannot help believing that had not Marmont
been so vainglorious Wellington might not have won the
battle, forcing the Emperor to continue fighting on two
fronts. It was not on the heights of Montmartre that Marmont
betrayed the Emperor, but in Spain.

"I no longer regret that I am childless. I do not share
Marmont's conviction that his action was justified. To me his
child would have been the child of a traitor. Have you yet
heard, dear Duchesse, the latest word the wits have coined
—*raguser*, to betray?"

Hortense's sobs were now coming so thick and fast that
her words were scarcely audible.

"I am the Maréchale Marmont but I am also Duchesse de
Raguse, and that now shameful title is the one I must bear
until I die."

Eugénie rose, unable to find words to comfort Hortense.
She could only press her hand in sympathy as she took her
leave from this painful interview, which had caused her
grave disquiet. Surely no one could accuse Charles of conduct in any way comparable with Marmont's yet the doubt in
her mind persisted, making her thankful that she had not
borne the child for whom she still longed.

That night, for the first time since her marriage, she denied herself to Charles in an act of defiance although unhap-
pily conscious that her rebellion would be of short duration;
in the end he would always exact her obedience. Obey
him she was obliged to do when he insisted on her appearance at the Tuileries; his position in the government demanded it, but it was for her mother's sake rather than for
his that she consented to make her curtsey to the royal family.

Eugénie was not alone in finding the newly restored
Bourbons unsympathetic. Louis XVIII, swollen with gout and

the excesses of the enormous Bourbon appetite, was a poor substitute for Napoleon. The Comte d'Artois possessed both the grace and charm his brother lacked but his exaggerated piety and reactionary ideas alienated all but the most faithful of his adherents. His elder son, the Duc d'Angoulême, was a nonentity, the younger, the Duc de Berri, the only member of the family to catch the popular fancy, not because of any outstanding merit but because the people were titillated by his many amours which reminded them of his ancestor, the *vert galant*, Henri IV.

Most disappointing of all was the Duchesse d'Angoulême. Everyone pitied the daughter of Louis XVI and Marie Antoinette as "the orphan of the Temple" but no one liked her. Her hauteur, her unyielding sternness, her awkward figure, florid face and eyes reddened by weeping attracted only aversion and a sense of guilt for her sufferings as a girl, no doubt responsible for the sterility of her marriage to her first cousin.

When first her father and then her mother and aunt were taken from the prison of the Temple to the guillotine Marie-Thérèse was left solitary, in hourly expectation of meeting the same fate. Every moment of the day the young girl was spied on by her savage jailers and she knew the agony of having her young brother torn from her, to be taught to call his mother the Austrian whore, to be fuddled with brandy and to die.

Remembering her own brief encounter with the revolutionary Committee of Public Safety, Eugénie chided herself for her failure to feel compassion for the infinitely more harrowing experiences of the Duchesse d'Angoulême but she was repelled by her arrogance. The Dauphine, as she was called, seemed to go out of her way to snub the Bonapartist ladies, patronising Maréchale Ney, whose mother had killed herself when she learned the death of her mistress, Marie Antoinette. For the Duchesse de Dantzig the Dauphine had nothing but contempt but, if Madame Sans Gêne had started life as a washerwoman, she had her own back on the Duchesse d'Angoulême, saying that of them both it was the

Dauphine, incongruously swaddled in white satin, who looked the washerwoman.

At the Tuileries where the bees and eagles of the carpets had been replaced by fleur de lys, Eugénie felt isolated, envying the women who stayed away but a chance remark, intended, she was certain, to be overheard, added to her irritation.

"That woman? Oh, she's a Maréchale, one of Bonaparte's cooks."

Why the Maréchales should be the special butt of those members of the old nobility who had greedily accepted everything the Emperor offered them, only when he fell to be the first to brush the Imperial dust from their skirts, Eugénie failed to understand. The majority of the Marshals' wives were of respectable birth, many like herself noble, almost all young, pretty, well educated and talented. Even those women of humble origin had learnt to "keep their rank," perhaps a little awkwardly, but with nothing either common or vulgar in their demeanour.

Eugénie approached the lady who had spoken with such contempt to say in a voice quiet but charged with fury, "You are mistaken, madame, in what you say. Mesdames les Maréchales were neither cooks nor serving maids but worthy wives of husbands who earned distinction and glory on the battlefields of Europe—for France."

"Oh, I was not thinking of you, Madame la Duchesse," was the gushing answer. "We know you are a de Coucy."

"Yes, madame, I am a de Coucy but I am also the Maréchale Oudinot, Duchesse de Reggio. I can assure you that I am as proud of my husband's title won by thirty-two wounds and great heroism as any Montmorency, Mortemart, Noailles or La Rochefoucauld is of hers!"

Shaking with indignation, though surprised by her defence of Charles, Eugénie bowed stiffly and walked away, to see out of the corner of her eye the lady whom she had addressed whispering to her friends. She would have wagered that she was saying, "Listen to the little de Coucy! So unlike dear Adèle de Chavanges."

Eugénie's lip curled. Adèle had been among the first to present herself at the Tuileries, parading not as the Maréchale Augereau, Duchesse de Castiglione, but as a Boulon de Chavanges in a gown so lavishly embroidered with fleur de lys as to leave no doubt of her royalist sympathies.

After a particularly dull evening at Court, as Eugénie took off the lappets and panniers the Duchesse d'Angoulême insisted on because they were worn at Versailles despite their absurdity with the Empire line of the dresses, she pondered on the contrariness of human nature. Instead of feeling at home at the Tuileries she felt disoriented; on her first appearance at Napoleon's Court she had felt strange, but the strangeness had quickly worn off. Even Charles was made to realise the difference in climate when the Prussian ambassador, denying him his title of Duc de Reggio, addressed him simply as Marshal Oudinot.

"And after all I did to preserve his country from the worst excesses of our army! Vanquished we may now be, but given the chance we would rout the Prussians time and again. If only I could get my hands round their necks . . ."

"But, Charles," Eugénie could not resist saying slyly, "did you not say that you told the Emperor making war was a bad thing?"

The Marshal's answer she thought it best not to have heard. Then he spluttered, "At that time I had known only what it was to conquer a country, not to be conquered."

Was it possible that he already regretted the consequences of those fateful hours at Fontainebleau; if he did he was not unique. Now that peace was an accomplished fact the nation as a whole showed only tepid enthusiasm for the Bourbons, while for them Eugénie had none. Only because it would please her mother did she attend the many balls and routs given to celebrate the Restoration, knowing how much Madame de Coucy herself would have enjoyed them, but to the British Embassy presided over by the Duke of Wellington the Maréchale Oudinot flatly refused to go, nauseated by the Marshals' wives who fawned on their husbands' conquerors.

"Charles, do you not accompany me this evening?" was

now her frequent question, meeting always with the same answer.

"Must I do so? Can you not go alone? You now have many friends in Paris so you no longer need feel shy. You know how little all this gadding about means to me, but if you insist . . ."

Eugénie did not insist; she knew better.

"No, of course not if you are happier at home smoking your pipe."

How horrified she would have been to know that, as soon as she left the house, Charles took himself off to indulge his passion for gambling at the Palais Royal of which Eugénie had heard only as the haunt of pimps, prostitutes and licentiousness in all its forms. She could not guess that the excitement of watching the fall of the dice was a substitute, if a poor one, for the excitement of battle. Always there would be much she did not understand about the character of a soldier.

To their mutual satisfaction, Eugénie because Paris no longer attracted her, the Marshal because he now assumed a more active role, the Oudinots' stay in the capital was cut short when he was given command of a corps of grenadiers and chasseurs, troops once part of the Imperial Guard. Ordered by his fellow Marshal Soult, the Minister of War, to live at his headquarters, the Oudinots packed their bags and moved to Metz.

Marshal Oudinot rose from his seat, reluctantly laid down his pipe, yawned, stretched himself and made ready to walk the short distance from his headquarters to the Oudinots' temporary home at Metz.

The thought of the ball they were giving that evening for the notabilities of the city bored him, a necessary courtesy but to him more fatiguing than a day spent on the battlefield. Once the ball was under way he promised himself escape to his study and his pipe, leaving Eugénie to entertain his guests. She was shaping well as a hostess—a pity that her shape hadn't yet altered, but no doubt it would in time; no one could accuse him of indifference to his marital duties!

Pleased with his jest, the Marshal was still laughing when a flustered orderly ushered in an estafette from Paris. Although tempted to let the despatch he brought lie on his desk until the morning, Oudinot felt it his duty to open it, only to stare incredulously at the few bald sentences: "Bonaparte has escaped from Elba, landed at Cannes on March 1 and is marching north in the direction of Paris. To block his advance Marshal Ney and the Comte d'Artois have left for Lyons but, should Bonaparte give them the slip, Oudinot must march with his Corps to stand between the ex-Emperor and Paris."

Had he, who knew Napoleon so well, ever really believed that he would be satisfied with being king of a petty island, Oudinot asked himself. They had all, the King, the government, he himself, been living for a year in a fool's paradise, but this was no time to dwell on their blindness; he had to reach an immediate decision on his own line of conduct. If he had not received the Minister of War's explicit orders his impulse would have been to march with, not against, Napoleon but only once had Marshal Oudinot disobeyed his orders, and that was at Wagram when his disobedience was decisive in winning the battle.

When facing the enemy the Marshal showed no hesitation but this was a moral not a tactical problem. Did his oath to Louis XVIII expunge the prior allegiance to the Emperor, the new loyalty override the old? Despite his admiration for the Emperor's bold venture, Oudinot came to the unwilling conclusion that it did, even though this decision should adversely affect his own future.

Of one thing at least he was sure, the need to keep this startling news secret until he had held a council of war with his senior officers. He had held his command long enough to suspect how tenuous was the loyalty of the old Imperial Guard to the Bourbons. Until the situation clarified itself any premature leakage of Napoleon's escape might lead to a dénouement to be avoided at all costs.

Eugénie was dressing for the ball when her husband entered her room, dismissing her woman with a jerk of his head. Intent on arranging her parure of diamonds she did not look up, only said reproachfully, "You're very late, Charles. You had better make haste or the guests will have arrived before you change your dress."

"That's of no importance. Listen, Eugénie! The Emperor has escaped from Elba and is marching towards Paris but, so long as the news can be kept secret, it must not be known.

Should anyone challenge you, you must deny all knowledge. I rely on you to see that the ball is as lively as possible without me for I have urgent problems with which to deal."

Charles rushed away, leaving Eugénie too dazed to grasp the full import of his news. Her heart had given a great leap to know that as his devotees had always believed, the Emperor had returned with the violets. But what did Charles feel? She did not expect him to confide in her; he never did so but she had been quick to notice that, unlike so many who now spoke contemptuously of Bonaparte, he still called him the Emperor. Was that a sign that he intended to align himself with Napoleon?

With this question agitating her the evening was a severe strain to Eugénie, who was obliged to animate the ball, explain her husband's absence as due to a slight indisposition and stoutly to deny as mere rumour the news which somehow or other had filtered into Metz and the ballroom. If only she had not been left alone, if there were among her husband's staff someone like Letellier to infuse some gaiety into the stolid Lorrainers but there was no one, no one to make her laugh as he did; he had vanished into thin air.

When, to Eugénie's great relief, the last guest departed and she sought out Charles it was to find him so absorbed in papers that she crept away, reluctant to interrupt him, hoping that his decision would answer her own wishes, but the Marshal's thoughts were very different. He believed he could rely on many, though perhaps not all, of the senior ranks to take the same stand as himself but about the men he had grave doubts; to the Imperial Guard the Emperor was their God as they were his children, unswerving in their mutual devotion.

Next day his fears were confirmed when he assembled his junior officers to demand what would be their response when he cried "Vive le Roi!"

With one voice they answered, "We shall shout 'Vive l'Empereur!' Monsieur le Maréchal," as they tore off the hated white cockade to replace it with the beloved three colours carefully preserved in pockets close to their hearts, an example eagerly followed by the rank and file.

--•◦•( )•◦•--

As the Emperor advanced steadily towards Paris so did the Marshals' personal dilemma grow. Ney, who had sworn to bring Bonaparte back in an iron cage, fell on the Emperor's neck when they came face to face, yet Ney had never liked Napoleon. Then, almost before anyone realised what was happening, the Emperor reached the Tuileries from which Louis XVIII, Marshal Marmont in his train, had fled incontinently. To a murmur of joyous disbelief, "Is it you? Is it really you, sire?" Napoleon was carried shoulder high by a weeping crowd into his palace where already the Bonapartist ladies were eagerly tearing from the carpets the fleur de lys imposed at the Restoration on the Imperial bees and eagles.

Covertly Eugénie watched her husband as his staff made known their decisions: General de Lorencez was for the King, Colonel Jacqueminot, his tirade in Russia against the Emperor forgotten, for his old allegiance. Although she knew that he had received affectionate letters from his old friends, Marshals Davout and Suchet, urging him to make his submission to the Emperor, so far Charles had given no sign of leaving Metz. The suspense became so unbearable that Eugénie was on the point of plucking up courage to ask his intentions, when he himself enlightened her.

"I have wrestled with my conscience, but always I return to the conviction that I cannot betray the oath of fealty I swore to Louis XVIII. My attachment to the Emperor cannot be doubted but he, as well as Suchet and Davout, will understand why I fail to range myself alongside him. Metz is a key fortress, the gateway into France. When the Allies invade us, as they surely will since at Vienna they have declared Napoleon an outlaw, they must take the traditional route of invasion, through Metz. For the sake of the Emperor and France the city must remain in hands friendly to him. Should he refuse to accept this reasoning and relieve me of my command, then we will return to Jeand'heurs and wait upon events."

Once Eugénie had told the Duchesse de Raguse that she could not, even if she would, influence her husband but she was deeply disappointed by his decision, especially as she failed to understand his reasoning. To her surprise, since she had been thinking of Hortense Marmont, she received a letter from her, guessing that she had written only because she had no one else in whom to confide. The Duchesse de Raguse, unlike her husband, had not rallied to the Bourbons but, on Napoleon's return, had gone to the Tuileries.

"In his abrupt way the Emperor told me," she wrote, "that he had no expectation of seeing my husband, but he was glad that one person who bore the name of Marmont remembered what was owed to her Emperor."

How dearly Eugénie herself would have loved to go to the Tuileries, if only to see Napoleon smile. Her hopes rose that she might be able to do so when Charles announced that he was leaving for Paris to explain in person to the Emperor why he could not join him. Secretly Eugénie was convinced that like Marshal Ney, when face to face with Napoleon, Charles would change his mind.

The Marshal's absence from Metz was short. All he repeated to Eugénie of his conversation with the Emperor was that he honoured Oudinot for his decision, invited him to dine at the Tuileries though they had not again met in private, but the Marshal's tenure of his command did not survive that one private interview. A little too casually he informed Eugénie that, as it would be too expensive now that he had lost the emoluments of his post, to reopen Jeand'heurs, they would find a quiet place near Paris in which to live. Though too schooled in obedience to Charles to question his motive, she was sure that he had other reasons for his anxiety to be nearer Paris than Lorraine, her suspicion confirmed when the Marshal returned to Paris to attend the Champ de Mai, the great ceremony held on the Champ de Mars where the Emperor presented new eagles to the army. This time Eugénie did question him, but all Charles would say was that the public was disappointed that, instead of wearing his familiar dark green uniform of his *Chasseurs à Cheval de la Garde*, the Emperor appeared in his theatrical Coronation costume, all white satin, gold lace and ostrich feathers, a mistake, the sole comment the Marshal allowed himself to make.

Ten days later, when Napoleon left Paris to meet the Allied armies massing in Belgium, Oudinot grew increasingly silent and morose, chafing at his enforced inaction, although it was his own decision which deprived him of the opportunity of fighting once again.

For a week Europe held its breath to give a great exhalation of relief when on June 18, 1815, Napoleon was decisively defeated at Waterloo. Those who loved him still hoped that he might escape the penalties threatened by the pitiless Allies, but their hopes proved vain. Tricked by the English into becoming their prisoner, *General* Bonaparte was sent to perpetual exile in an island in the South Atlantic, whence there could be no escape as from Elba.

With Louis XVIII once again installed at the Tuileries superficially life in France resumed its normal course, but beneath the surface the nation seethed at the hardship of a colossal war debt and the bitter obligation of maintaining an army of occupation, nor was that all. Those who had supported Napoleon were subjected to a veritable witchhunt, exile and proscription, but the most prestigious to be caught in the net was Marshal Ney, Duc d'Elchingen, Prince of the Moskowa, the bravest of the brave.

"What a fool Ney was," Oudinot exclaimed irritably when the Marshal's capture was known, "not to escape when the means were offered him. As if that were not folly enough, he now refuses trial by us, his colleagues, who would be in honour bound to acquit him of the high treason of which he is charged. The trial by the Chamber of Peers which he prefers is a foregone conclusion—the Chamber is stuffed with émigrés who will show him no mercy."

Eugénie, though deeply distressed by Ney's fate because at their one meeting in Berlin she had taken a great liking to *Le Rougeaud,* was thankful that Charles had been called as a witness for the defence not the prosecution. She pitied poor Hortense Marmont when Marshal Marmont, Duc de Raguse, sitting with the peers, voted for the death sentence on his fellow Marshal.

For subservience to the régime Marmont's reward was

command of the Royal Guard, together with Marshals Victor, Macdonald and Oudinot, but Louis XVIII's gratitude was not shared by France. Marmont's company was known as the Company of Judas.

Marshal Oudinot, happily for Eugénie's peace of mind, was in a different category; in addition to his share of command of the Royal Guard he was given command of the National Guard, but she frequently felt that the favour of the Bourbon Court and an administrative command were small compensation to him for the loss of glory and the perilous excitement of the battlefield.

This new appointment obliged the Oudinots to leave their own house for the official residence of the National Guard in the Rue de la Grange Batelière where once again, as in the early days of Eugénie's marriage, the house was filled with the young officers of his staff, but she was conscious of the great difference in herself since that time. She was only twenty-four, but she supposed that, living with a man so much older than herself, insensibly she had matured quickly. No longer was she little Eugénie de Coucy who nourished romantic dreams about Eugène de Villers but a woman who had learned, however painfully, to accept her responsibilities and adapt herself to a great position.

Although she was not reconciled to her sterility Eugénie had almost given up hope of bearing a child when to her surprised joy she discovered that she was pregnant. At first she refused to believe it, dismissing the physical fact as imagination, product of wishful thinking but, when three months had passed, all her doubts were banished. She was indeed pregnant! On Charles she now could look with a kindlier eye since he had at last fulfilled her greatest desire. Love him she still could not but she could and would be grateful. She saw her future as one of peace, relieved of the anxieties she had suffered during the war, with the happiness of rearing a son or daughter but such a prospect was not to be her lot. The tranquillity she expected proved to be a mirage.

Shortly before their child was due to be born, Charles,

smiling broadly, entered Eugénie's boudoir where she was contentedly stitching a little dress. He planted a kiss on her forehead as he announced triumphantly, "I have just been informed that, when the Duc de Berri marries Princess Marie Caroline of the Two Sicilies, the King intends to appoint you as her Lady of Honour."

Eugénie stared at her husband in amazement, then burst into tears.

"What are you crying about? Ah, I see, you are overcome at this signal favour, the exceptional mark of confidence shown you at your age in being invited to act as Lady of Honour to the wife of the heir to the throne! What would my old father have said had he known!"

Eugénie raised her head to see through her tears that Charles was not jesting but was perfectly serious. Since to a de Coucy honours came naturally she was shocked that Charles appeared to regard as extraordinary that the wife of a man of humble origin should be singled out for this post. Her indignation mounted as she exclaimed, "What do I want with such an honour? All my comfort would be ruined if I accepted this offer which to me is wholly distasteful. If you have fogotten what the Duchesse de Montebello said to me, I have not! She told me that acting as Lady of Honour to the Empress was gilded slavery. I refuse to be a slave! I want to be free!"

For a moment Eugénie could not remember why these words sounded familiar until she recollected that she had said the same thing on the day that Marie Louise had passed through Vitry when she had questioned her mother about the duties of a Lady of Honour. How delighted Madame de Coucy had been and what vicarious pleasure she had taken in Eugénie's attendance at the Tuileries even though it was not at Versailles, but how distressed the Comtesse would be to know that her daughter had been happier at the Imperial Court! Madame de Coucy, who believed the sole object of existence to be service to God and the King, would have been outraged to learn that Eugénie regarded acting as Lady of Honour to a royal princess as slavery!

--◦◦❦{ ❧}◦◦--

Eugénie's sobs came faster as she contemplated her future in the shadow of the Duchesse d'Angoulême's cold formality. The words of refusal were on her lips and she was ready to cross Charles's will until she saw his deep frown and the displeasure manifest on his face.

"Is it your wish, Charles, that I sacrifice myself?"

"You cannot refuse." His tone brooked no contradiction.

Eugénie set her lips, still ready to rebel, but the habit of obedience to her husband was too strongly ingrained.

"Come, come, Eugénie." The Marshal was now more conciliatory. "It is not good for you to get upset now; you will find that what you call slavery is mere imagination due to your state. We shall both be together in Paris and you will be in the inner circle of the Court where you can be very useful to me. Not bad for one of Bonaparte's cooks, eh?"

Eugénie avoided her husband's eyes lest he should see the contempt in her own that he rated so highly this proffered honour to her so empty and distasteful. She was ashamed for him that he seemed content to hang on his wife's skirts for the favour of the King and for what King? One who had ousted the Emperor whom Charles had served faithfully, even affectionately, for so long. Suddenly Eugénie felt herself all de Coucy and Charles the parvenu she had never consciously thought him.

She would not listen as he dwelt on the political aspect of the appointment, of the Court's anxiety to repair its mistakes with regard to the Bonapartist ladies, of the King's realisation that some gesture was essential to reconcile the Imperial and royal entourages. Whatever the Marshal might say, Eugénie knew very well that, had she not by birth been an aristocrat, the royal choice would have fallen elsewhere. Why, oh, why, had it not done so? She wished she knew whose was the advice which had persuaded Louis XVIII to select a Marshal's lady instead of a member of the nobility which, through all the vicissitudes of the Bourbons, had remained devoted to their cause, but after all what did it matter?

Given Charles's excited pleasure and insistence on her

acceptance Eugénie saw no alternative but to submit to this dreadful charge thrust upon her, a charge she viewed with alarm and deep disgust. Yet had she not for four years been a slave, a slave to Charles's will? She had not loved her chains but within her body a slight stir reminded her that he had served her purpose as now she supposed she must serve his, even if it meant her isolation in a Court ruled by prejudice.

Charles's voice was now so imperative that it forced its way through her reverie.

"Eugénie, you must at once go to thank the King for the honour he has done you."

"No, Charles," she protested. "I am too near my time. Our child may be born at any moment, perhaps in the Tuileries itself if I am obliged to go there."

"All the more reason," he retorted jovially, "for going immediately."

Eugénie wanted to tell him that he refused to understand, that all through her pregnancy she had been in terror of a mishap but, knowing he would only laugh at her fears, she merely said coldly, "Whatever *you* may say, Charles, *I* do not relish the prospect of going to Court in my condition."

"What's wrong with it? You're a respectable married woman not a light of love."

For a fleeting moment the coarseness of Charles's remark made her hate him, yet she was less disturbed by it than knowing that he, who had once sought renown only against France's enemies, should show such eagerness to bask in her reflected glory—and what glory! To be at the beck and call of a girl of seventeen, so much younger than herself, but who would have the power to rule every moment of her Lady of Honour's existence! Her thoughts flashed back to Eugène de Villers, who once accused her of republican ideas. What would he have thought of her reluctance to serve the future Duchesse de Berri?

"Very well, Charles, as this is your wish, please ask for an audience for me as soon as possible. I repeat that I have no desire that my child should be born in the Tuileries. I am quite content to give birth in my own home."

Eugénie was always intimidated by the King, his vast bulk squeezed into a wheelchair, his enormous gouty legs wrapped in felt boots and flannel, but she had never disliked him so much as when he cast a salacious eye over her own swollen figure, yet he did not invite her to sit down in his presence.

"I have approved this choice, Madame la Duchesse, but I did not myself make it—my nephew alone has decided on the household of his future bride."

And what, Eugénie thought furiously, had she ever done to the Duc de Berri that he should impose this monstrous task on her?

"You appreciate, madame, that it is a very great thing to be appointed Lady of Honour."

Eugénie, teetering on legs weary with supporting the heaviness of her body, looked Louis XVIII full in the face, expecting to see some sign of humour, but there was none; he was as gravid with the importance of service to the royal family as she herself.

The King nodded. The audience was over.

With great relief although with difficulty Eugénie curtseyed herself three times out of the royal presence, angrily hoping that now Charles would be satisfied that she had done her duty, duty as a wife, duty as a subject of King Louis, duty to her own aristocratic birth and the traditions of her caste.

One further audience Eugénie was required to seek, with the Duc de Berri, but unlike his uncle, he showed her every consideration, bidding her be seated and assuring himself that she was comfortable. To her polite enquiry when the Princess was expected to arrive from Naples, she was astonished by the doleful reply that he had only two months of freedom left to him, adding hastily, "Please do not be surprised, Madame la Duchesse, by my unhappiness. Only the obligations of my position force me to marry which I have no wish to do. I shall do my best not to let the poor girl realise what a sacrifice I am making—and may I say how grateful I am to you for making the same sacrifice to accede to my request that you act as my future wife's Lady of Honour."

Although disconcerted by the Duc's frank avowal of his reluctance to marry, Eugénie was a little comforted to know that she was not alone in deploring the curtailment of her liberty. If de Berri showed himself so understanding perhaps the future might not be so wretched as it appeared.

Then the future Duchesse de Berri, the King and all his Court were forgotten in Eugénie's happiness in giving birth to the child so eagerly awaited, even rejoicing in her intense and prolonged suffering since it led to the ineffable moment when in her arms she held her daughter Louise, but her recovery was slow. She was obliged to remain in Paris while the other members of the Duchesse de Berri's household travelled to Marseilles to await her arrival. Only when the doctors decided that she was strong enough to make the journey did they permit her to leave.

"Bon voyage," Charles called gaily as he helped Eugénie into her carriage, but his gaiety struck a false note. In spite of her gratitude that he had given her a child, she had been out of charity with him since he had insisted on her accepting the appointment as Lady of Honour. His too vocal satisfaction continued to irritate her and, even though it meant leaving Louise, she was glad to be parted from him, however briefly.

"It is all very well for you," she reproached her husband, emboldened by the baby in her arms. "*You* have not risen from a severe lying-in to take the long journey to Marseilles alone, merely to welcome a young girl on her arrival in France."

"What you say is true, but must I remind you how often I rose from a bed of suffering to perform a duty considerably more dangerous? And the 'young girl' you are to meet is not *any* young girl, but the bride of the Duc de Berri, heir to the throne of France."

Eugénie always felt contrite whenever Charles made one of his rare references to his wounds but, although she knew she should be the last person to accuse him of indifference to pain, her farewell to him was cool as reluctantly she handed Louise back to her nurse.

During the long journey to the south accompanied only

by her woman, Eugénie had ample time for reflection and self-pity. While resentful that no one had suggested that she need not travel to Marseilles, perversely she would have refused if she had been offered this indulgence; it was her duty to go and do her duty she would. She was sure that, were she able to consult the Duchesse de Montebello, her answer would be, "Did I not warn you, Madame la Duchesse de Reggio, not to accept a Court appointment? If you have been so foolish as to ignore my advice it is useless to bewail your acceptance now."

"Foolish I agree," Eugénie would have replied, "if I had considered my own wishes alone, but what about my husband? How could I refuse that which manifestly gives him so much satisfaction? You may say that I should not have allowed him to persuade me but, however much I resent his domination, since our marriage his will and pleasure have been mine—he is so much older than I that I have no alternative!"

Eugénie could not resist the fancy that, wherever Madame de Montebello might now be, happily released from her gilded servitude, she would smile contemptuously at Eugénie's apologia, deploring her lack of willpower.

Seeking support for her rebellious mood, Eugénie wondered where she would find it, certainly not from Madame de Coucy, then from whom else?

"The Emperor! He would have understood."

Only when her woman asked her solicitously if she were feeling quite well was Eugénie conscious that she had spoken aloud. Despite her assurance that nothing was amiss, the woman still eyed her mistress nervously, but Eugénie was again absorbed in her own fancies. Yes, she was certain that, although in general Napoleon held women in little esteem, he would have understood her grief at being torn from Louise; mothers of children he regarded with respect. *He* would appreciate her feeling the more since he, too, had been forced to leave a dearly loved son, but in his case no doubt for ever.

Eugénie gave herself a guilty shake. What right had the Lady of Honour to the Duchesse de Berri to think of the Emperor. What Emperor? There was only an outlawed General Bonaparte in exile on the remote island of St. Helena where his enemies fervently hoped his very existence would be forgotten and not his enemies alone. With what ease had the Marshals and their wives, strutting about the Bourbon Tuileries, fawning on the returned émigrés, sloughed off the Empire—and Charles was one of them. She had never been able to forgive his prompt disavowal of the Empire. Did he not remember that his present honours derived from those bestowed on him by Napoleon? Eugénie had long since realised that his true feelings he never revealed to her. About the past he talked freely enough, although always about the campaigns in which he had fought, the cities he had governed. The Emperor's name rarely crossed his lips.

When she arrived at Nevers, Eugénie remembered that she was following the route taken by the Emperor to Elba, that here he had been acclaimed by the populace. Did the citizens of Nevers cherish his memory still? In the bustle of arrival all other considerations vanished until at the inn where she was to spend the night to her surprise she came face to face with Jules de Montendre, brother of her dear Pauline.

"Eugénie! How delightful to see you again!" Then, with a sweeping bow and mock apology, "Forgive my informal address, Madame la Duchesse."

"How can you be so foolish, Jules! To you I hope I shall always be Eugénie."

"Believe me I shall never think of you as anything else, particularly as I can see little difference in you now and the girl I used to know, not so very long ago. Perhaps Eugénie de Coucy was not so elegant, but that is the only change."

Eugénie was sufficiently cheered by Jules's flattery to answer demurely but with a twinkle in her eye.

"You disappoint me! I hoped you would say that I had changed so much for the better that you scarcely recognized me!"

Their mutual laughter carried away much of her ill-humour, before she enquired for news of Pauline.

"She is happy," her brother replied tenderly. "We do

not, of course, see her, but from time to time we are permitted to have news of her."

Shortly after Eugénie's marriage Pauline entered on her novitiate in an enclosed Order; she would never now send her friend a golden ring, but in her last letter she wrote:

"When I am clothed as a nun and put on the silver ring which weds me to Christ, my last worldly thought will be of you, dear Eugénie, and our friendship. Your diamond spray will decorate the statue of the Virgin in the convent chapel."

Between Jules and Eugénie silence fell as they thought of their merry childhood companion who for the life of the spirit had renounced the world. Jules was the first to speak.

"This evening the officers of my regiment are giving a ball—we are quartered at Nevers. Will you honour me by coming as my guest? Surely I need not ask if you care to dance! Eugénie de Coucy could never keep her feet off the dance floor."

"That, dear Jules," Eugénie sighed, "was in my girl-hood. Now that I'm an old married woman with a daughter my dancing days have come to an end."

"Old married woman indeed! You're no older than I. Do come to our ball, Eugénie, my brother officers would be enchanted to meet you."

Jules de Montendre did not know with what regret Eugénie held fast to her refusal. She was reminded of the day, not really so long ago, when de Bourcet sat down at the pianoforte and Letellier asked her to dance, but the Lady of Honour to the Duchesse de Berri must observe a decorum even more formidable than the Maréchale Oudinot.

"Do not tease me, Jules. It *must* be no."

He accepted her final refusal with good grace, kissed her hand and was gone, taking with him what she felt to be the last vestiges of her youth, yet this meeting and the brilliant sunshine had a beneficial effect on her spirits. Hitherto all her journeys had been in the cold unfriendly north so that she was astonished and entranced by the wealth of flowers blooming at this season and by the honey-coloured Greek and Roman ruins among which she would have liked to linger, but her delay in leaving Paris required her to make haste if she were to arrive at Marseilles in time to meet the Princess.

Although Aix-en-Provence was a mere thirty kilometres from Marseilles, Eugénie decided to spend the last night of her freedom there; on the morrow her gilded slavery would begin. As her carriage drew up at the hostelry of the Roi René a traveller descended from another carriage, his hat pulled well down over his eyes, his face muffled in a scarf. When the stranger turned to pass by her, she recoiled in alarm, to be reassured when she heard an exclamation of joyous disbelief.

"Madame la Maréchale!"

There was no mistaking the voice which rang so often in her ears, but what was Letellier doing in Aix? Recollecting herself, she held out her hand for him to kiss while he raised his eyes to look at her.

"You do not change," he murmured, "only more beautiful."

Despite her confusion at this unexpected meeting, Eugénie could not help smiling. True, she had blossomed since her marriage and Louise's birth, her girlish figure now elegantly formed, but she had never regarded herself as beautiful, blushing with pleasure that he should think her so.

How long they stood silent neither knew until Letellier said, "Will you not enter the inn? You must have come a long way and be sorely in need of rest and refreshment."

He followed her as she stepped over the threshold, to be welcomed by the innkeeper who showed her to a private parlour while her woman mounted to prepare her bedchamber for her. While his coachman bespoke a room for him, Letellier stood out of the light. Only when he and Eugénie were alone in her parlour and he was removing his hat and scarf was she able to observe his face. Sadly she saw that he looked much older with bitter lines about his mouth. To break the constraint Eugénie explained her presence at

Aix and that only at the last minute had she decided to spend the night in the town.

"But what brings you here, Colonel Letellier? It is a long way from the Vendée."

Without answering her question he said in a low voice, "Once you called me Michel. Will you not do so again?"

Eugénie was unconscious of how tender was her smile as she responded.

"Then, Michel, tell me why you are here."

"I am on my way to India, to Pondicherry, where I have friends who will help me to make a fresh start in life. Tomorrow or the next day I embark at Marseilles. Why do I go? May I tell you, Madame la Maréchale?"

"Why not Eugénie?"

In his eyes she saw that which made her lower her own.

"Thank you. It is as Eugénie that I think of you and you cannot guess how often that is." As if afraid of saying more, Letellier embarked on his story.

"You may have heard that at Leipzig I was taken prisoner by the Austrians and sent to Hungary. My attempts at escape failed and I was obliged to remain in prison until the peace of '14 when I had to make my own way back to France to find that all was over, but I was not one to lick His Most Christian Majesty's felt boots—and anyway who was General Letellier?"

"A very honourable gentleman," Eugénie murmured, allowing the hand he caught and pressed gratefully in his own to remain for a long moment before withdrawing it.

"So I returned to the Vendée—my father had died—and I tried to make something of what little was left, but I was not happy, how could I be? Then came the incredible, the glorious news of the Emperor's escape from Elba. I rushed to Paris to join him . . ."

"Why did you not come to see me—to see the Marshal?"

"Do not think I did not long to see you, but with the Marshal it was different. For seven years I served him loyally as aide-de-camp and he gave me my step up in rank, but I soon discovered that he had not rallied to the Emperor."

What could Eugénie say without showing disloyalty to her husband?

"I fought at Waterloo—that English duke was right, damn his eyes—we should have won, we should have won," he repeated fiercely. "The rest is simple—with so many others I was put under police surveillance, my every movement watched, impotent to do anything, furious to see France occupied by the enemy, forced to pay an infamous tribute to her conquerors, worst of all to know the Bourbons' rancorous treatment of the army. Death seemed the only solution, but that is the coward's way. I decided to leave France for ever, France as she is now so that I need remember France only in the days of her glory, in the days of the Emperor . . ."

"So you, too, Michel, keep the Emperor in your heart?"

"*Too*, Eugénie?"

"Yes, I, too, Lady of Honour to the Duchesse de Berri I am forced to be, but I do not forget Napoleon."

Conscious of the dangers of their conversation, Eugénie rose.

"We must both be in need of our dinner. I will change my travelling dress, then we will dine together and you shall tell me how you eluded the police and more of your plans."

As Letellier held the door open he bent towards her and her heart beat faster to find him so near. She dared not stop nor look at him for fear of what she might precipitate.

When she entered her room her woman was surprised that, instead of the simple evening gown laid out for her, she was told to take out of a trunk the splendid dress of white satin intended for wear at the official reception of the Duchesse de Berri. Eugénie lingered over her dressing, fussing over her hair and the set of her dress but, when the woman offered her the case containing her diamonds, she pushed it aside. This evening she wanted neither to think of Charles nor wear his gifts.

When at last Eugénie descended the stairs to find Letellier awaiting her in the shadows her face was so radiant that he drew in his breath sharply as he led her to the table.

At last, when the exquisite indulgence of a dinner alone with her could not be prolonged, he threw down his napkin.

"The night is yet young. Will you not walk with me a while in the Cours Mirabeau to crown an unforgettable memory of my last night in France?"

Even had Eugénie been able to resist the voice which had always cajoled her into laughter, she would not have spoiled this evening for him—nor for herself. With her hand resting lightly on his arm they strolled together through that most beautiful of all malls, speaking little. When they exchanged a few words, they were unimportant, nothing mattered but their harmony, more poignant because there would be no tomorrow.

As the night air became cooler Eugénie shivered a little, but she did not resist when Michel put his arm about her shoulders and they turned back to the inn where now no one stirred. Hand in hand they mounted the stairs together to pause outside her room. Michel raised her hand to his lips, murmuring,

"You must know, must have guessed that I have always loved you, that I love you still . . ."

For a moment as Eugénie looked up to his face she hesitated then, opening the door, she drew him inside.

In the morning she found herself alone; it was better for them both that he had gone with no farewell, but he had left her filled with a happiness she had never before experienced. She had thought that she would never know a joy greater than holding her child in her arms, only to realise that love was not, as she had believed, indivisible. Insensibly her love for Letellier had grown with the years and its fulfilment, beyond her remotest dreams, was of a nature entirely different from her love for Louise. Love, she now knew, wore many faces nor did one kind of love exclude another.

She turned to the pillow where Michel's head had rested, as if to feel again the warmth of his presence but the warmth had gone with him. Never again would that warmth, that ineffable glow of happiness, revive. Between them there would be no communication, only the cold silence demanded by the fact of her marriage to another man. She must even deny to the privacy of her thoughts picturing what his life might be in the Indies, following him day by day in fancy. One indulgence alone she permitted herself. When she reached Marseilles she ordered her coachman to drive to the port to wave to the white sails of a ship hull down on the horizon. That was all.

Perhaps it was as well that Eugénie's duties began immediately with a daily visit to the Princess Marie Caroline in the lazaret; not even for a princess were the quarantine regulations relaxed. As the Lady of Honour talked through the grille to her charge she was able to form some opinion of the girl who would henceforward rule her life. She was not precisely pretty but her large blue eyes and flaxen hair had their own appeal.

"Do you think he is handsome, the Duc?" Marie Caroline asked wistfully. "Perhaps his portrait does not flatter him?"

How soulless were these dynastic marriages where bride and groom were known to each other only by an exchange of portraits! Eugénie was unwilling to confess that de Berri's neck was so short that his head seemed to rest on his shoulders.

"We do not think Monseigneur to be outstandingly good-looking, but he is so gay and has such charm that I am sure, madame, that you will not be disappointed in him."

When her visit to the Princess ended, Eugénie was obliged, though with reluctance, to join the other members of the household, nearly all of them émigrés on terms of familiarity with the Duc de Berri whose exile they had shared in London. She could not avoid the feeling that they resented the intrusion into their staunchly royalist circle of the wife of one of Napoleon's Marshals. Only when they recollected that she belonged to their own caste did they unbend slightly towards her, but she was conscious that, unless she conciliated her new colleagues, her life would be uncomfortable indeed.

The journey to Paris was exhausting, leaving Eugénie little time to think as Louis XVIII had decreed that the Princess Marie Caroline's progress should follow the same ceremonial as for other royal brides from foreign countries, involving a succession of receptions, balls and fêtes, culminating in the meeting between the Duc and Duchesse de Berri, already man and wife by their marriage by procuration at Naples.

The Princess and her entourage arrived punctually at the clearing in the forest of Fontainebleau where Louis XIV had met his Spanish Infanta and Louis XVI his Austrian Archduchess Marie Antoinette, pomp and ceremony easing the awkwardness of the moment when the Duc and Duchesse de Berri met each other face to face for the first time. Despite her pity for the little Duchesse Eugénie smiled when the Duc de Berri, awakening from the nightmare he had created for himself, whispered to her, "You have brought me someone incomparably better than I thought she would be." As if her Lady of Honour had fashioned the bride with her own hands!

Longing though Eugénie was to be reunited with her daughter, she could not leave Marie Caroline, who clung to her, feeling more at home with someone near to her in age than with her formidable Mistress of the Robes and elderly ladies in waiting. Only when the nuptial mass had been celebrated at Notre Dame and the couple solemnly bedded by the whole Court led by the King himself was Eugénie at last free to return home.

Towards Charles she had no feelings of guilt, refusing to believe that loving and being loved was a sin. Ever since her marriage she had submissively fulfilled all the demands he made on her, but hers had been lip service only; never had her heart been involved. Yet, if Charles knew that she had consummated her love for Michel Letellier he would consider his honour smirched. For this alone she was ready to make amends. Henceforward she would sink the two separate entities, Charles and Eugénie, in one, the ménage Oudinot, but, in spite of this brave resolve, her heart ached at the bleak future which lay ahead with only the memory of the night at Aix-en-Provence so vivid in her mind and vibrant in her body.

--◦◦❦ ❧◦◦--

# ❧ 10 ❧

"How barbarous a custom this is," Eugénie exclaimed indignantly as with Charles she drove away from the Tuileries. "My heart goes out to the poor little Princess, obliged to endure publicly what for any bride is a terrible moment."

"You found it very terrible, did you not, little Eugénie? How frightened you were—you're blushing—wait till we get home and I'll see that you have something about which to blush."

Long since Eugénie had schooled herself to accept without flinching the broad remarks it amused Charles to make. Ignoring him, she urged the coachman to drive faster; so great was the press of carriages leaving the Tuileries that the Oudinots seemed to be proceeding at a snail's pace.

"Such impatience is gratifying—and unusual."

"Please, Charles, a little less of the grenadier. You know how I long to see my darling Louise—tell me about her, quickly."

For the remainder of the drive to the Rue de la Grange-Batelière Eugénie succeeded in diverting the conversation into paths less dangerous to herself, surprised nevertheless by the new assurance she felt in dealing with her husband but, when she reached home and held her baby in her arms, everything but her joy in the child was forgotten.

Eugénie was not given long to enjoy a respite from her

duties, nor had she the heart to leave the little Princess alone among so many strangers, remembering her own home-sickness in the early days of her marriage. How much worse to find oneself in a foreign country married to a man un-known.

Charles was gratified by the way Eugénie was fulfilling her duties but she refused to be praised.

"I do my best by being perfectly natural and I have pro-fited by what you used to talk about, organization and ad-ministration, as I find that both are part of my duty."

"Still determined to be my little grenadier, Eugénie?"

"Yes, Charles, if you like to put it that way. You have always found me, and always will, obedient to your orders."

If, as Charles kissed her hand, he had any idea why she had thus expressed herself what would he have done, but that he never would know, Eugénie vowed.

At the beginning of the New Year when Eugénie an-nounced that she was expecting another child Charles's de-light knew no bounds.

"So you've learnt the trick at last? This time you'll make me a son."

Some echo awoke in Charles's mind at these words. Of course it was the Emperor who had bidden him make him sons for his Grande Armée, but there was neither Emperor nor Grande Armée, both better for one's peace of mind forgotten.

"Yes, Charles, I promise you the child will be a boy."

Her certainty was justified; the child was indeed a boy, whom Eugénie hoped, if Charles agreed, to call Henri. Happy at having a son to carry on his name and inherit his honours, Charles raised no objection.

"You may call him by what first name you like."

"Even Napoleon?" murmured Eugénie under her breath, although in this moment so ineffable for Charles she was unwilling to provoke him.

"All that matters is that his surname is Oudinot, but the boy doesn't take after you or me," he remarked as he dan-dled the baby in his arms.

---

"No, he's pure de Coucy, the image of my grandfather," was the composed reply which gratified the Marshal, puffed with pride that the grandson of a brewer should resemble a Comte de Coucy.

Henri's birth was quickly followed by that of a second daughter named Caroline after her sponsor, the Duchesse de Berri. Eugénie had now worn her harness for three years and was accustomed, if not wholly reconciled, to the division of her life into public duty and private inclination. She longed to devote her time wholly to her little family but knew it was hopeless to expect Charles to agree to her resigning her appointment. Of him she saw little. He was happily occupied with his command of the National Guard while Eugénie spent a large part of her time with the Duchesse de Berri at the Elysée. At least between her and her husband there was now the mutual interest of their children. Although Eugénie nursed a secret in the innermost places of her heart, the marriage was now to all appearances conventionally happy.

Ever since that night at Aix-en-Provence and the birth of her children, Eugénie had found a new serenity, had blossomed in looks and behaved in her onerous post with such charm and tact that the initial hostility her colleagues had shown her melted away. Even those royalists who had been the first to decry the choice of a Marshal's lady to attend the Duchesse de Berri were forced to admire the calm dignity and affability with which she exercised her duties.

The withdrawal of the Allied army of occupation and a return to prosperity brought a welcome change in the atmosphere as France looked forward to a period of peace and progress, but the nation was shocked out of its newly found complacency on Sunday, February 13, 1820, by an event no one had foreseen.

At the Elysée, now the residence of the Duc and Duchesse de Berri, the household, and particularly the Duc himself, was in high spirits as he indulged in his favourite pastime of tossing fresh eggs across the breakfast table to his gentlemen in waiting who had to be extremely dextrous in catching the missiles if they wished to avoid ruining their uniforms in a shower of egg yolk. So fast and furious was the fun and laughter that they were nearly too late for the King's mass at the Tuileries. For Eugénie her day's duties were now at an end and she rushed away to play with her children until it was time to dress for a ball given by Maréchale Suchet, Duchesse d'Albuféra, at her mansion almost next door to the Elysée.

Eugénie was chatting to friends when a gentleman came up to whisper in her ear, "A terrible thing has happened—the Duc de Berri was stabbed as he entered the Opéra, but the blow is not thought to be mortal."

But the blow *was* mortal! When Eugénie arrived breathlessly at the Opéra it was to see the Duc de Berri, only this morning so impishly gay, with life seeping out of him. Blood was everywhere, staining the little Duchesse's white satin dress as she knelt beside her husband on the mattress on which he had been laid on the floor. The Duc's pallor was ghastly; it was obvious that his life was measured in minutes not hours.

"Speak only in a whisper," the Duchesse murmured to her Lady of Honour, "because he hears everything."

Silence was absolute but for the Duc's painful gasping for breath until the surgeon announced that he must open the wound which had now ceased to bleed, so heartrending de Berri's cries as the operation was carried out that Eugénie covered her ears with her hands to drown them, but the intervention achieved its purpose.

"A priest! Bring me a priest!"

The priest, already summoned, bent over de Berri to hear his final confession and grant him absolution when he succeeded in raising his head from his wife's knee on which it was resting, murmuring faintly to everyone's amazement, "I wish to see all my children."

*All* his children? Only one was known to the witnesses of this tragic scene, the daughter born to the Duchesse at the same time as Eugénie's third child. The Duc turned his head painfully to look at his wife, confessing that he had several children. In disjointed phrases, punctuated by pauses as he fought for breath, de Berri told of his exile in London when his longing for a home and family led to his liaison with Amy Brown who had borne him the two daughters to whom he was deeply attached.

"Charles, why did you not tell me?" cried the little Duchesse whom until now no one had credited with much sense or heart. "I would have adopted them as my own."

A wraith of a grateful smile crossed the Duc's face until the two little English girls were brought hastily to receive his blessing. Not until he had embraced Mademoiselle, his legitimate child, did the Duchesse lose her composure, throwing herself in an agony of grief on the floor beside her husband.

"Take care," he begged, his voice now a mere thread, "not to hurt the child you are carrying."

Even at this poignant moment there was room for an emotion other than sorrow, for thankfulness that France might still have an heir. Mingled with prayers for the Duc de Berri's quiet passing and ultimate salvation was the fervent supplication to the Almighty that this posthumous child would be a son.

Though failing fast, the Duc was making a supreme effort to remain alive until the arrival of Louis XVIII, to whom he uttered his final words.

"Sire, as the last favour that I beg in this world, I ask the life of the man . . . Uncle, make haste . . . grant me the life of the man who . . ."

A terrible groan escaped the Duchesse as she was gently led away, but she shook herself free to return to her husband's side, too late. Throwing herself on her knees to the King, she cried, "Charles is dead, is dead, is dead! Oh, sire, let me go home to Naples, let me go!"

This cry from the distraught widow pierced Eugénie's heart who knew that one day she too might cry, "Charles is dead." With something of a shock she now realised when the time did come for her to echo those words, she would mourn the Marshal. Michel was a dream but Charles, the stable factor in her life, was reality. Above all she would be thankful that her husband would not die on some distant battlefield. Together with all France Eugénie recognized that with the Bourbons had come peace; as she prayed for the repose of the soul of Charles-Ferdinand, Duc de Berri, his widow and children, she added the passionate petition that never again would men slaughter one another—to what end?

The King's words, as he raised the little Duchesse up to clasp her to his heart, brought Eugénie back to the present.

"My daughter, you will stay with us, you and your children. It would have been his wish."

Painfully Louis bent to close his nephew's eyes and kiss his hand as one by one everyone, bowing low before the dead Duc, left that place of tragedy.

Only after the solemn obsequies at St. Denis, final resting place of the Kings of France, was it borne in on Eugénie how much the Duc de Berri's death meant to her. The year of mourning demanded her almost permanent absence from her home but, so helpless was Marie Caroline in her grief, that all thoughts of self were banished.

The Duchesse de Berri, her life now infinitely precious, was installed at the Tuileries which offered greater security than the Elysée. As if grief must be made evident, the ducal apartments were hung with black crepe from floor to ceiling, obscuring the mirrors and the gilding, the huge windows letting in barely enough light by day, while however many candles were lit in the evening the darkness seemed as impenetrable as the tomb in which the Duc de Berri lay.

The Duchesse's bedroom, as a concession to her pregnancy, was hung not with black but with grey draperies, but the deep mourning worn by her household intensified the gloom. Black woollen dresses, unbearable in the summer heat, replaced silk and now no laughter was heard in Marie Caroline's apartments; in keeping with the dismal atmosphere everyone spoke in whispers.

Only once since that fatal Sunday had Eugénie been able to snatch a brief moment to visit her children, yet she could not complain, reminding herself how much more fortunate she was than the little Duchesse, now more than ever an object of pity. At a time when a woman wished to withdraw from public gaze, she was obliged to parade her body as the royal family dared not risk the hostile allegation of a false pregnancy.

--◄[ ]►--

Even her child's birth caused the Duchesse great distress. She was already in labour before the official witnesses could arrive and the only person at hand to confirm that the baby was not a warming pan child was the sentry on duty. So great was the confusion that not until the officials rushed in was it seen that the child was the boy so greatly desired by the royal family.

Eugénie was the last to leave her charge lying wan and still in her vast bed with her baby son beside her, infinitely pathetic with no proud husband to take her in his arms. Did she, alone at last, Eugénie wondered through her own tears, allow herself to weep? She could not guess.

To give thanks to God for the birth of her son, the Duc de Bordeaux, the Duchesse de Berri went on a pilgrimage to Notre Dame de Liesse, a shrine not far from the Château de Coucy, Eugénie's ancestral home, but when Eugénie told her the story of Raoul de Coucy and the Lady of Fayel, Marie Caroline shuddered.

"But he was a monster, this Seigneur de Fayel! I should not have been able to do what his lady did. Would you, Madame la Duchesse?"

"It is a question I have frequently asked myself, madame, but never yet have I succeeded in finding the answer."

"Then let us think of it no more."

But Eugénie could not so easily forget the Lady of Fayel; all her life she had admired her fortitude and constancy, but it was to her lover not her husband she had been constant. While Eugénie continued to doubt her own ability to equal the lady's fortitude, she could claim to be as faithful to her lover without being put to any cruel test. Only when her longing for Michel became unbearable did she now think of the Lady of Fayel. From him no news came, but she expected none. If only she had known where to reach him she would have yielded to the temptation to write to him; there was so much she wished to tell him, but communication between them could only be in her thoughts.

At last the trying year of mourning ended and Eugénie was free to return to Jeand'heurs, especially lovely in the spring when her greatest pleasure was to drive with her chil-

dren through the forest rides thick with violets and prim-
roses. Even when spring turned to summer to her joy she
was permitted to lengthen her leave of absence.

Now it was too hot to venture far afield. Eugénie was
playing with the children in a grove of trees near the house
when she saw her husband striding across the park at a pace
as rapid as if he were pursued by Cossacks.

"Louise, my love, go into the house, find Pils and ask
him if Papa has had any bad news," but, before the child
could do as she was bidden, Pils himself emerged, a crum-
pled newspaper in his hand which silently he held out to
Eugénie, startled to see tears on his weather-beaten face as
he pointed to a paragraph tucked away in a corner of the
*Quotidienne:*

> News has been received in England that Napoleon Buonaparte died
> at St. Helena on May 5, 1821. The cause of death is said to be
> cancer of the stomach.

The paper dropped from Eugénie's hands as she and Pils
stared at each other, neither able to utter a word, their deep
feeling visible only on their faces.

Eugénie rose hastily from her seat, her impulse to try to
overtake Charles although he was now out of sight but, di-
vining her intention, Pils shook his head.

"No, Madame la Maréchale, it is better to leave the Marshal alone."

Grateful that Eugénie shared his own grief, Pils took her
hand and kissed it respectfully before with bowed head making his way slowly back to the house, but several hours
passed before Charles returned and when he did he made no
reference to the Emperor's death, then or later.

How regretful his thoughts must be Eugénie could only
guess. Her own grief was less for the fallen sovereign than
for the man, so alone in his captivity, bereft of wife and son,
yet in a curious way Napoleon's death was a relief. Now
Charles need suffer no more about a dual allegiance, to the
Emperor over the water and the King in the Tuileries.

When at summer's end the Oudinot family returned to

Paris Eugénie told Marie Caroline that she was expecting another child.

"I am so pleased for you, dear Duchesse," the Princess sighed wistfully. "It is a happiness I myself will never know again."

Eugénie's joy at the birth of a second son, named Charles after his father, was shadowed by the grief of losing her beloved mother. She was thankful for her sake that Madame de Coucy had lived to see the Bourbons reestablished on the throne of France and for her own sake that her mother had never guessed her daughter's true feelings but believed that she shared her happiness in Eugénie's office as Lady of Honour.

The birth of her son and her deep mourning for her mother released Eugénie for some time from her duties but shortly after her return to Paris the calm security she had built up in her life was shattered. So far from being years of tranquillity the period following the end of the wars was one of turbulence, not in France but in other European countries struggling to free themselves from the constriction of absolute monarchies, causing Metternich, now more than ever dominating the diplomatic scene, to exclaim, "The world was in a perfect state of health in 1789 compared with today."

With this opinion Eugénie Oudinot heartily agreed when a French army was ordered to cross the Pyrenees to suppress the revolution which had broken out in Spain against the dictatorial rule of the Spanish Bourbon King. The mere idea of war in Spain frightened Eugénie since it was ultimately in Spain that Napoleon's downfall had its origin. In Russia she had seen for herself that the weather was the prime cause of the débâcle, but in Spain it was undeniably the high-nosed Duke of Wellington.

Charles laughed at his wife's fears about the outcome of a Spanish expedition as gleefully he told her that the Duc d'Angoulême had been given titular command of the expeditionary force and that he himself confidently expected to command a corps.

"I'll lay you odds that I am right."

"You may be a gambler, Charles, but I am not. Marshal

Marmont would be a far better choice since he fought in Spain while you did not."

But it was Marshal Oudinot not Marshal Marmont who was given command of the First Corps.

"I suppose I can say without false pride that the choice fell on me because of the two I am the better general."

Eugénie was not mollified; in her view Marmont, childless and separated from his wife, was expendable. She regretted that since she had taken up her appointment as Lady of Honour she had little leisure to cultivate her friendships. If, during Charles's absence, she found herself with any free time, she determined to call on the Duchesse de Raguse, whom she had not seen for many months, partly, it was true, because much of her time was spent at her château at Viry.

Not for a long time had Charles been as happy as now, which once again made Eugénie realise how much he had missed the active service which had been his whole life. For hours at a time he pored over his maps and busied himself with recruiting his personal staff, anxious to have as his officers men who had previously served under his command and who would be proud to march again under the prestigious banner of the Grenadier Oudinot.

He had forgotten none of them but, as he checked through his lists, he sighed deeply as he crossed through the names of those who had fallen in battle; others had attained high rank, yet others had retired from the army, unwilling to serve the Bourbons. Few were left of his companions of those last three terrible campaigns, the invasion of Russia, the battle of Leipzig and the final disaster of the battle of France.

Sitting quietly in Charles's study, from time to time Eugénie heard a name, only for her heart to miss a beat when he looked up from his papers with a frown.

"Letellier? What became of Letellier? Ah, I remember now—when I gave him his brigade he went to Victor's Corps. I believe he fought at Waterloo, then retired from the army—a pity—he was an excellent officer."

Charles hurried on to the next name, but his thoughts were busier than his pen. The scene at Lübbenau when he and Letellier parted company was not one he cared to recall but how happy they had all been before that fatal quarrel! A few years ago on a sudden impulse he had invited Charlotte von Kielmansegge to visit Jeand'heurs, an invitation she refused much to his relief. With time she grew dim in his memory until, after the Emperor's death, he heard from her.

She wrote a heartbroken letter, saying that as the Marshal had been present at her last meetings with the Emperor, he would understand that the world for her was now like a darkened room where all the lights were extinguished. Since that fatal day of May 5, 1821, which had proved to her that Napoleon was mortal, she had worn mourning and in her will she had left instructions that she was to be buried in black with a black cap on her head.

Her letter ended with a few words which puzzled Oudinot: she was deeply distressed that the packet which the Emperor entrusted to her at Dresden had mysteriously disappeared so that she had been unable to carry out his last instructions to her; she could only hope that the packet had reached its destination.

Oudinot had not answered that letter, embarrassed by her devotion to Napoleon which he felt was exaggerated. At this distance in time the Marshal bore Charlotte von Kielmansegge no ill-will for rejecting his advances, was even in a shamefaced way grateful that she had saved him from the only occasion on which he was tempted to be unfaithful to Eugénie. About *her* loyalty he need have no fears—no wife could have been more dutiful—nor need she have fears about him. Bound for Spain he might be but without the smallest wish to imitate the conduct of the Spanish Marshals!

As the day of Charles's departure approached, Eugénie by no means shared his enthusiasm for this new campaign. She dreaded a repetition of the anguish of being called to his bedside to find him seriously wounded or smitten with illness or even that he might be brought back in a coffin, although her four children would ensure that his loss would be less keenly felt than if she were the childless widow she had once feared she might be. Since that night at Aix-en-Provence, so long ago it now seemed, Eugénie had struggled to come to terms with her life with Charles. Her serenity had

210

been hardly won but now she was satisfied that it would endure to the end.

With Charles gone, Eugénie at last had a little leisure to pay the visit to Madame Marmont she had long promised herself, to her surprise finding Hortense in a gay mood.

"I have been thinking about Marmont," she chuckled, "and his absurd attempts to make money. Like your husband, only a quarter of his year is occupied with the Royal Guard, but he is still too young, too energetic and has too fertile a brain to be content with idleness. In common with so many soldiers he has not the remotest idea of how to live as a civilian; it is a new trade they have to learn and Marmont's trade involved him with sheep."

The Duchesse de Raguse laughed so much that she had difficulty in continuing.

"Even Marmont realised that, if sheep are sheared during the cold weather they would suffer, but only he would have conceived what he thought was the brilliant idea of having coats made for them, coats for sheep! What made the project even more ridiculous was that he dressed his sheep in artillery colours, red and dark blue! What a sight I missed— Marshal Marmont commanding a flock of sheep! Naturally his scheme of getting two fleeces a year failed. Anyone but Marmont would have guessed it."

Eugénie had joined in Hortense's laughter but now her mood changed.

"Of course I only heard this story from someone else. My husband and I are now total strangers, we have not even met for years, but he does not lack consolation. Women are essential to Marmont to feed his vanity; their admiration compensates him for the neglect and slights of which he believes himself to be the victim."

Scornful Hortense Marmont might sound but to Eugénie, naïve in some things as she still was, it was obvious that she was still in love with her husband. Perhaps her fault had been to love him too well while paradoxically Eugénie's own marriage, in the eyes of the world at least, was successful because she loved her husband too little!

A few days after her visit to Madame Marmont a courier

arrived from Charles, asking for some papers to be sent to him which Eugénie would find in his desk, where everything was arranged with his usual scrupulous neatness; she was surprised when she found one drawer so jammed that she was able to open it only with difficulty, the fault a roll of bills which had got stuck in the back.

Idly she unrolled the package to find it contained not bills but drafts of letters written by Charles in 1815 to Marshal Davout and others at the time of the Emperor's return from Elba. A little guiltily Eugénie began to read, her consternation growing as one letter after another revealed what had been sedulously kept from her.

She had known that Marshal Davout had written to Oudinot, inviting him to renew his allegiance to Napoleon. Of this letter he had told her but his reply that he could not break his oath to Louis XVIII she did not find. Now she realised that it had never been written. Charles had lied.

Every one of his own letters expressed his eager desire to be restored to the Emperor's good graces. He had bombarded his old friends, Marshals Davout and Suchet, even his former aide-de-camp, now General Jacqueminot, with requests to intercede for him with the Emperor.

"Tell me that I have been restored to favour—it is the best news that you can give me."

Any doubts Eugénie had that these letters had been sent were dashed when she discovered that Charles's reason for electing to live near Paris was not voluntary, but an order of exile imposed by the Emperor who not only steadfastly refused to offer him a new command but even threatened to strike him from the list of Marshals. Napoleon did not forget that at Fontainebleau it was Marshal Oudinot who had uttered the word "abdication."

More than any other, the letter which most distressed Eugénie was one written to Marshal Suchet.

"Say that Oudinot has never forgotten what he owes to Napoleon, that if Oudinot has made mistakes, as soon as he knows what they are, he will correct and expiate them. I need you to do this for me for the sake of my wife and family and all who share the misfortune which has overtaken me."

Oh, no, not for her sake! How cowardly to pretend thus! Eugénie had been ready to accept that Charles's refusal to join the Emperor was inspired by the new obligations he had assumed and to which he remained loyal. Now she understood why he had gone to Paris to see the Emperor not, as he had declared, to explain his reasons for failing to rally to him, but to beg for reinstatement.

With hindsight Eugénie knew that whether or not Charles had thrown in his lot with Napoleon it would not have affected the final issue. What came as a violent shock to her was that her husband had posed as loyal to the Bourbons while in fact he was ready to turn his back on them had not the Emperor turned *his* back on Oudinot.

Avidly now Eugénie read on to discover that, after Waterloo, Charles was involved in a plot to bring the Bourbons back again, turning the tables on Marshal Davout by urging him to speed the Second Restoration. In this at least Eugénie, however grudgingly, was obliged to concede that Charles was actuated by the imminent arrival in Paris of the Russians and Prussians, whose thirst to avenge the sack of Moscow and defeat at Jena was still not assuaged. Only the King's return offered any hope of security for Paris.

When Eugénie came to the end of the batch of letters she sat back, staring into space. She had believed so implicitly that Charles, who had shown himself capable of so much chivalry, was incapable of deceit. For one thing only was she grateful to him; he had acted alone, not making her a party to his intrigues. At last Eugénie knew why the Emperor's name so rarely crossed his lips. Still she puzzled about his actions. Had he acted as he did because he bitterly regretted his advice to Napoleon to abdicate only, now he wished to repair his error, to find that he had lost the Emperor's confidence? Or, and this was most distressing of all, had Charles been moved by self-interest, by the desire to follow the rising sun, only when that sun finally set, to range himself eagerly again on the other side.

Even if she had not previously been aware of it, this revelation of Charles's conduct in 1815 showed the fundamental gulf between Eugénie and her husband. In his public dealings his courtesy and chivalry matched the quality of the de Coucys but, as a private individual, he lacked the aristocratic sense of the point of honour. He had acted like a parvenu, clinging tenaciously to his offices and his honours. How mistaken Eugénie herself had been, oh, so long ago, when she protested to Eugène de Villers that aristocratic behaviour was not the privilege of one class alone, and how right he was to insist that the Emperor could create nobles but not aristocrats. She was struck by a sudden distasteful thought. Was her appointment as Lady of Honour to the Duchesse de Berri Charles's reward for loyalty which was no loyalty? Why had he not taken her into his confidence? Did he think her still too immature to understand the struggle between two opposing loyalties?

Charles had deceived her, but she had deceived him. There could never be a confrontation between them, but Eugénie was comforted that if she had her secret from him, he had his from her. On his return from Spain she would meet him with the same composure as on her own return from Aix-en-Provence. Carefully Eugénie replaced the telltale letters where she had found them and left the study.

All the veterans of the Napoleonic wars who had looked forward to the combat they had missed so much were disappointed. Few battles were fought in this Spanish campaign and no laurels won in a war of pen and ink rather than guns. Nevertheless, Charles, entrusted with the difficult but bloodless task of subduing Madrid, was obliged to prolong his stay in Spain for some months.

When the Marshal finally returned to Paris and resumed his commands the Oudinots quickly fell back into the old routine. Secretly Eugénie marvelled that of all the surviving Marshals Charles should be the one most highly esteemed by the King. She did not believe that the Emperor rated him among the best and greatest of his Marshals but, of course, Louis XVIII was no soldier and had never seen the face of war.

Soon it was obvious that the King's health was failing, although he might say with his sardonic wit that a king must die but he must never be ill. When Eugénie returned from sea bathing with the Duchesse de Berri at Dieppe she was shocked by Louis's appearance. He had shrunk into his coat, the epaulettes affected by one who had never held military rank drooped on his shoulders. As he was wheeled into the dining room where the household, as etiquette demanded, stood to receive him, they were conscious of an aura of decay.

Louis XVIII's reign ceased on September 16, 1824. During his last moments the ladies and gentlemen in waiting withdrew from his bedchamber to leave the King alone with his family. Standing in rigid silence in the great Galerie de Diane, now so familiar to Eugénie that she passed through it daily without noticing her surroundings, today, her emotions heightened in the neighbourhood of death, she recalled the first time she had entered the gallery. So vivid was the memory that, when the door leading to the private apartments was flung open, she almost expected to hear a voice announcing:

"Madame la Duchesse de Bassano to present Madame la Maréchale Oudinot, Duchesse de Reggio, to his Imperial Majesty the Emperor."

The illusion vanished as, not the Emperor's usher, but the First Gentleman of the Bedchamber in a voice stifled with grief uttered the traditional words:

"The King is dead! Long live the King!"

Few among those waiting had heard those words before and a shiver ran through the ranks of the household as the Comte d'Artois, his handkerchief pressed to his face, rapidly left the King's room for his own apartments in the Pavillon de Flore, as the household took up the cry:

"Vive le Roi!"

Momentarily the Comte d'Artois, whom they must now learn to call Charles X, looked startled before, bowing briefly, he was gone.

The accession of a new King was for France a big question mark. Would he be as successful as his brother in holding the country's diverse elements in check? Time alone would yield the answer. Now the grisly ceremonial of a royal death had everyone in its grip.

--◦❦|❧◦--

# 11

"Madame la Maréchale has given strict orders that she is not to be disturbed."

The caller took no notice, brushing past the servant as he threw over his shoulder, "Inform her that Marshal Marmont wishes to see her urgently."

Eugénie, busily packing to join her family at Jeand'heurs, was extremely annoyed when she was told that the Marshal had forced an entrance into the house. She disliked the man himself, unable to forgive his behaviour to his wife and perhaps as much what he had done in 1814 to the Emperor, once his dearest friend, then acting as Napoleon's worst enemy.

Sighing, she supposed that she must see Marmont lest he had indeed something of importance to communicate but she had barely crossed the threshold of the salon when Marmont burst out, without the courtesy of a greeting, "I hear you are leaving to join Oudinot in Lorraine. Tell him what I have told him often, that he is the happiest and I the most wretched of men."

Was it for this that Marmont had contravened her orders? Eugénie's indignation was shown by her cold invitation to him to be seated which he ignored, pacing furiously up and down the room.

"Oudinot may have told you of the measures the King plans to quash the opposition, measures which I personally consider abhorrent to the nation and fatal for the dynasty. During the next three months when I am in command of the Royal Guard it will fall to me to support the King with armed force."

Still Eugénie could not understand the purpose of Marmont's visit. No doubt Charles was equally aware of the King's intentions and stood in no need of a reminder.

Irritated by her silence Marmont glared at her.

"You may also tell Oudinot that, if by some lucky chance I escape this agonizing responsibility, I shall request a long leave of absence to escape from France and the fatality which has always pursued me."

Marmont was so obviously distraught as he now stood biting his lips that Eugénie refrained from retorting, as she would dearly have liked to do, that the fatalities were of his own making. Instead she said quietly, "Perhaps you are mistaken, Monsieur le Maréchal. I cannot believe that if the Duc de Reggio considered a crisis imminent he would have left Paris."

"No, madame, I am not mistaken, though I wish to God I were! My final message to Oudinot is that in a mere matter of weeks there will be a coup d'état, with what consequences I shudder to think."

With these words Marmont departed as unceremoniously as he had come, leaving Eugénie even more puzzled as to the purpose of his visit and his messages to Charles. If his prediction was correct what did he think Charles could do to avoid a clash between King and people? The Oudinots, intimately connected with the Court, had for some time been uneasily aware of the misguided course followed by Charles X; the nation at large detested the reactionary policies of the close circle of émigrés who had shared the King's English exile but only to their advice did he listen.

Charles had been angry enough when the King arbitrarily dissolved the National Guard, his grief and rage such that Eugénie feared that he might fall into an apoplectic fit as he strode up and down, cursing and swearing as she had not heard him do since that day, long ago, when they entered Berlin.

"Blind, those damned courtiers, blind!" Oudinot spat out. "Around the King there are still men of goodwill, men who know what the nation needs more than those poltroons of émigrés ever will. Can no one make him realise that fear of revolution makes it inevitable?"

As a man born of the people Oudinot understood the feelings of the nation far better than the King who had spent twenty-five years of his life in exile, but Charles X's evil geniuses were in full command.

As she returned to continue her packing Eugénie concluded that, so discredited was Marmont, in Paris he could find no one to unburden himself to as the Marshals who shared his command had all, once their tour of duty ended, retired to their country estates. She herself was the only one in any way connected with the Royal Guard remaining in Paris. Despite her dislike of Marmont, she could not help pitying him.

Immediately on her arrival at Jeand'heurs Eugénie told Charles of the Marshal's presentiment.

"He may well be right." Oudinot nodded. "Poor devil, he seems to attract these terrible crises of conscience as once again it will fall to him to be the arbiter of a dynasty, bearing the brunt and contumely of performing an intolerable duty. He should, of course, resign his command but Marmont's hands are tied to his pocket—he cannot afford to forego his pay."

To Eugénie it was obvious that Charles did not share her opinion of Marmont's conduct in 1814, but she heartily agreed with him when he continued:

"You and I, Eugénie, may thank Heaven that by an accident of timing it will be not I but Marmont who will be forced into taking fateful decisions because the way things are going I agree that this summer will see trouble in Paris."

That Charles did not consider it his duty to return to

Paris in an attempt to make his moderating influence felt was a great relief to Eugénie; he had served and suffered for France long enough and now was surely entitled to some peace, to escape responsibility for whatever disasters might be looming.

As June gave way to July the feeling of expectancy in the air of Paris where in the hot summer heads began to boil penetrated even to peaceful Jeand'heurs. News of the King's latest rash move, rescinding the liberties granted by Louis XVIII, intensified fears of unavoidable bloodshed in the capital, although at Jeand'heurs all that was known for certain was that fighting had broken out in the streets of Paris.

The danger threatening the Duchesse de Berri convinced Eugénie that she should rejoin her at the Elysée, her wish to do so endorsed by Charles.

"You are attached to the person of your Princess, my dear Eugénie, your duty therefore is to go to her and, should the situation worsen, remain. Anxious though I myself am to obtain the King's direct orders, until I receive them I am obliged to stay in Lorraine to preside over the electoral college of Verdun."

After some consideration the Marshal decided that Eugénie should travel under an assumed name but he would send with her an aide-de-camp who should masquerade as a merchant, even though it entailed the sacrifice of his military whiskers.

Remembering the dangers of previous journeys she had taken Eugénie made light of any possible hazards, but the nearer they came to Paris the more alarming was the information they gathered: in street-fighting the populace had overwhelmed the Royal Guard but the travellers scoffed at the absurd rumour that the guns had been loaded with human bodies including that of Marshal Marmont, whose despair continued to haunt Eugénie.

"Madame la Maréchale," suggested the aide-de-camp nervously, "I believe it to be inadvisable to continue our journey to Paris," but Eugénie would not agree although she was stunned to learn from some travellers that Charles X had abdicated in favour of the Duc d'Angoulême, Louis XIX for as long as it took him to sign his name, before he abdicated in favour of his nephew, the little Duc de Bordeaux, to reign under the regency of their cousin, Louis Philippe, Duc d'Orléans. This news made Eugénie even more desperately anxious to join the Duchesse de Berri but she was able to discover only that the royal family had left St. Cloud and were thought to be at Rambouillet.

Sent to reconnoitre, the aide-de-camp returned with a grave face.

"Further progress is, I fear, impossible, madame. The Parisian mob is streaming along the road to Rambouillet, blocking it completely. Our only course seems to be to return to Lorraine."

Eugénie was sickened by the thought of the Parisians' march, with its sinister reminder of 1789 when the mob dragged Louis XVI and Marie Antoinette from Versailles. God grant that their fate did not overtake the King and his family!

Reluctantly Eugénie, though deeply anxious about her little Princess, saw no alternative to returning to Jeand'heurs, to tell Charles all she knew and discuss the future with him. There was no doubt in her mind that her duty lay in seeking the Duchesse de Berri wherever she might be found. Unlikely though it was that a letter would reach the Duchesse, Eugénie wrote a hasty note, assuring the Princess of her loyalty and her firm intention not to desert her post. Then, bitterly distressed at the failure of her mission, she ordered her coachman to turn his horses towards Bar-le-Duc, only to find on arrival that the Marshal was better informed than the travellers themselves.

"They are calling these days *Les Trois Glorieuses* as if it were glorious for Frenchmen to fight Frenchmen, " he exploded with the soldier's horror of civil conflict. "And the wretched Marmont had to be the one to open fire on his countrymen——it is all far far worse than in '14. Then we were fighting a foreign enemy on French soil and students helped to man the guns turned on the Prussians and the Russians while now Marmont was forced to mow down the boys from the Polytechnique and the Sorbonne."

"We must thank God that this terrible duty did not fall to you."

"I do thank Him but I cannot forget that, if this catastrophe had arrived a month ago, it would have been I who was forced to do as Marmont did with only six thousand troops under his command against the whole population of Paris."

For Marmont Eugénie now had no pity to spare, all her feeling reserved for the family in whose intimacy she had lived for so long. She was a little comforted to know them safe in England but saddened that the King must renew his occupation of the gloomy palace of Holyroodhouse which had sheltered his earlier exile.

"Do you remember, Charles," Eugénie asked, struck by a sudden recollection, "that at the last fancy dress ball during carnival the Duchesse de Berri insisted on appearing as Marie, Queen of Scots, although we did our best to dissuade her from assuming the dress and character of that unhappy Queen? She laughed saying that the coif was so becoming. I can only pray that she does not meet the same awful fate."

Eugénie's fear was so real that Charles could not help smiling.

"Come, come, that is highly unlikely—we live in more civilized times. After all this is the nineteenth not the sixteenth century. You may rest assured that no royal heads will roll."

Very shortly after Eugénie's return to Jeand'heurs Charles announced that he would go to Paris to cast his vote in the Chamber of Peers in favour of the Orléans regency for the Duc de Bordeaux, since he judged Louis Philippe the only man capable at this juncture of saving France from the mob rule of a republic. That power should rest in the hands of the son of a regicide was repugnant to Eugénie but her indignation knew no bounds when Louis Philippe, coolly disregarding his pledge to act as regent, had himself proclaimed King of the French.

Now, she thought, Charles would resign his various of-

---

fices to live as a private citizen, peacefully busying himself
with his property and enjoying watching his children grow
up. He was much calmer and, as he grew older, the demands
he made on her had lessened considerably so that she found
it was possible to live with him without the revulsion of the
earlier years of her marriage. The future looked more pleasant than for a long time but Charles was still able to surprise
her.

When he returned from Paris he announced defensively,
"As the only possible course I have taken the oath to Louis
Philippe who represents the sole constituted authority.
Whatever a soldier's personal feelings may be, his duty is to
submit to authority. I am not prepared to discuss this matter
further."

Try as she would, Eugénie failed to understand the fine
point of "submission to constituted authority." She remembered only that in every change of régime since 1814 Charles
had always opted for the winning side, but she had never recovered from the shame of knowing that, while insisting on
his loyalty to Louis XVIII, behind his back he curried favour
with Napoleon. As in so much else she realised how far apart
they still were. Her motive in determining to join the Duchesse de Berri was not affection alone; to abandon her now
would, in Eugénie's eyes, be an infamous dereliction of duty,
but it was a sacrifice the Duchesse refused to accept.

When Eugénie showed Charles the Duchesse de Berri's
letter he told her somewhat impatiently that she had done all
she could.

"If you continue in this way you will worry yourself into
illness—do you imagine that I do not know how you toss and
turn during the night?"

"Why do you so wilfully refuse to understand? My duty
is to a woman whose husband conferred on me the honour of
inviting me to act as guide and companion to his wife, a trust
that for many years I have done my best to fulfil—and may I
remind you that, in spite of my reluctance to assume this
charge, it was you who urged, indeed insisted, that I accept
it. So far from relieving me of my responsibility, the Duc de

Berri's death made it impossible for me to abandon his widow then and especially now. I should be deserting my post in the face of danger and that is something I should certainly not expect you to approve."

Charles must have felt the force of her argument as he made no attempt to dissuade her from writing again to the Duchesse, renewing her request to join her, to meet with the same refusal.

"Well, Charles, you must be satisfied that I shall abide by the orders I have received; at least I cannot be called a deserter. Had the Duchesse bidden me to go to Edinburgh I would have gone, whatever it cost me to leave you and the children. Now my only obligation is to you all, but why do I speak of obligation when being with my family is my greatest joy?"

The routine into which the Oudinots now settled fulfilled all Eugénie's wishes. Three of the winter months were spent at the Hôtel Oudinot in Bar, the remainder of the year at Jeand'heurs which she had come to love. The boys came and went from school, each declaring, to Charles's satisfaction, his intention when old enough of joining the army, while the two girls, Louise and Caroline, were pupils at the same convent their mother had attended. Did they, she sometimes wondered, indulge the same romantic fancies she had shared with the two Paulines?

When the Duchesse de Berri left Holyroodhouse for Italy and shortly afterwards Charles X and the Duc and Duchesse d'Angoulême exchanged the unkind Scottish climate for Austria, all communication between the Maréchale Oudinot and the royal family ceased, little known of their movements until the Duchesse de Berri descended on the faithfully royal Vendée to raise the standard for her young son. Oudinot was proved right in predicting that the enterprise was doomed to fail; the Duchesse was arrested and imprisoned. Without this time consulting Charles, Eugénie wrote offering to share her captivity to meet a final refusal, the reason she learned when she found her husband chuckling over a report in the newspaper.

--❦❦--

"Your little Duchesse," he told Eugénie, "a widow of twelve years' standing, is pregnant, there's no doubt about it because her state cannot be concealed any longer. Well, well, who is the happy man responsible I wonder?"

Eugénie was deeply offended by Charles's amusement. Gay little Marie Caroline had lived without love until she could no longer endure the sterility of her heart. During her stay in Italy she had married a childhood friend, the Count di Lucchesi-Palli, but perhaps her pregnancy had come at the wrong moment. Nevertheless it secured her release from prison, the government by no means displeased that her gallant escapade had ended in ridicule.

"I hope that now, Eugénie, you will put aside the foolish idea of trying to resume your old duties with the Duchesse de Berri or rather the Contessa di Lucchesi-Palli. By her marriage she has ceased to be a member of the French royal family and your days as Lady of Honour are finished."

Charles was, of course, right. Eugénie had become accustomed to subordinating her life to Marie Caroline's, but she was honest enough to admit to Charles, "It is strange; I have long since ceased to think of my post as gilded slavery, even though I once did so but, though I regret my little Princess, I am so happy not to be torn between my duty to her and to you all, to be able at last to live the life I love best, here at Jeand'heurs with my family."

Eugénie's period of peace lasted for seven years during which she did not even spend a day in Paris until early one morning Charles burst into her boudoir, brandishing a letter.

"Read this, Eugénie. I have been invited to become Grand Chancellor of the Legion of Honour, a post reserved for Marshals of France. I am gratified to know that so much prestige attaches to the name of Oudinot. We shall have to leave Jeand'heurs, of course, and take up residence in the Palace of the Legion, the old Hôtel de Salm."

Eugénie, loath to leave the calm of Lorraine, did not share her husband's enthusiasm, reluctant to live in Paris again and fearing the exertion of his new office for Charles. She wished that another Marshal had been chosen, but how few of the twenty-four created by Napoleon survived and one, Marmont, lived in penurious exile in Italy, unable to return to France to face a court-martial and a long term of imprisonment.

During her long absence from Paris Eugénie had lost touch with Hortense Marmont but, now that she would again reside in Paris, she hoped to renew her friendship with her. Thinking of Hortense reminded Eugénie of something Madame de Coucy had once said to her.

"Perhaps in this world we are granted only a certain sum of happiness, for some concentrated in a short period while for the lucky ones it is spread over their whole lives."

Hortense's period of happiness must have been very short but not, Eugénie thought not without bitterness, as short as mine. Joy in her children she certainly had but of pure happiness one night only, one night in a whole lifetime!

To her relief there was little ceremonial attached to Charles's new position; Eugénie had witnessed too many ceremonies during her years at the Bourbon Court not to have had her fill of them, but the ceremony which took place in December 1840 was one she would not for the world have missed.

Since his death in 1821 Napoleon's remains had lain in a grave in Geranium Valley on St. Helena, unmarked because the British, unswerving in their refusal to recognize him as other than General Bonaparte, would not allow the single name "Napoleon" to be engraved on his headstone. To bring the Emperor's remains back to France was Louis Philippe's great gesture of conciliation to the Bonapartists who remained hostile to his reign. In defiance of the law forbidding the Bonaparte family to enter France, the Emperor's nephew, Prince Louis Napoleon, made an abortive attempt at a coup d'état, but this did not deter the King from decreeing that the greatest of the Bonapartes should return to his good city of Paris.

Under the command of the Prince de Joinville, one of Louis Philippe's sons, the *Belle Poule* sailed for St. Helena, among her passengers the men who had first journeyed there in company with the Emperor, General Bertrand, Baron Gourgaud, the young Las Cases and Napoleon's valet, Marchand. While Paris waited for the Emperor as so often they had waited for his triumphant return from one of his glory-laden campaigns, his old companions had the moving experience, when his coffin was opened, of seeing him, recognizable still, in his uniform of a colonel of the *Chasseurs de la Garde*, the crosses of the Legion of Honour and the Iron Crown untarnished on his breast.

Then the coffin was again closed, to be carried by soldiers of the English garrison to the ship which set sail for France, anchoring at Cherbourg, where a black catafalque ship waited to proceed slowly up the Seine, its banks crowded with troops of the line. Could the Emperor but have woken from his long sleep he might have fancied himself still in the camp, hearing the sound of bugle calls and seeing the bivouac fires lit by his veterans who kept a night-long vigil to watch their Emperor pass.

When Eugénie woke on the morning of December 15 Charles was no longer by her side but, only when she discovered that he had left the house at first light, did she begin to feel anxious.

"Did the Marshal say where he was going?" she asked her maître d'hôtel.

"No, Madame la Maréchale, but Pils was with him."

To know that Pils was with him relieved some of Eugénie's fears; Pils would see that Charles came to no harm but he had still not returned home by the time she herself was obliged to leave to take her place with the other surviving Marshals' ladies at a window overlooking the great Esplanade des Invalides. She went reluctantly, ever more anxious about her husband who was to take part in the ceremony at the Invalides, but go she must or otherwise she would never be able to force her way through the crowds.

The bitter weather reminded Eugénie of the terrible days of 1812 but it did not deter the mass of people lining the route from Courbevoie where the catafalque ship was moored. Deferentially the civilians made way for the veterans of the Grande Armée, old men now in their once so familiar and now so strange faded and threadbare uniforms donned for the last time to do honour to their Emperor.

Headed by lancers and cuirassiers with standard, drums beating and bands playing solemn music, the great procession passed through the Arc de Triomphe de l'Etoile which Napoleon had left unfinished, down the Champs Elysées and across the Pont des Invalides, at last to come into view of the watchers eagerly waiting for it. All eyes were fixed on the funeral car drawn by sixteen black horses, their white plumes nodding, their saddlecloths embroidered with the Imperial arms, eagles and laurels. On the purple pall strewn with golden bees lay the Imperial crown, the sceptre and the hand of justice, while immediately behind the car the Emperor's charger furnished with the First Consul's saddle and harness was led by a groom in the Imperial dark green livery.

Eugénie craned her neck perilously out the window as the procession moved slowly into the Esplanade, seeing to her great relief the four pallbearers marching to the right and left of the coffin—General Bertrand, Admiral Roussin, Marshal Molitor—and Marshal Oudinot. As the coffin moved into the great courtyard of the Invalides Eugénie realised why Charles had slipped out of the house while she was still asleep. He had gone to Courbevoie to march beside the coffin on its six-mile journey to the Invalides, and Charles was seventy-one. He was limping badly—since he was wounded in the thigh in Russia he avoided walking any distance—but she saw that Pils marched discreetly near, ready if need be to give the Marshal a helping hand.

What surprised Eugénie even more than that her husband should have undertaken the painful march was that he wore, not the dress of a Marshal of France, but the dark blue of a Marshal of the Empire, the dress coat heavily embroidered with laurels and oak leaves he had worn at their wedding. The broad red ribbon of the Legion of Honour slashed his chest, but today no Cross of St. Louis adorned it, only the crosses of the Legion and the Iron Crown. She was just able to make out that on his hip rested not the baton decorated with the lilies of France but the one of dark blue velvet embroidered with laurels in gold thread, a star in golden paillettes in the centre, the baton which bore the legend, "Oudinot Nicolas-Charles, nominated July 12, 1809." At his side she recognized the magnificent sword, its hilt encrusted with diamonds, presented to him in 1811 by the city of Amsterdam.

Was this uniform, these honours, a silent tribute to the Emperor on whom Charles had turned his back in 1814, a sign of his shame at the choice he had made? Eugénie realised how much about him she still did not know even after so many years of marriage. Passionately she wished that Napoleon could know that the flame he had kindled in the hearts of the men whom he had so often led to victory still burnt so brightly, the flame in her own heart—and Michel's. How he would have rejoiced to be here today, but since he could not be, she would gather him into her own rejoicing. Now it was time to move with the other ladies into the church of St. Louis des Invalides to take her place on the stands draped in black velvet which surrounded the catafalque nine feet in height, crowned with an immense golden eagle.

As the coffin was borne down the aisle to rest on the catafalque the whole assembly dropped to its knees, but no prayers offered up for the Emperor were more fervent than those of his old moustaches, unbelievers though they might be. Not one of them, Eugénie thought with some bitterness, had a troubled conscience for deserting his Emperor; none had wavered in his allegiance.

Now General Bertrand advanced to place the Emperor's sword on the coffin, followed by General Gourgaud with the poignantly familiar black beaver hat, then, as the four pallbearers ranged themselves on both sides of the catafalque, standing stiffly at attention, the solemn mass began, intoned by the choir.

At the end of the service a solitary cry reverberated

through the church, to be taken up by the whole assembly. The voice was that of Marshal Oudinot and his cry, *"Vive l'Empereur!"*

Then it was over.

In his own way Charles Oudinot had made his amends.

Eugénie pushed through the crowds to find Charles and take his hand in hers.

"Come, dear, it has been a long and tiring day for you."

No other words were spoken between them as slowly they left the Invalides where four old soldiers of the Imperial Guard stood guard with drawn swords by the coffin and the first of hundreds and thousands of people began to file past to pay their final respects to the Emperor lying at last, as he had wished, by the banks of the Seine among the French people he had loved so well.

Three years later Marshal Oudinot returned as Governor to the Invalides, the last and greatest honour bestowed on an old soldier. If Eugénie missed the peace and beauty of Jeand'heurs Charles was happy among his old comrades in arms; some, who had served in his "infernal column" of grenadiers, welcomed him as an old friend while others were pleased to be under the orders of so distinguished a hero— Marshal Oudinot had always been known for the fraternal ease of his relationship with his men.

Although so many years had gone by since the Marshal had last commanded in war, Eugénie realised that he whose youth and maturity had been spent in the camp, had never wholly reconciled himself to life as a civilian. She herself found the Invalides gloomy, only from time to time stealing away to the chapel of St. Jerome where the Emperor's coffin lay until it found its permanent resting place—to pray for him, for Charles, for herself and for Michel wherever he might now be.

One day, walking down the Rue de l'Université which leads into the Esplanade des Invalides, Eugénie was tempted to call on the Duchesse de Raguse. She had heard that she was ill and had long since left her home in the Rue de Paradis but, after many years spent mainly in her château at

Viry, she had returned to Paris to the Rue de l'Université, living the life of a recluse. Perhaps she would relax her solitude to see Eugénie?

Although she told herself there was nothing about which to be apprehensive, Eugénie could not help feeling nervous as she knocked on the door which, after what seemed a long time, was opened by a stern-faced woman.

"Please inform Madame la Duchesse de Raguse that the Duchesse de Reggio would like to see her."

The woman eyed Eugénie up and down, then said reluctantly, "Wait here, Madame la Duchesse."

As she had not been invited to enter the house, Eugénie had perforce to wait on the doorstep until the woman returned with a message.

"Madame la Duchesse de Raguse sees no one."

Eugénie felt she had received a blow on the face from a woman for whom she had always had the kindest feelings. Another chapter in her life had closed. Sadly she turned away to walk the short distance to the Invalides.

# ⸱⸱❦{ 12 }❧⸱⸱

Eugénie Oudinot sat busily writing at the table Pils had
placed for her in the shade, from time to time raising her
head from her work to gaze at the Jacqueminot roses now in
full bloom. Although Charles's aide-de-camp had never been
a great favourite with her, she did not forget that he had
helped to bring them away from Vilna nor that at Waterloo
General Jacqueminot had fought on the side of the Emperor.
It was in tribute to that fidelity that she had planted the roses
named in his honour.

Gradually her writing grew slower until at last she laid
down her pen to study every tree, every flower and the great
house itself to imprint on her mind every detail of the
Jeand'heurs from which she had once fled but which she
loved dearly. She could not quarrel with young Charles's
decision to sell the domain nor would she let him know what
a wrench it would be for her to leave Jeand'heurs. Would
Henri have sold Jeand'heurs knowing how much it meant to
her when, as the elder son, he inherited the estate and
Charles's honours? Idle to ask herself this question since

Henri, her first-born son, was dead and young Charles was the heir. Eugénie wiped away a tear as she remembered her conversation with her younger son.

"You know, *maman*," young Charles had said, "it was my hope that you would be able to live here as long as you wished, but I must confess that the upkeep of Jeand'heurs is a great drain on my resources. After Papa lost his dotation when the Empire fell he was not really a rich man and the calls on him were very great."

"Of course, dear Charles," Eugénie had answered her son brightly, anxious to conceal from him how shattered she was by his decision, "you must not let me be a burden to you. I shall be very happy in the house at Bar, indeed it will be more convenient for my work."

Since the Marshal's death Eugénie had devoted herself to the cause of the poor and suffering in Bar-le-Duc, earning for herself the title of which she was most proud, "the good Duchess," as once Charles had gloried in being not the Marshal but the Grenadier Oudinot. He had fought with his usual courage against failing health, but even he could not withstand the tale of years. When the waters of Plombières, so beneficial in the past, proved of no avail he insisted on taking the long painful journey to Paris and the Invalides.

"Grenadier Oudinot must be found at his post when the bugles sound '*Reveil*,' " he declared but his voice was the merest whisper.

They buried him not as the simple grenadier but as a Marshal of France alongside all the other great commanders who had served their country so well. Eugénie's own wish was that he should lie at his "paradise" of Jeand'heurs, but the honour of burial in the Invalides was one neither she nor her children could refuse.

As the organ rolled out the stirring sounds of the "Marseillaise" and the impressive funeral service at St. Louis des Invalides came to a close, Eugénie, leaning on the arm of young Charles, now the second Duc de Reggio, wistfully asked her son, "Will he be happy here? Leaving him alone makes me feel desolate."

232

"Dearest *maman*, he is not alone. He lies among his old comrades near the Emperor whom he served so faithfully as long as he could—and, who knows? Perhaps when we have left them in peace, the marshals and the generals relive their old battles, waiting for the summons to the clash of arms in some soldiers' heaven. No, dear *maman*, do not fear that Marshal Oudinot will feel lonely among his peers and, remember that, so long as we are here and so long as the great deeds of those who fought for France remain in her memory, he will live on in our hearts and hers."

Even through her tears Eugénie smiled at young Charles's whimsy, intended she knew to comfort her; her grief for her husband was real. Habit is a very strong force and during those last tranquil years of his life she had grown closer to Charles. He had long since ceased his attentions to young girls, which she had always assured herself were because he loved youth so much; only occasionally did a round oath escape him and his gambling was a thing of the past.

"My only vice is now my pipe," he said as he looked proudly at his great collection of pipes and shells displayed in cases in the library at Jeand'heurs, the room which belonged so specially to him and where Eugénie had bravely talked to young Charles about his father's actions in 1814 and 1815.

"You must not misjudge, *maman*," he said gently, taking her hand, "what Papa did in 1814. I was not even born, but he told me that in that crisis he genuinely came to believe that only a Bourbon Restoration offered any hope for France. Better than many others, he appreciated the truth of the military situation; the men were just not there nor, above all, the horses. Had the Emperor been able to repair the losses of the Russian campaign there would have been no Leipzig and he would still have been at the Tuileries. Perhaps if Marshal Marmont had acted differently there might have been a chance for Napoleon, but it was only a slender chance because we now know what few then knew, that he was already a sick man, that his powers of decision, his great genius, were wavering, that his star had set."

Even though his arguments failed to convince her, Eugénie was glad that young Charles championed his father but when a nervous enquiry about the Marshal's conduct in 1815 revealed that his son did not know of those damning letters she was immensely relieved; young Charles must never know. But, when she went to look for them in the desk which had been brought to Jeand'heurs from Paris, she found they had gone. So Charles had destroyed them, unaware that she had read them! She was content that she had never given him the smallest sign of her knowledge of his conduct in 1815, nor had he ever suspected her own defection.

Eugénie shook herself out of her memories; there was still so much to do, the accounts of the Children's Clothing Fund to check and to study the reorganization of the charity closest to her heart, the Fund for the Veterans of the Grande Armée. So absorbed was she in her work that she gave a start to find Pils, bent and white-haired now, standing beside her.

"What is it, Pils? I thought I gave orders not to be disturbed?"

"So you did, Madame la Maréchale, but a gentleman has called and begs you to receive him."

"Why did you not tell him that I am too busy to see anyone?"

The old man looked crestfallen.

"But, Madame la Maréchale, he said that he had come a long way in connection with a charity so I knew you would not refuse to see him."

Eugénie rose, annoyed that an unknown gentleman should force himself on her but Pils was right, an appeal for charity could not be refused. She collected a sheaf of papers, saying, "I'll finish these in the library. Show the gentleman into the salon and say I will be there directly but, Pils, you must tell him that I can spare him only a few minutes."

When a little later Eugénie entered the salon she said with a touch of asperity, "Pils says you have come a long way to talk to me about a charity. I trust that it is not you yourself who is in need of help."

The man standing with his back to her looking out of a window swivelled round at the sound of her voice.

"But I am in need, greatly in need as I have been for so many years, Eugénie, in need of you."

Eugénie's hand went to her heart. Although his face was burnt black by the sun and his brown hair was liberally streaked with grey, she could not be mistaken. Still upright and soldierly in his bearing, it was Michel who smiled at her with great tenderness as he crossed the room to take her hand.

"You could not think I have forgotten, Eugénie? As soon as I learnt of the Marshal's death I left Pondicherry to come home to France. I hope my unceremonious arrival has not given you a shock, but I had the feeling that, if I announced myself, you might not wish to receive me—after all, it has been so long. I was a little afraid that Pils might recognize me, but perhaps I have changed a great deal though never in what I feel for you. Tell me at least, Eugénie, that you are glad to see me!"

Eugénie could find no words until, after a few minutes which to Letellier seemed endless, she repeated his own, "It has been so long, Michel—so long."

"Just how long for me you could not guess, nor how lonely, but now at last I am here and nothing stands in the way. Eugénie, will you marry me?"

The hand which had been holding hers found its way to her shoulders while, as he drew her to him, the other caressed her hair. Eugénie trembled as she said in a low voice, "But, Michel, I am an old woman."

"Never to me! I see you always as the girl with whom I danced and you ran away because the Marshal was angry. To me you will always be a young girl, that is how I have thought of you, how I think of you, but always it is as you were at Aix that I think most often. My feelings have never changed. When I led you out of that Russian hell my concern was not for the Marshal's safety but for yours. I always wanted you. I want you still."

—◦◦⊰ ⊱◦◦—

With a touch of his old humour, Letellier added, "I have heard that you are most charitable. Will you not include me among your good works?"

Silently Eugénie disengaged herself from Letellier's encircling arm. With a look of anguish he stepped back. Had he been living all these years in a fool's paradise, believing that her feelings for him were what his were for her? Lonely and unhappy in his Indian exile, had he forgotten what time can do? But Eugénie spoke softly, "Come with me; there is something I must show you."

He followed as she led the way upstairs to a little oratory where over a vase of fresh flowers hung the portrait of a young man. As he gazed at it he was puzzled by a look he could not quite place. Although certain that he had never before seen the portrait, yet about the features there was something familiar. With a question in his eyes he turned to Eugénie.

"You have seen the likeness." Her voice faltered to a whisper so low that Letellier had to bend his head to catch her words. "Charles never guessed, never knew, he worshipped the boy and Henri adored him." Suddenly she laid her head on Letellier's breast. "He is dead, Michel, he died as you would have wished, fighting for France but so young, oh, so young—in Africa, in an expedition against the rebels. His body has never been found. The most heartrending moment of my life was the arrival of his baggage and his bloodstained sword."

"Why did I never know, why did you not tell me, Eugénie?"

"I wanted to, so much I wanted to, but it was part of the penance I imposed on myself for deceiving Charles to deny myself that joy, even if it meant denying it to you also. I think I paid in full for that brief moment at Aix when in our chapel we celebrated mass for the repose of Henri's soul. I still hear those terrible sobs from Charles at the loss of his dearly beloved son, Henri was always his favourite, but he was not his son. I called him Henri because it is one of your names but in my heart he was always Michel and when he died my last link with you was broken."

Eugénie could no longer control her own tears when from Michel she heard a great sob, quickly stifled as he turned her to look at the portrait.

"Don't you see, Eugénie, that he is smiling to see us together for the first time? Do we not owe it to him to come together at last, to cherish his memory together?"

But, with a final look at her son's portrait, Eugénie led Letellier away, shaking her head.

"How can I do so? There are the others. 'Young Charles,' as we called him, Charles's son, and my two daughters who all revere their father's memory. They would be grievously hurt if I quit their father's name." She paused briefly. "Even though it must hurt you, Michel, in the end I became reconciled to being Charles's wife. When I returned from Aix I made a vow that I would be a good wife to him and I was—it was easier when he grew older. He never knew that my heart he did not have, had never had."

Between them silence fell, a long silence when Letellier would not meet Eugénie's imploring eyes. At last he faced her and it was she who turned away.

"Loath though I am to go, I shall leave you now, Eugénie. I see that I was wrong to have forced my way in, I was too abrupt, too careless of the effect my unexpected arrival might have on you. I thought only of the years when I yearned to see you again. While wishing the Marshal no harm—we were good friends once—he was so much older than I that I knew that at some time you would be left alone and I convinced myself that then my chance would come, but perhaps I was mistaken."

With a touch of bitterness he continued:

"I failed to realise how full your life was with the Marshal and your children, while I thought only of my loneliness, every day of my life reliving the hours I spent with you, the days in Vilna and your heroism during the retreat—and then that unlooked-for, unforgettable meeting at Aix. Eugénie, only you can decide whether I am to be as alone as I have been, even lonelier now that I know all that I have missed."

Nothing could stop the flow of Eugénie's tears as on a gentler note Letellier went on.

"I see that I am asking you to give up much, to dwindle from the Maréchale Oudinot, Duchesse de Reggio, to plain Madame Letellier. I have done well in the Indies—we could travel, do whatever you wished. I entreat you, do not send me away for ever. Until I hear from you I shall stay at Bar, but I shall not try to see you again before you have made your decision." Under his breath he murmured, "Please let it be soon and let your answer be what I have so long and so passionately wished it to be."

Abruptly, without a further glance at Eugénie, Letellier left her to find Pils hovering in the hall.

"You know who I am, Pils?"

"Yes, *mon colonel.* When you came in I thought that I knew your face but I am getting old and my memory is not as good as it was, then suddenly it came back to me. I'm glad to see you again, sir."

"Some other time we'll talk about the old days, Pils, but now please tell my coachman to meet me at the bottom of the drive. I'll walk down."

Sighing deeply, Pils watched Letellier stride down the drive until he disappeared from view, then he went to the salon where he found the Maréchale sitting staring into space with the tears running down her face, but she managed to smile at the old man.

"Did you recognize Colonel Letellier, Pils?"

"Not at first, Madame la Maréchale, but when I had a good look at him I remembered. He was Monsieur Henri's father, wasn't he?" he asked simply.

"How did you know?"

"Forgive me, Madame la Maréchale, if I have been indiscreet, but I have been so long in the Marshal's service and now in yours. You know I am an artist—I was always sketching, in bivouac, even on the battlefield. One day I did a sketch of the Colonel and then—when Monsieur Henri was still with us—I was turning over my drawings and I was struck by the likeness. When he grew up I knew I could not be mistaken."

"But the Marshal did not guess?"

"No, madame. He was so happy with his first-born son, as he thought, and Monsieur Henri loved the Marshal as if . . . as if he were his own father."

The old man crossed over to Eugénie to take her hand in his.

"We all loved you, Madame la Maréchale—it was an honour to serve you—it still is. Even if the Marshal had doubted, which he never did, it was your secret and I kept it."

"Thank you, Pils." Eugénie was deeply moved. So even Pils! How, Eugénie asked herself as the old man hobbled out of the room, had she deserved such love? She had deceived her husband, denied her lover knowledge of his son. Had she any right to enjoy the happy future offered her? Suddenly she felt very weary; surely she was too old, too tired to begin a new life. Her years as Lady of Honour had taken a greater toll of her than she realised. Michel might still think of her as a young woman but, if she married him, he would soon discover his mistake—and the children? What would they feel? How explain, without revealing her own weakness, that their mother wished to marry a man of whose very existence they were unaware?

Despite her depression and fatigue Eugénie remounted the stairs to the oratory to fall on her knees in front of her son's portrait.

"Now that for the first time you have seen your parents together do you think, Henri, that I should marry your father? Am I still capable of giving him the happiness he deserves for his love and faithfulness? Do you think that I should disappoint him, that he has been living a dream which will not bear reality? And your brother and sisters, Henri—your half-brother and sisters—should I not lose their respect and love if they knew the truth about you. Wherever you may be, my son, pray for me, pray that I do what is right."

But from the portrait there was nothing but the same steady gaze.

Rising to her feet Eugénie walked through the house, particularly every room most closely associated with Charles, the armoury with its historic arms and armour, the great gallery lined with the busts of marshals and generals, his own among them, the broken shoulder long since repaired. Her lips moved though no sound came as now she addressed the cold marble.

"Charles, what would you have me do? You had the best of me, all the years of my youth. If you did not have the love I gave to Michel you had my submission and you fathered three of my children. Yes, Charles, three only because I deceived you once, but only once and so long ago. I never reproached you for your own deceptions. In the eyes of God I may be a sinner, but to me you were something worse, you betrayed a different trust put in you, the trust of the Emperor who showered you with honours, yet you survived to die an honourable death."

What response did Eugénie expect from that impassive face? Yet she continued her appeal.

"May I now not dedicate what is left of my life to a man who kept his oath of allegiance, who remained loyal to his Emperor? I know you would say that he deceived you, that in one night he stole your honour but do you not remember, Charles, how truly he served you for seven years? Have you no pity for his lonely exile while you were adding to your honours and enjoying the blessing of a happy family life? And, Charles, did not Michel Letellier put honour before honours as you did not?"

A joyous young voice interrupted Eugénie's soliloquy, "Maman, maman, where are you?"

"Charles! When did you arrive?"

"A few minutes ago—I've got some leave and, of course, I came to spend it with you." He hugged her warmly. "How are you, dearest maman?"

"A little distressed, dear," Eugénie confessed, conscious of the tearstains on her face. "I've had a visit from an old friend"—she hesitated for a moment but sooner or later she must say his name—"from Colonel Letellier, who was one of your father's aides-de-camp, oh, for a long time."

"Was he? I do not recall hearing the name. Wait a moment, was it not he who led you out of Russia? Of course I must see him. Where is he? He's staying with us naturally."

"No, dear, he has gone to an inn at Bar."

"But, *maman*—an old comrade of Papa's—why did you not invite him to stay?"

Already Michel's appearance was presenting Eugénie with problems. She had not expected young Charles to arrive without warning and of course he would be delighted at meeting one of his father's aides-de-camp.

"I did not think of it," was her lame reply.

"Never mind, *maman*, I'll send Pils to rout him out and get Madame Thiers to prepare a room for him. Goodness knows there are enough rooms at Jeand'heurs and, even if there weren't, there would always be a place for one of Papa's old comrades."

"Wait a little, Charles." Eugénie laid a restraining hand on her son's arm. "I want to talk to you and a stranger—a visitor—would be in the way."

"As you will, *maman*."

He tucked his arms in hers.

"Come into the gardens—it's much too fine to stay indoors—and *I* have something I want to say to you."

"Very well, but let me get my shawl . . ."

"Nonsense, don't pretend you're an old lady; you won't catch cold."

So forthright, dear Charles, just like his father, yet Charles had never loved the boy as much as he loved Henri.

"I can't wait to tell you, *maman*. I proposed to Marie and she accepted me. Are you happy about it?"

"I'm delighted, dear Charles. Your father and I always hoped you would marry Marie, such a suitable marriage in every way."

"I'm glad you're pleased and that I'm marrying into the marshalate. I myself will never rise to such heights, no more wars, that's the pity, but it is very appropriate for the son of a Marshal to marry a Marshal's granddaughter, don't you think?"

"Yes, I do think, but what is more important is that you are in love with each other."

Lovingly Eugénie smiled at her son's happy face, but the thought obtruded how ridiculous it would be if young Charles and his mother married at the same time. Fortunately he was too busy talking of his Marie's beauty, her virtues and her graces to see the startled look his mother wore. Had she then already made her decision, made up her mind so impulsively to marry Michel without giving herself time for reflection? Absorbed now in her own thoughts, Eugénie heard only snatches of what Charles was saying, that he'd like to be married soon and at Jeand'heurs before it was sold. His fiancée and her mother were perfectly agreeable that the marriage should take place there and it would be a fitting farewell to the Oudinots' occupation of the old abbey.

Faintly Eugénie agreed, but young Charles was too carried away by his own excitement to notice how lacklustre was her response yet how could she cast the slightest shadow on her son's joy? She could not. In her life she had sacrificed much, with her subservience to Charles and her long gilded servitude to the Duchesse de Berri. It seemed that one more sacrifice was asked of her, but would it indeed be a sacrifice? In all honesty Eugénie admitted to herself that, during their long separation, Michel's image had faded; at times it had been an effort to conjure up his face. Certainly he was her one great love but in default of her lover she had lavished all her tenderness on her children, especially on Henri but on Henri because he was Michel's son. For one moment Eugénie thought of seeking the advice of her confessor, but it was too late. How could she, so many years later, admit her sin and justify her failure to do so long ago? If only she knew what she really wanted!

As these thoughts agitated her, she and young Charles were still strolling about the gardens, when suddenly he stopped to ask:

--◦◦◦◦--

"Did you not say, *maman*, you had something you wanted to say to me?"

"Later, dear. It is not important."

Was it after her first big lie that she had got the habit? No, her first lie was letting Charles believe she loved him when all she wanted was for him to give her a child, but what was young Charles saying?

"Goodness, I'd forgotten about Colonel—what did you say his name is?—Papa had so many aides-de-camp. The only one whose name I remember is General Jacqueminot but that's because of the roses."

Helplessly Eugénie watched young Charles run into the house in search of Pils, calling him to take the carriage to drive into Bar to bring back Colonel—Colonel—

"Letellier," Pils supplied the name young Charles could not remember.

"Yes, Letellier. Tell him that the Duc de Reggio and the Maréchale would be delighted if he came to spend a few days with them at Jeand'heurs. No, on second thoughts you'd better bring him back with you. Now, if you will excuse me, *maman*, I'll go and change my dress."

Eugénie and Pils were left alone.

"Pils," she began but the old man shook his head.

"Leave it to me, Madame la Maréchale. You will see that it will all turn out right."

He said no more but made his way to the stables, grumbling at the stable boys for taking their time in putting the horses to. It would take him an hour to drive into the city and an hour to return, even if he found Michel immediately. Two hours to decide her whole future was Eugénie's agitated thought, her future—and his!

When Pils, who had gone from inn to inn in search of Letellier, entered the inn where he was putting up, he found him staring out of the window of his private parlour, the *Quotidienne* lying neglected at his feet.

"Pils!" Letellier started up eagerly. "The Maréchale has sent for me!"

"Not exactly, *mon colonel*, but if you will allow me to sit down—my legs don't carry me as well as they once did—I will explain everything to you. It was Monsieur le Duc, the young Duc as we call him, who sent me to fetch you to Jeand'heurs. He is very excited at the prospect of meeting the man who helped to bring his parents out of Russia . . ."

"I see. And the Maréchale?"

"May I be frank with you, *mon colonel?* You were Monsieur Henri's father, were you not? It is not for me to ask why or how, but I grieve that you never knew him. We all adored Monsieur Henri and we mourn him greatly. I must tell you, sir, that the Maréchale's life has not been easy—no one better than you knew the Marshal's temper—but he valued her. She is always so cool, so correct, that although we are all devoted to her, we have never known what her feelings were, but this I can tell you she did her duty and more than her duty."

Letellier nodded but Pils had more to say.

"Did you know that she became Lady of Honour to the Duchesse de Berri? Perhaps you did not out there in the Indies. She did not want the appointment but the Marshal insisted that she accept it."

"Yes, I did know, Pils, because it was when she was on her way to meet the Princess and I was bound for Pondicherry that I met the Maréchale at Aix-en-Provence."

He had no need to elaborate; it was clear from Pils's face that he understood, but he gave no other sign, continuing with his story.

"The Maréchale became fond of the little Princess, but she hated the Court, particularly after the Duc de Berri was assassinated, it was so dreary she said, so unlike the Emperor's court. I believe, *mon colonel*, that like so many of us, although her family belonged to the old noblesse, she was always for the Emperor."

"Yes, yes, Pils, but what of now, what of *now?*"

"Please do not be impatient with me, *mon colonel.* Let me tell you in my own way. You would like to marry the Maréchale, would you not?" It was a statement, not a question. "But she does not know her own mind, of that I am sure—she thinks only of her children and her respect for the

Marshal's memory, never of herself; it is time she did so."

"So *you* think, Pils, that the Maréchale should marry me?"

"I do, sir. Mademoiselle Louise and Mademoiselle Caroline are married and the young Duc soon will be. She will be very lonely but most of all she will miss Jeand'heurs which the young Duc is obliged to sell. Naturally he is in the army and rarely able to come to Bar."

"Then what should I do, Pils?"

To neither did it seem strange that the officer should seek the grenadier's advice but after all Pils, who had spent nearly all his life with Marshal Oudinot and his family, knew them better than anyone else. Far better than I, was Letellier's bitter thought, who have been away for so long.

"What I think you should not do, sir, is to accept the young Duc's invitation. It would be too great a strain for the Maréchale to have you as a guest at Jeand'heurs before she has made up her mind what to do. Give me, if you please, a note for the young Duc, thanking him for his offered hospitality but saying that urgent business calls you to Paris and that you look forward to meeting him at some later date."

"But I want so desperately to go to Jeand'heurs to see the Maréchale again."

"And so you shall, sir, trust old Pils. Believe me, she will be grateful for your patience. When the young Duc has left— he has only a few days' leave—then I will let you know that it is time to come to Jeand'heurs."

Letellier rose from his chair to pace about the room.

"It is difficult for me to be patient. In all these years I have exhausted my patience."

The old man trotted up to him to pat him gently on the shoulder.

"We all had to be very patient climbing up Ponary, you remember, *mon colonel*. One false step and the carriage turned over or your horse stumbled and you were thrown into the murderous snow. I sat on the box then and, if you permit me, sir, I'll hold the reins again."

Impulsively Letellier took the old man in his arms.

"You've always been a good friend, Pils. How often did you stand between me and the Marshal's anger! You remember how he picked a quarrel with me at Lübbenau and tried to throw a dish at my head?"

"Do I not, sir! But a junior officer does not fight a Marshal of the Empire as you wanted to do. He bade you to get out of his sight although a few days later he had you nominated general of brigade—though fierce, his rages never lasted long. Indeed, *mon général*, I apologise for not giving you your correct title, but the old one was more familiar."

"That doesn't matter, Pils, I'm just plain Monsieur Letellier now.

After a few moments' hesitation he asked, "Does the Maréchale know—about Lübbenau?"

"That the Marshal was jealous which was really why he picked a quarrel with you?"

"It wasn't my fault," murmured Letellier a little awkwardly. "You knew the Gräfin von Kielmansegge, how lovely and attractive she was. She could have had any one of us she wanted and we were soldiers for whom there seemed little future. Wherever our real affections lay we were always ready to grasp any opportunity offered us, there might never be another. I had always believed the Marshal to be a faithful husband but even he succumbed to the Gräfin's charm. She told me so, but it was I she wanted. What choice did I have or to be honest want? That I could ever have the Maréchale at that time I believed impossible and I'm a man as well as a soldier."

"You don't need to tell me, *mon général*. I saw the Gräfin's eyes whenever she looked at you. Any of them—Colonel Jacqueminot, Captain Lachaise, Captain de Bourcet, the Marshal himself—would willingly have taken your place."

"Yes, she was lovely, the Gräfin—and kind. You may know that I was taken prisoner at Leipzig, eating my heart out for a year in Hungary until peace was signed in '14. I had lost everything but the burning desire to return to France. My way back lay through Dresden where the Gräfin was then living and I saw her again. She urged, begged me to stay, but I could not. In France there was the Maréchale and, even if fate did not permit me to see her, we would at least be in the same country. When she realised I would not stay with her the Gräfin did everything possible to help me to return. I shall never forget her kindness but I did not, do not, want to become involved so I have never attempted to see her again."

Certainly he had been fond enough of Charlotte von Kielmansegge, perhaps flattered by her preference for him and to refuse what she offered so eagerly for the sake of a distant and unattainable dream would have been foolish. He was no saint; in the Indies there had been other women but it was always one woman alone he held in his arms, a mirage which faded with the daylight, *maya*, an illusion. Now at last there was the reality of Eugénie but would she still be the loved and lost?

"How can I, Pils, plain Monsieur Letellier, expect the Maréchale to give up all her titles and state to become my wife?"

"I don't think, *mon général*, that consideration would weigh with her at all. The Maréchale was born a de Coucy which has always meant more to her than the name she now bears. With the Marshal it was different, he was the son of a brewer and even more than in the marshalate he gloried in his title of Duc de Reggio."

"I know."

"The Maréchale won't be rich—the Marshal didn't leave much money and their children must have their share."

Pils paused. He had picked his words with care with a purpose in mind, but Letellier laughed.

"It wouldn't matter to me if she were beggared, and not merely because I'm now a rich man. It was difficult at first, starting a new life and one which was wholly foreign to me, but I worked hard—there was nothing else to do—and I prospered. I can give the Maréchale whatever she wishes—even buy Jeand'heurs for her if she wants it."

Pils watched nervously as Letellier moved purposefully to the writing table and picked up a pen.

"I'm going to write to the young Duc, Pils, telling him

what you suggest, but I shan't go to Paris. I'll wait here until the Maréchale sends for me—if she does. You had better give her that message—no. On second thoughts I'll write to her myself."

For some time he wrote busily, rising with a sigh to hand his letters to Pils.

"Thank you for everything, old friend. Assuredly we shall meet again."

"Surely we shall, sir. And thank you for listening to an old man's advice."

Letellier grasped his hand warmly before Pils slowly left the room, following him in fancy on the road to Jeand'heurs.

Pils ordered the coachman to drive slowly; he had much about which he wished to think. His visit to Letellier had not been as innocent as he had declared. Anxious always to protect Eugénie, he had wanted to satisfy himself that Letellier was no fortune hunter, eager to repair his damaged finances by marriage to a well-to-do woman. Of this anxiety his mind was now relieved, while of the sincerity of the General's feelings he had no doubt. It remained for him only to convince the Maréchale that she should do what to him at least was clear, marry the man who had loved her so devotedly and, instead of a lonely widowhood, enjoy the happy marriage which had never been hers, but how easy would be his task?

When at the gates of Jeand'heurs he saw Eugénie waiting for his return, a broad smile broke over Pils's face; there would be no task!

"Alone, Pils?"

He heard both disappointment and relief in her voice, but disappointment was the louder.

"Yes, Madame la Maréchale. The General—I had forgotten that the Marshal had him promoted general before Leipzig—has written to excuse himself to the young Duc. I have his letter here."

"But you have two in your hand."

"Yes, madame, one is for you."

Pils handed Eugénie the letter destined for her, adding tactfully, "I will go to deliver this to the young Duc."

Although he would dearly have loved to see the

Maréchale's face as she read General Letellier's letter, he dismissed the carriage to hobble up the drive, leaving her staring at the paper in her hand. How many letters had she not received in the course of her life bringing her news of disasters! She could scarcely bring herself to open this one, but she must.

"Once, Eugénie," she read, "you told me the story of your ancestor, Raoul de Coucy, and that his love, the Lady of Fayel, was forced to eat his heart. For me the situation is reversed. Must I eat my heart out for my Lady because I am as faithful as Raoul de Coucy?"

Standing at the gates of Jeand'heurs, Eugénie re-read the letter several times. Soon Jeand'heurs would be only a dear memory as once Michel had been but, even if it were no longer hers, the château would still be there, perhaps for hundreds of years, but he? If she now sent him away he would never return. Had she not done her duty by Charles, had she not loved her children dearly? Charles was dead and her children lived far away. Once her mother had told her that her husband must come first, that her children would not love their mother less, but the largest place in their hearts must be filled by their husbands and their wives. Now Eugénie had no husband, only an empty heart but, since Charles had never filled it, that heart had always been empty until Michel had taken possession of it.

At last Eugénie began to move slowly back to the house, her thoughts, had she but known it, those of Pils who had told Letellier that her concern was always for everyone else, never for herself. It was true still. It was not of herself she must think, but of Michel. Would she have him eat his heart out when it rested with her that it should beat strongly again? Let him but give her a little time, only a little time! She could not let him eat his heart out.

---